Linda's story unravels so cleverly, and Raabe keeps you
questioning what's fact and what's not right to the end,
ratcheting up the tension at the same time . . . A genuinely
griping debut. I had to keep reading until I'd finished!'
Debbie Howells, author of *The Bones of You*

'You won't be able to resist'
Elle

'A very clever, mind-bending thriller'
Woman & Home

'A fast, twisty read for fans of
Paula Hawkins and Gillian Flynn'
Booklist

'A must-read for thriller lovers'
Essentials

'Blurs the lines of justice deliciously'
Dead Good Books

'A page-turner in the very best sense of the word.
It's clever, devious, and driven, and twists the reader
inside out until it reaches a terrific ending'
Ian Hamilton

THE STRANGER UPSTAIRS

Melanie Raabe grew up in Thuringia, Germany, and attended the Ruhr University Bochum, where she specialized in media studies and literature. After graduating, she moved to Cologne to work as a journalist by day and secretly write books by night. Her debut novel, *The Trap*, was an international bestseller. Her second, *The Stranger Upstairs*, remained on *Der Spiegel*'s bestseller list for almost six months when it was first published in Germany in 2016.

Imogen Taylor is a literary translator based in Berlin. Her translations include *The Trap*, Sascha Arango's *The Truth and Other Lies*, and *Fear* and *Twins* by Dirk Kurbjuweit.

Also by Melanie Raabe

The Trap

THE STRANGER UPSTAIRS

MELANIE RAABE

Translated by Imogen Taylor

PAN BOOKS

First published in English 2017 by The Text Publishing Company Australia

First published in the UK in paperback 2018 by Pan Books
an imprint of Pan Macmillan
20 New Wharf Road, London N1 9RR
Associated companies throughout the world
www.panmacmillan.com

ISBN 978-1-5098-8622-7

Typeset by J&M Typesetting
Printed and bound by CPI Group (UK) Ltd, Croydon, CR0 4YY

Visit **www.panmacmillan.com** to read more about all our books
and to buy them. You will also find features, author interviews and
news of any author events, and you can sign up for e-newsletters
so that you're always first to hear about our new releases.

Sarah

The world is black. The sun above me is black.

I stand, head thrown back, eyes wide open. I try to drink in the moment, to commit it to memory, to block out any other thought. The trees are rustling softly, almost ceremonially. Only the birds high in the branches seem unimpressed: they sing as if to spite the darkness, as if singing is all that matters. The sun is black and I stand and bask in the sight. There is no more warmth. No light.

This is not the first eclipse of the sun I have witnessed. When I think of the first, I have to smile, in spite of everything. Philip had wanted to get out of town and go to the woods—he thought the birds would suddenly stop singing when the sun went dark and wanted to know if he was right. I wanted to stay in town with our friends—all of us together, young and silly and keyed up, with our special glasses on our noses. I talked him round. It wasn't hard—back then he was happy to let me talk him into all kinds of things. He made one last attempt to persuade me, saying how much more romantic it would be in the woods, just the two of us, but I said, 'Don't be soppy!' and he laughed and we ended up staying in town with the others.

The strange thing is that I can't remember the eclipse itself. I remember all the rest—our friends' chatter, the music coming from the radio, and a smell of burning because someone had put sausages on the barbecue and forgotten about them. I remember Philip's hand in mine. I remember that we ended up taking off our glasses because they got in the way of kissing. We held each other's hands and must have missed the moment. For the first time, though, we talked about the future. I had always refused up until then—the future wasn't something I believed in. But someone had said that the next eclipse of the sun we'd see would be in 2015 and that there wouldn't be another one until 2081, and that was real—I could believe in that. We worked out that Philip would be almost forty at the next eclipse and I'd be thirty-seven. We laughed at the sheer madness of the thought that we would one day be that old, but we promised one another we'd be more careful next time, that we'd see the black sun and that we'd see it together—in the woods, so that Philip could find out if he was right about the birds.

And here I am now, thirty-seven years old, standing in a small clearing alone in the middle of the woods. I am staring at an enormous black sun and it stares back at me and I wonder if Philip can see it too—if it's visible wherever he is. Our son will be seventy-five at the next eclipse—I will no longer be around and Philip will no longer be around. Today was our last chance. As I stand here watching the moon edge its way across the last sliver of sun, I realise that Philip was wrong—the birds around me aren't any quieter at all. I wonder whether he would have been disappointed or pleased and tell myself that it no longer matters. Philip isn't here anymore, I think. Philip has gone. Philip has disappeared. Philip has fallen off the edge of the world.

And at that moment the birds stop singing.

The hairdresser has a beautiful face with prominent cheekbones. His hands are slim and feminine. I was hesitant to enter the salon and deliberately walked past a few times before pushing open the door. Now I am sitting here in a swivel chair, at the mercy of this man.

Fingers spread, he runs his pianist's hands through my hair, which is so long now I can almost sit on it. He does it once, twice, three times, all the way from the roots to the tips, making admiring noises, and a colleague who introduces herself as Katja comes over and does it too. The physical contact embarrasses me—it is far too intimate. For so many years there was only one person allowed to touch my hair, and that person loved it. He rested his head on it, dried his tears with it. But I let the two of them have their fun and pretend to be pleased at their compliments. Eventually they stop oohing and aahing and Katja goes back to dealing with her customer's extensions.

'So,' says the hairdresser, his fingers already twining through my hair again. 'You want the ends trimmed?'

I swallow drily.

'I want the whole lot off.'

The hairdresser—his pretentious name has slipped my

mind—gives a brief giggle, but falls silent when he realises that I'm not laughing with him, that this isn't a joke. He looks at me. I am prepared. I rifle through my handbag, produce a page torn out of a fashion magazine, hold it up and point.

'Like that,' I say. And then, as if to reassure myself, I say it again: 'Like that. That's what I want.'

The hairdresser takes the glossy page from my hand and studies it. At first he frowns, then the steep line bisecting his forehead vanishes. He looks at me, looks at the magazine again, and eventually nods.

'Okay.'

I breathe a sigh of relief, glad not to have to argue with him. I'm a grown woman, and I hate it when other people think they know what's good for me. Patrice—the hairdresser's name has suddenly come back to me—is enough of a pro not to challenge me. He sets out his equipment on the little table in front of the mirror: scissors and combs, brushes, liquids and sprays, and a hair dryer with an assortment of nozzles. A hand mirror, which he will presumably use later to show me what my hair looks like at the back, is lying on a stack of magazines. But it slides off the slippery surface of the tower and falls to the ground. Patrice curses and bends down to pick it up. The glass is lying in smithereens on the floor.

'A broken mirror brings seven years' bad luck,' I say.

The hairdresser looks at me, startled, his brown eyes wide, and gives a nervous laugh. How wonderful to be afraid of bad luck— it means, after all, that it hasn't yet found you. I could smash up an entire hall of mirrors and it wouldn't make the slightest bit of difference to me.

Seven years ago my husband disappeared without trace on a business trip to South America. I've been waiting for him ever since, my life on hold—seven years of hopes and fears and a lost feeling so intense that sometimes all I wanted was to wipe every last memory of Philip from my mind.

I've already put seven years' bad luck behind me.

Patrice fetches another mirror without a word. Then he carefully gathers the biggest pieces and sweeps up the rest. I keep quiet and let him get on with it. I close my eyes and run my hands through my hair, very tenderly, as if I were fingering precious lace. Like my mother, many years ago. Like Philip, once upon a time—and no one since. Philip, playing with my hair.

I think of our first night together, water all around us and stars overhead, my wet hair draped over my naked shoulders like a cloak, drops of water glistening on Philip's skin. No sound, apart from our breathing. Darkness. The world suddenly tiny, shrunk so small that there's no room for anyone but us. A cocoon of silence and stars. And Philip's hand in my hair.

'Okay,' the hairdresser says. 'Ready?'

He has cleared away the broken glass and is standing behind me, a pair of scissors in his hand.

I nod.

With his other hand he grasps a hank of my hair and lifts it, then he catches my eye in the mirror.

'Sure?' he asks.

I swallow.

'Sure,' I say.

He puts the scissors to my head and starts snipping.

I can hear my hair screaming. It is a frail, silvery sound, like a whimpering child, like a whisper. I close my eyes.

The hairdresser works in silence, swift and efficient. Soon there is nothing left—nothing to run your fingers through dreamily.

I mourn my hair with three big, silent tears that fall to the ground as softly as the first snow of winter. Then I dry my eyes, get up, pay and leave the salon. Life goes on—at last.

That roller-coaster feeling you get in your stomach when you've done something you can't undo—deliberately smashed up a priceless family heirloom, finally spoken a terrible truth, broken with the past—that feeling is still with me when I get home. I can't put it any better—I'm not good with words. But there's a warm heaving and churning in the pit of my stomach, as if I'd been drinking homemade liquor. My footsteps echo off the walls. This house, rather a grand one, left to me, if you like, by Philip, has been my home for many years, and yet I still feel out of place here. Its cool elegance suits me as little as the long, straight hair I've had hanging down my back all my life, like a fairy princess in a storybook. Maybe it's time to move out, I think—find a place that suits me better. For Leo and me.

I push the thought aside.

One thing at a time.

I go into the bathroom, wash the dust and dirt of the outside world off my hands and look at myself in the mirror over the basin. Since carrying this secret around with me, I have the feeling that everyone must see it in my face, but it's nonsense. My face looks the same as ever. I hazard a smile at the woman with the short brown hair who suddenly looks boy-like rather than fairy-like, and she smiles back. I leave the bathroom, take my shopping bags into the kitchen and am about to start getting dinner ready when I remember something: the plastic bag the hairdresser gave me.

I find my handbag in the hall, open it and take out the bag of hair. I have no idea what to do with it, but I'm certainly not going to hang on to it like a sentimental idiot. There are enough ghosts in this place as it is, and they don't need hair to play with. Without stopping to think, I go out the back door to the covered area where we keep the bins. It feels strange carrying my hair in my hand, holding something that was once part of me.

Telling myself to be strong and get on with it, I undo the loose knot tied in the bag and slide my hair into the compost bin. I close my eyes for a second. There it is again—Philip's hand in my hair, in the small hollow at the base of my skull. My chest suddenly tightens and my cheeks flush warm. For a moment I can't get my breath, but I soon chase away the thoughts I must have brought back from the clearing with me—taunting woodland sprites who go off reluctantly, murmuring and giggling—and then I can breathe again. The lid of the compost bin is still in my hand, and when I look down I can see my hair, lying there among the wilted flowers, coffee filters, potato scrapings, orange peel and eggshells. I look away, clap on the lid and go back inside.

I had been dreading today—the day of the eclipse. For so much of my life I have been steering towards it, and I often wondered what I would feel when it arrived. On that day, I was convinced, all the hurt I had buried, the questions I had forced down, would be washed to the surface as if by a ravaging flood. And now that day has come and almost gone, like so many other days. It hasn't swept me away. I am still here, and the pain and bitterness have subsided. Since leaving the hairdresser's, I feel as if I'd done something thrilling and forbidden, like a teenager who's just smoked her first cigarette on the sly: a little queasy, a little dizzy—but free.

I sort out my shopping, packing everything for Mrs Theis next door into a big paper bag and putting it to one side. I'll get Leo to take it round later. Our old neighbour isn't as steady on her feet as she was and doesn't have a car—I've been doing her shopping for about a year now. Usually I like to have a chat with her when I drop it off, even if she is a funny old stick, but today I don't feel like getting caught up in a conversation.

I have a lot to do. Have to get everything ready for the dinner party and then pick Leo up from Miriam's. I'm hoping to catch my best friend on her own—I need to tell somebody what I've done. Or rather, what I haven't done.

Better hurry then. I take the chicken I bought earlier—free-range, organic—and lay it on the kitchen counter, almost dropping it on the floor. I'm ridiculously nervous. I tell myself it's no big deal. Just a few friends to dinner. No big deal. At least, it shouldn't be. Unless, of course, it's years since you last had any friends round to the house.

Things change, I tell myself. I turn on the oven and take out the olive oil, salt and pepper, the bunch of fresh thyme I went specially to the market for, a few stalks of parsley, a bulb of garlic, a tin of fennel seeds and two lemons, setting everything out on the bench as if preparing for some elaborate game. I examine the chicken, wrapped tight in its plastic packaging. It's years since I cooked a chicken. Leo doesn't like eating meat of any kind. He takes after his father in that respect—Philip turned vegetarian when he was still a teenager, and I followed suit when we moved in together. My guilty conscience pricks me for a second, but I shake it off. Doesn't matter now. I've got guests coming and they're not vegetarian, so we're having chicken—chicken with salad and potatoes.

I take a deep breath, smooth a non-existent strand of hair behind my ear and unpack the chicken. It looks sad and somehow ridiculous, its flesh exposed, with no head and no feathers. At first it's hard even to touch its dead skin—I feel nothing but coldness, the coldness of a corpse. The life that once inhabited this strange little body has long since flown from it, who knows where. It seems bizarre that I am standing here, planning to cook something that once ran about, pecking grain, but I pull myself together and push the thought aside. It's time I stopped thinking Philip's thoughts, it really is.

I take the chicken in both hands, give it a quick rinse under running water and pat it dry with kitchen paper. I cast an eye over the recipe I found in one of my old cookbooks and make sure I haven't forgotten anything.

Then I strip the thyme leaves from the stems, put them in the mortar with a little salt and plenty of olive oil and begin to crush them. When I've finished, and the kitchen has begun to smell of herbs, I dip my hands in the marinade and begin to rub it into the chicken's skin. It feels strange to be doing this, like some archaic, occult ritual: herbs, oils and dead animals. Witchcraft. I watch myself performing these rites as if I were an actor in a film.

When I've rubbed oil all over the chicken, I cut the lemons, crush the garlic and chop the parsley for the stuffing. Once, many years ago, when roast chicken was my favourite food, I could stuff a bird without thinking about it. Now I hesitate, but eventually I grit my teeth and push the lemon, herbs and garlic into the cavity until no more will fit. The chicken is cold on the inside, too, cold and dead, and it couldn't care less what I'm doing to it. What's dead is dead. What is dead feels no pain. What is dead doesn't

11

suffer. What is dead is invulnerable.

I have so often wondered whether Philip is dead, but I could never really imagine it. Sometimes, on particularly dark nights, I have almost wished he was dead. So I could be sure—so I'd know it for a fact. To have it over with.

I put the chicken in the hot oven and begin to peel potatoes. Then a word comes to me.

A word for this feeling of newness coursing through my body.

Afresh. I'm beginning afresh.

The summer is back. In the sky above me, swifts are jousting with the wind. Miriam's front garden reminds me of my beloved gran's—a hotchpotch of marigolds and morning glories, sunflowers and honeysuckle, roses, poppies, delphiniums and dahlias. On the little patch of lawn is a child's bike. Martin's car isn't in its usual spot outside the house, so I'm in time to catch Miriam on her own. I press the bell. Beneath it, a sign decorated with a hedgehog reads in clumsy letters: *Mum, Dad, Justus and Emily.* The second I take my finger from the bell, Miriam appears in the door, looking tired but happy. Her ash blond hair is pulled back into a short ponytail. Behind her glasses, her eyes are slightly red from lack of sleep.

'Oh my God,' she says impulsively. 'Look at you!'

I'm not surprised—I knew she'd be shocked.

Then Miriam gets a grip on herself. 'Sorry, I didn't mean it like that. You look…' She pauses. 'You look great. Different. Older somehow, but at the same time younger. I don't know how to describe it, but I like it.'

I smile at her.

'Thanks.'

'Come on in,' she says. 'The boys are upstairs.'

I adore Miriam's lovely, rather chaotic house, home of the M&M's—Leo's nickname for Miriam and Martin—and their children. There are always toys lying about, always a vase full of brightly coloured flowers from the garden. A faint smell of cooking wafts towards me, and from upstairs come the usual rumbustious sounds of boys at play.

'Calm down, boys!' Miriam calls, but gets no reaction.

She rolls her eyes and I have to smile. I love being here, in this completely normal house with this completely normal family. Emily, Justus's six-month-old sister, will be sleeping peacefully in her cot, oblivious to the antics of her eight-year-old brother and his best friend.

'Is that Sarah?' I hear Martin's voice, and a moment later he is rounding the corner, a drill in his hand.

I hastily swallow my disappointment. Maybe it's for the best.

'Whoa!' says Martin. 'Love the hair!'

I laugh.

'Really?' says Miriam, pretending to be annoyed. 'I only have to say I want my ends trimmed and you launch a major protest, but when Sarah gets all her hair cut off, you love it?'

Martin chuckles. Then he remembers the drill in his hand.

'Oh yeah,' he says. 'I dug this out for you. As promised.'

He holds it aloft for a moment, then deposits it by the front door so that I'll remember to take it when I leave.

'Great,' I say. 'Thanks.'

Martin is always keen to lend a hand when I need something done around the house, but I prefer to take care of things myself. I like banging nails into walls and drilling holes. You perform a simple action and get a clear, predictable outcome. You create order. You get things under control. I love order and control.

14

'So?' Martin says, grinning. 'Have you got something to tell us?'

'What do you mean?' I ask.

'Don't they say that when a woman cuts her hair, there's a man involved?'

'Martin!' Miriam exclaims in horror.

She knows I've been alone since Philip's disappearance. She thinks I need protecting.

'It's all right,' I say. ' Martin's never known when to mind his own business.'

He grins again. 'How's the training going?' he asks.

'Fine.'

I trained for my first marathon with Martin. Since then he's stopped running because he has trouble with his knees, and I've progressed to triathlons.

'You're amazing,' he says.

'Oh, give it a rest.'

I glance at Miriam. Sometimes I worry that it might bother her, Martin showering me with attention the way he does—but she actually seems to like it. I think she feels sorry for me, even now, after all these years. In fact she probably told Martin to be especially nice to me back when we first met, and to offer his help with DIY jobs around the house.

'Will you stay for dinner?' Miriam asks.

'No, I have guests of my own tonight,' I say. 'I can't stay long.'

'Ah yes, of course, the dinner party with your friends from work,' Miriam replies.

I immediately begin to feel nervous. Miriam doesn't notice.

From upstairs comes the sound of muffled laughter.

'I'll go and fetch Leo,' says Martin, starting off up the stairs. He looks back at me, winks and is gone.

Miriam rolls her eyes as if she were annoyed, but really she loves Martin just the way he is. She knows where she is with him. He's not an adventurer or a romantic or a seducer. He's Martin the joker, Martin who likes manning the barbecue, Martin who still wears T-shirts of his favourite rock bands even though he's pushing fifty, who loves to play with the kids, who's fond of telling jokes and then laughs at them louder than anybody else, but without getting anyone's back up, because he's just so nice—because he's Martin. Miriam sometimes complains that he never buys her flowers or springs romantic surprises on her. Privately, I always think, *Not every man can be like Philip*, but out loud I say, 'What do you want with florist's bouquets when you have a whole garden full of the most beautiful flowers?'

'Hello, Mum,' Leo calls from the top of the stairs. He runs down and gives me a hug, oblivious to the fact that I've had all my hair cut off.

Then he discovers the drill and abandons me again.

'Cool,' he breathes, holding it in front of him like a laser gun, taking aim at an imaginary enemy and firing. 'Pew, pew! Pew, pew!'

'All right then,' I say, giving Miriam a kiss. 'We'll be on our way.'

'Take care!' she says.

I smile at her and wrest the drill from my son.

'Bye, Martin!' I call.

Martin's head appears on the landing.

'See you later, alligator,' he calls after me.

I can't see Miriam, but I know she's rolling her eyes.

I feel light as I speed through town with Leo in the back seat, even though I didn't manage to get anything off my chest. I probably couldn't have done it anyway. Some things are just so hard to get out.

My dinner guests all turn up together: my colleagues Claudia and Mirko, and Claudia's husband, Werner. It's strange seeing them here. They look a little out of place—in fact they *are* out of place. They belong at school, not in my house. Mirko has come bearing flowers, Claudia and Werner have brought wine.

All three seem slightly ill at ease. I don't know why. Is it the grand old house that makes them uncomfortable? Do they sense the presence of the ghosts of the past that live here with my son and me? Is it as strange for them as it is for me to see each other here, and not at school—as people rather than colleagues?

'It's lovely and cool in here,' says Claudia. 'The heat's unbearable, isn't it?'

The men agree, and we begin to chat. The ice is broken. They compliment me on my new haircut, which doesn't seem to surprise any of them—unless they are hiding it very skilfully. I take the flowers and wine from my guests and thank them, noticing in passing that Mirko has decided on red roses, which I find strangely inappropriate, although I do not, of course, remark on it. I show everyone into the dining room, where I give them an aperitif. Then I excuse myself, going to put Mirko's roses in water and check on dinner. Leo ate earlier in the evening and is playing in his room. All is well.

When I bring in the food, my guests are engaged in a lively debate about the most recent episode of *Crime Scene*. I realise how much the walls of the old house have longed to be filled with life. It's been a while.

Over dinner, we talk about school—it's hard not to—and eventually we end up discussing one of our colleagues, Katharina. 'Her behaviour's completely unacceptable,' Claudia says. 'The woman is constantly off sick, and when she does come in, she's not prepared. For her, teaching biology means letting the children watch old David Attenborough documentaries on an endless loop.'

She gives a snort of disgust.

'Why is she off so much?' asks Werner, who has no idea who we're talking about but seems happy to join in the conversation anyway.

'Oh, last year she was off for a whole six months. *Burnout*, apparently,' says Claudia.

'You say that as if it didn't exist,' Mirko says.

Claudia shrugs.

'Of course it exists. But seriously, I feel burnt out too—it doesn't mean I sit at home on my backside. Or take Sarah. If anyone has it hard, she does! A single mother and then that terrible business with her husband. But Sarah makes it to work every day!'

Claudia looks at me for approval. I say nothing.

'Don't you agree?' she persists. 'Her behaviour's outrageous.'

'I'm not sure,' I say. 'I don't think I know enough about Katharina's situation to be able to judge.'

Claudia smiles.

It's amazing. Since 'that terrible business with my husband', as Claudia puts it, no one argues with me anymore. No one tells me I'm wrong—I'm never questioned. As if I'd become a moral authority simply because I've suffered and managed to survive. Even argumentative people like Claudia let me say what I like. It sometimes drives me round the bend.

'You're just too good,' says Claudia. 'I don't know how you do it.'

When I've cleared the table and return with the pudding, I find 'Two Truths and a Lie' in full swing, a game that's very popular right now with the children at our school—and apparently with their teachers, too.

'My turn,' Claudia is saying. 'Let's see. Okay. Number one: I've been skydiving. Number two: I once had sex with a rock star after a concert. Number three: I have six toes on my left foot. One of those is a lie.'

'The rock star's a lie!' I say.

'No,' Werner replies with a wry look. 'The rock star's true.'

Everyone laughs, and as Claudia slips off her shoe to show us the tiny sixth toe on her left foot, I realise how much I'm enjoying the evening.

'That was pretty impressive,' says Mirko, when we've all calmed down a bit. 'But yeah, now it's my turn.'

He thinks for a second, glancing in my direction.

'Number one,' he says, running his hand through his blond hair, 'I speak fluent Japanese. Number two: When I was a teenager I rescued someone from a burning car. And number three: I'm in love. One of those is a lie.'

His gaze brushes my cheek. I avoid his eyes.

Werner and Claudia cheer. I open another bottle of wine.

'Hmm,' says Werner. 'Say something in Japanese.'

'What?' Mirko asks.

'Anything,' says Werner.

Mirko spreads his arms in defeat.

'Got me,' he says.

'You can't go falling in love,' Claudia tells him. 'You'll break the heart of every girl in the sixth form!'

I fill everyone's glasses. Out of the corner of my eye I see Mirko looking at me with a smile.

'Your turn, Sarah!' says Claudia, but then I hear a little voice behind me.

'Mum?'

It's Leo, barefoot and in pyjamas.

'What is it, darling?' I ask, putting the wine down.

My son stares wide-eyed at the grown-ups at the table. Claudia and Werner both smile at him, but Mirko gets up and goes over to Leo. He bends down to him, gives him his hand and calls him the 'man of the house', which I find silly—until I see the smile on my son's face.

'Go on up. I'll come and put you to bed in a second,' I say and watch Leo pad off.

Then I turn to my guests to excuse myself, promising to be back down soon.

'To be honest, Sarah, we need to head off soon anyway,' says Claudia. 'Werner has an early start tomorrow.'

'Oh,' I say, 'okay.'

I glance at the clock. It's only now that I realise how late it is. Time really has flown. So I must have had fun. The evening must have been a success.

'It's been wonderful,' says Werner.

'Yes, really wonderful,' says Claudia. 'You'll have to come to our place next time. I'll make my boeuf bourguignon.'

They get up and kiss me on the cheeks. Mirko gets up too. I

lead the way to the front door, say goodbye to Claudia and her husband, thank them for coming, tell them how lovely it was to see them, realise as I say it that I mean it—and watch them disappear into the darkness.

'Such a strong woman!' I hear Werner say to Claudia, and I suppose he means me. I hate it when people say that. *Strong woman.* As if women usually weren't. Strong, I mean.

I turn to Mirko. I thank him for the lovely evening and the flowers. Mirko looks me in the eye and gives me an awkward pat on the shoulder.'

He was the only one who knew it was the first time in seven years I'd had guests in my house. You can tell Mirko that kind of thing.

We're silent for a moment.

'It was about time,' he says and I nod.

Leo is waiting for me. He's sitting in bed, his knees drawn up to his chin, the quilt pulled right up despite the warm night. Leo loves stories. It's a deal we strike every evening—sleep in exchange for a story—but while I pretend to read to Leo for his sake, our nightly ritual is in fact my favourite part of the day. I need the fairytales just as much as my son does. After working our way through the Brothers Grimm last year, we've now started on Hans Christian Andersen. I don't like him much—don't like his strange, dark stories. They're so different to the Grimms' fairytales, where good and evil are so clearly delineated. I find the clarity and certainty of the Grimms' tales comforting, and I'd be happy to read the story of the goose girl again, or even good old Cinderella or Sleeping Beauty, but Leo is obsessed by Andersen's 'Snow Queen' at the moment. At first I thought he was fascinated by the mysterious figure of the queen herself, but what really enthrals him is the enchanted mirror at the beginning of the story.

I sit down on the edge of the bed. Leo says nothing, just looks at me in that calm, unruffled way of his. Sometimes he's so like his father it's almost unbearable. I smooth a damp strand of hair from his face.

'Aren't you hot, darling? Would you like a lighter quilt?'

Leo shakes his head. I suppose he's imagining he's in the Snow Queen's palace, all built of snow and ice, and needs his heavy quilt, even if it is the middle of summer.

'What would you like me to read today?' I ask, though I know the answer already.

'The Snow Queen,' says Leo.

'Right.'

I open the book and begin. I know the words so well by now that I tell the story rather than reading it. I tell Leo how the devil once fashioned a mirror that made all the beautiful things reflected in it dwindle to almost nothing, while all the bad things reflected in it got worse and worse. Leo looks at me with wide eyes that grow wider still when I say the word *devil*.

'But,' I continue, 'one day the mirror shattered, and the little splinters went flying and anyone who got one in his eye saw everything twisted, or only had eyes for twisted things. Some people even got a splinter from the enchanted mirror in their hearts, and those people's hearts turned to lumps of ice.'

It moves me every time to see Leo instinctively clutch his heart at this point and blink like mad, as if he wants to make sure that his heart is not a lump of ice and there's nothing wrong with his eyes.

'Mum!' he says.

I look at him.

'How do you know if your heart's turned to ice?' he asks.

At first I don't know what to say.

You don't feel anything the way you used to, I think. Joy is no longer a frenzied whirl, more a faint smile. Anger is no longer boiling hot, but at most lukewarm. Colours fade to grey, and you no longer know what people mean when they talk of happiness.

I lay my hand on my son's chest and feel his little heart beating, fast and alive. Tears well up, I don't know why, but I blink them back before Leo can see them. He looks up at me intently, his earnest little face close to mine, waiting to see what I'll say.

I force a smile. 'Lumps of ice don't throb.'

Leo nods, apparently convinced. Then he lays his hand on my chest. For a second I have the irrational fear that he won't feel a heartbeat—that one of the splinters from the devil's mirror has caught me unawares, and that I no longer have a heart in my chest—only a lump of ice as big as a fist. My son frowns, pressing his hand down a little more firmly, and then his face brightens. He says nothing—just withdraws his hand and sinks back onto his pillow, satisfied. I fight back the tears rising in my throat.

'Keep reading, Mum,' Leo says.

So I do as he asks, and we set off together through a cold and treacherous winter's night, our hearts pounding.

The silence has returned to my big empty house. Leo has fallen asleep at last—I have breathed a careful kiss on his forehead, switched off the light, left his room and closed the door noiselessly behind me.

I am lying in bed when I hear it.

A strange, indefinable sound.

A...rumbling.

Someone is in the house.

I'm on my feet at once, groping for my jeans, which I've only just taken off, and for my mobile, until I remember that it's on the dining-room table. The landline handset is in the charging dock, at the other end of the house. Damn.

I open the bedroom door cautiously and stop and listen. I stand there as if frozen, all my senses sharpened, but I hear nothing—only my breathing and the familiar creaking of the house. I'm exhausted. I close my eyes for a moment, take a deep breath—and hear it again: a rumbling sound. Now I'm having trouble breathing. Only the wind, I tell myself, but I don't believe it.

It probably isn't wise and I don't know why I do it, but I set off down the dimly lit passage towards the sound. Again I stop, uncertain which way to go, but this time I don't have to wait long before I hear it again. My scalp contracts painfully. I'm scared. The sound is coming from the living room—there's something there, just behind the door, only a few steps away. I hold my breath, rigid with fear, and suddenly all is quiet. I don't know what to do, but I know I can't just turn and walk away. I don't know how I know, but I have to open the door—I have no choice.

Again there is a rumbling, horrible and indefinable. Whatever is on the other side of the door, it's waiting for me. I grasp the doorhandle and push it all the way down. I know I mustn't see what's behind the door—that it will kill me to see what's behind it—but I can't stop myself. As I fling it open, the rumbling sound rolls over me like thunder. I hear myself scream—and at last I wake up.

For a moment I stare breathlessly into the darkness. Don't think about the dream, I tell myself. Go back to sleep. But I can't. I never can. I'm so much more susceptible to black thoughts at night. They creep up on me as I lie here. I think of solar eclipses—the first one, all those years ago, and today's. I think of my son's damp little hand pressing against my chest, trying to find my heart to make sure it hadn't turned to ice. And I think of all those doors, and lurking behind them, all the dangers I can't protect myself against—and certainly can't protect Leo against. I think to myself that the world is a dangerous, dangerous place where I can't survive alone.

It's a long time since I dreamt of the rumbling noise behind the door, and I wonder what it was that triggered the nightmare again—especially now I think I know what's on the other side. I toss and turn in bed, as if the dark thoughts can be scared off like ravens, with a sudden movement, but they are here to roost.

Number one, I think: I'm a cheat.
Number two: I have killed someone.
Number three: I have a tattoo in a secret place.
One of those is a lie.

Summer 2008

The moment just before it happens, he thought—that moment when you know it's going to happen, but before it actually does. That moment is everything.

It was like the fluid, apparently effortless movements that take ballerinas years of practice to master—and at the same time entirely spontaneous. As if by some secret and unspoken arrangement, they began to turn their heads, his blond head one way, her dark curls the other. Then their lips met.

It was their first kiss—he saw that at a glance. The thrill quivering between the two of them was palpable.

He's amazed at how soft her lips are, Philip thought, looking out of the corner of his eye at the young couple sitting across from him. Whenever you kiss a woman for the first time, you can't believe how soft her lips are. No matter how many women you've kissed before, it never fails to astonish.

The two of them were alone in the world. For them, there was no boarding area filled with people sneaking looks at them, no terminal and no airport. No Hamburg, no Germany, no world— only the two of them, only warmth, moisture, breath, lips.

It was, of course, only biochemical processes being played out. The two of them were merely entering into an intuitive exchange of saliva to check for genetic compatibility—that was all there was to kissing. Anything else, thought Philip, averting his gaze at last, is mysticism—romantic nonsense. At once the airport noises around him grew louder, as if somebody had turned up the volume: people talking, announcements, clacking heels, ringing phones, laughter. Philip left his seat by the gate and went for a wander.

Today is my eleven thousand, eight hundred and seventy-fifth day on earth, he thought. Eleven thousand, eight hundred and seventy-four times he had woken up and opened his eyes, always with the same question at the back of his mind: what kind of day will it be today? Then he had lived through the day and gone to sleep again, and eleven thousand, eight hundred and seventy-four times he had lain and dreamed.

An old friend of his had once chosen to celebrate his eleven thousand, one hundred and eleventh day on earth instead of his thirtieth birthday, and since then Philip sometimes did the sums.

As he watched the planes taking off and landing, he took stock of his life. It was important to do this from time to time, so you knew where you'd been, and where you were going.

I had a moderately happy childhood, he thought. I got through my teenage years without any major disasters. I fell in love seven times before I met my wife. I studied business, buried my father, married, fathered a child. I'm the head of a large enterprise and good at my job.

A successful life—a fulfilling life.

But that isn't all, he thought. I've done something else.

Philip ran his hand through his hair, suddenly craving a cigarette although he hadn't smoked for years.

He bought himself a packet and joined the other mute figures in the smokers' lounge.

He couldn't stop thinking about the way he had left Sarah.

He should have told her—should have told her before now, certainly—but he hadn't, and this had been his last chance. He'd drunk his coffee and watched the baby, steadied by Sarah, padding across the kitchen on those fat little legs that never failed to draw squeals of delight from elderly ladies. He'd watched him almost trip over the edge of the cream rug, catch himself, carry on. It occurred to him what a miracle it was to have a wife and a healthy child. He knew he should be grateful, but he wasn't.

This is my punishment, he thought. I knew I'd be punished one way or another for what I did.

Sarah had turned to him, as if she'd felt his gaze on her back, and forced a smile.

Ask me, he thought. Ask me whether I'm all right, how I'm feeling—anything. Ask me one of those stupid questions you always used to annoy me with.

But Sarah had just busied herself with the baby and hadn't given him another glance. He could still see the kink left in her long, loose hair by the hairband she tied it back with at night. He would have liked to touch her hair. On the table, there had been brightly coloured flowers—ranunculus, if he was not mistaken— the only dab of colour in a monochrome room done out all in cream.

The entire house was so awfully beige—almost completely drained of colour—but he hadn't noticed until now. His mother, Constanze, had decorated it entirely to her own taste: beige upholstery, lots of antique wood and, on the walls, framed prints of nautical motifs. They had made very few changes out of respect for the old woman, who after moving to a smaller and more manageable place had been in the habit of inviting herself to tea and deploring so much as the slightest change in 'her' house. After a while, he supposed, they must simply have given up and acclimatised themselves to its cold restraint, the cream-coloured elegance that suited Constanze, but not her son—and certainly not his down-to-earth wife with her love of vibrant colours.

The flowers Sarah bought at the market every week were the only thing that gave the rooms life. He was surprised that she still found the time for such details—for agreeable, pointless activities like buying flowers and trimming them and arranging them in vases. But perhaps it was precisely such small, unimportant details that kept Sarah going.

From the outside, their marriage looked the same as ever, but things between them had changed. He had forgotten the simplest things: how to stroke your wife's hair or kiss her goodbye, how to play with your year-old baby—sometimes even how to breathe. When had they begun to slip out of control? Was it really on that fateful night? Or had it started before that?

As the time approached for him to leave, Philip had struggled with his conscience. Should he tell her? He'd watched the hands on the kitchen clock jerk forward, minute by minute, until it was too late to broach the subject. He'd given Sarah a kiss on the forehead and turned to go.

Sarah had always come to the door with him and watched him leave when he was setting off on a long journey. Countless times she'd stood in the doorway, waving until he was out of sight. He'd felt her gaze on his back as he got in the car—seen her grow smaller and smaller in the rear-view mirror as he drove away. At first he'd thought it sweet, then he'd come to regard it with indifference. At some point he'd started to find it silly, and in the end he'd stopped noticing. But on this day he was glad of the ritual. It meant that she still loved him, and he knew now he couldn't take that for granted.

And somehow it had been nice to know what was coming as he set off on his trip. That small, loving gesture that said: no matter what accusations we've hurled at each other, no matter how many spanners Constanze has thrown into the works, no matter what has happened, we can keep going. He had been grateful, and it had pleased him to know that he was still capable of feeling some kind of emotion.

He had gone out the door, feeling Sarah's gaze on his back as always, and resolved to do something he had never done before because it had always seemed faintly ludicrous to him. He resolved to get into his Mercedes as usual—and then lower the window and wave to Sarah. She would see him wave and know that he still loved her. And she would smile. Unselfconsciously. The way she used to.

Philip had gone down the front steps, turned to face Sarah and smiled—just in time to see her close the door and disappear into the house. That was it. No wave, no ritual, no comfort. Only the milk-white front door, flanked by a number eleven.

As he got into the car, he could taste autumn in the air—tiny particles of the first frost and rotting leaves—the way cats supposedly smell approaching death in the fatally ill. On the way to the airport it began to rain. Grey rods, as thick as bars, connected sky and earth.

Queasy from the cigarette, Philip stubbed it out and returned to the gate to sit down—this time as far as possible from the smooching couple. Most of the black vinyl seats were occupied by businesspeople, grey men like him, tapping away at their laptops or phones. Only a handful of obligatory tourists were scattered between them, as garish as exotic birds.

Earlier, rummaging around for his ticket, he'd discovered that Sarah had put an apple in his bag. He didn't know whether this pleased or annoyed him. If he'd wanted an apple, he'd have taken one himself. His wife's strange mixture of patronising solicitude and coolness—what was it all about?

He watched the people in the terminal building, each hurrying towards an uncertain fate, and as so often of late he was overcome by the thought that free will was a mere illusion. He wasn't moving freely through life, but travelling on tracks that led him this way and that, regardless of what he wanted. It wasn't up to him to take this turning or that, to choose between right and wrong, kindness and malice, love and hate. All he could do was hold on tight when the train took a bend, and occasionally stick his head out of the window and enjoy the feel of the wind in his face. Everything was hurtling towards some predestined end. He himself, Sarah, Leo—everything, everyone.

He'd never had thoughts like these in the past—none of this had started until that damn night. But maybe he was deceiving himself. Maybe it had all begun much earlier. He went over the situation again, step by step, as he had so many times in the past few months, and as always he felt overwhelmed by the force of what had happened. It was as if a freight train had crashed into him at full speed—a train he had had no chance of stopping. He searched his memory, but found no moment when he might have acted differently from the way he did. When had the train been

33

set in motion? Was it when they'd left home that fateful evening? Or before? He found no answer to these questions.

Still, he should have told Sarah. Even if she didn't deserve it.

Philip took out his phone and called Sarah's number, but then hung up straight away and put the phone back in his pocket. You didn't deal with that kind of thing over the phone.

He would tell her—of course he would—as soon as he was back.

My eleven thousand, eight hundred and seventy-fifth day, he thought. A day I'll be spending almost entirely on an aeroplane.

From his seat in departures, Philip could see the planes taxiing to the gate and taking off. He leant back and watched them shoot along the runway and slowly overcome gravity. The summer rain had stopped, and the sky was a mixture of dirty grey and streaky blue.

I could stay, Philip suddenly thought.

For weeks, he'd wanted only one thing—to get away—but now the thought of boarding a plane that would take him further away from everything that mattered to him with every passing second was almost unbearable. South America—what the hell did he want in South America?

I could stay, he thought again—not board the plane, not run away, but do the right thing for once.

The smooching couple had vanished. He looked across at their empty seats as if they held the answer.

I could take a later plane, Philip thought. Or none at all.

Eleven thousand, eight hundred and seventy-five days, he thought.

I have a lot. I have a lot to lose.

What do I want?

What kind of day will it be today?

He still hadn't made up his mind when his flight began to board.

Sarah

The lions are tired. They lie sluggishly in the summer sun, their bellies slowly rising and falling with their breath. My son looks at them for a few minutes, then pulls me away towards the meerkats, who are more entertaining than the boring old lions. At least the meerkats do something.

I hate zoos—hate looking at caged animals,—but Leo begged and cajoled me for so long that I ended up caving in. He's off school for the summer and most of his friends will be going away with their parents, so a trip to the zoo is the least I can do. Besides, it does me good to get out of the house. I can't stand being bored, so I need some way of occupying myself in the summer holidays. I never say it out loud because I don't want to be thought strange, but I don't look forward to the holidays. I like the rhythm my work gives the days and weeks and months. I like the discipline, the knowledge that when I get up I'll go jogging, have a shower, make breakfast, take Leo to school, go to work—that I teach German and English from Monday to Friday and art too on a Friday. That when I come home, I'll help Leo with his homework, tidy up, clean, cook, and then, depending on the day of the week, help out in the refugee shelter, meet up with Miriam or work out.

Leo tugs impatiently at my hand, bringing me back to the present. I see what he's pointing at and have to smile at the teeming bustle of meerkats.

'Mum,' he says, after we've watched them in silence for a few minutes, tightly wedged between the hordes of visitors who flood the zoo at this time of year, 'can I have an ice-cream?'

'Of course, sweetie.'

To get to the ice-cream van we only have to walk round the elephants' enclosure to where the children with pink and brown smeared mouths are streaming from. The queue is a throng of excited children and weary parents. By some miracle I discover a free bench only a few metres away. I give Leo some money and sit down while he queues up by himself, nervous but proud. I close my eyes for a second, enjoying the feel of the sun on my skin. The horrors of last night are already far away.

I open my eyes again and find myself staring at the elephants. They are in a kind of dusty yard, a small group of them huddled together like dejected smokers whose break is coming to an end, their unloved work beckoning. To my left, a solitary elephant stands in front of the wall, swaying its head back and forth, shaking it from left to right, over and over again. It's as if it were in permanent denial of its situation: I am on the African savannah. I'm not here in this tiny, dusty enclosure—no, I'm not—no, no, no, no, no. I tear my eyes away from the distressing spectacle and look around for Leo, who has moved forward in the queue but is still a long way off being served. I catch his eye and he smiles at me, all gappy teeth and dimples. If I had a lump of ice instead of a heart, like in Leo's favourite fairytale, it would melt on the spot.

I turn my attention back to the animals. Being locked up is the worst, I think, and I picture myself coming back at night and opening the enclosures. I imagine the animals leaving their cages, pouring out of the zoo and filling the town—baboons attacking cars stuck in the rush-hour traffic; leopards silently climbing the trees in city parks and fixing their gaze on unsuspecting joggers, their eyes narrowed to slits; elephant families tramping side by side along the broad shopping streets, reflected in the shiny glass of the shop fronts; giraffes, their big eyes wreathed by long lashes, staring in at the upper windows of office blocks as startled workers spill black coffee over their white shirts.

'Mum, your phone's ringing,' Leo says at my side. I jump slightly—I hadn't noticed him sit down beside me, a cone piled high with soft ice-cream in his hand. He licks at it diligently, his face serious, as he concentrates on winning the race against the implacable sun.

I fumble in my handbag for my phone, expecting it to be Miriam, or possibly one of yesterday's guests—maybe Claudia, who left her silk scarf behind, or perhaps Mirko. But it's a number I don't know.

I'm immediately uneasy, though I know it's foolish. I don't like to answer the phone when I don't know who's calling. You never know who's on the other end and what they might be about to tell you. For a moment I toy with the thought of letting the call go through to my voicemail, but then I remind myself that Leo is with me, that Leo is all right—very much all right even, with his enormous ice-cream running stickily over his fingers—and that as long as Leo is sitting next to me, grappling with his ice-cream, there can be no catastrophe. I take the call.

'Hello?'

'This is Wilhelm Hansen,' says a sonorous, official-sounding voice. 'Is that Sarah Petersen?'

I frown.

'Speaking,' I say.

'Mrs Petersen, I work for the Foreign Ministry. I'm so glad I've managed to get hold of you. I've been calling your landline all morning while we tried to track down your mobile number. We have some important news for you and didn't want you to hear about it from the press.'

My mouth is suddenly very dry.

'You didn't want me to hear about it from the press?' I repeat.

I know what he's going to say. This is the call I've waited seven years for. I know it is, and yet I can't believe it. It feels like a dream. Any minute now I'll find myself, trembling and fearful, before a closed door from which a dull rumbling sound is emanating.

'Mrs Petersen, are you sitting down?' the voice asks.

'I'm sitting down,' I say.

I've had seven years to prepare for this call. There's nothing this man can tell me that I'm not ready for. There's no scenario he can confront me with worse than the ones I've thought up as I lay awake night after night. He will tell me, and then, at last, I'll be able to start over again. Start afresh—wasn't that the word?

I swallow.

'Tell me,' I say.

There is a very brief pause before he speaks. I listen to him in silence. When the call is over, I put the phone back in my handbag, do up the zip, put the bag down beside me and begin to vomit.

'm sitting in the garden under my favourite apple tree. I know it must be hot, but I feel cold. The world looks so different, as if someone has dropped a filter over it that makes everything more intense. Everything dazzles me: the sky is bluer, the leaves on the trees fluorescent green, and the sun so bright it hurts my eyes, even through my sunglasses.

Philip used to have the same effect on me: bringing colour to my sometimes drab world, lighting up grey days or gloomy moods with his lust for life and his humour and enthusiasm, colouring in my life the way a child colours in pictures in a book with thick wax crayons.

I'm glad there's nobody here—Leo playing inside, my neighbours nowhere to be seen—because I need a little time alone to give my brain the chance to process everything. I sit under the apple tree as if I were waiting for enlightenment, like Buddha under the Bodhi tree. Three words go round and round in my head like a mantra.

Philip is alive.

He's alive.

A ginger and white cat skirts the fence. It stops for a moment, throws me a glance, then decides to ignore me and disappears into the next-door garden. I wonder where its twin is—there used to be two cats, playful little things from the same litter. I never found out who they belonged to, but Philip used to like them.

I'm sitting here, trying to get my head round things, when suddenly something swells in my chest, a feeling too big for my body, too big for my narrow ribcage. I'm bursting—this is unbearable. I can't sit here any longer, so I get up and head back to the house and go to the phone. I can't keep it to myself any longer. I have to tell somebody—tell somebody or explode.

But as soon as I have the phone in my hand I'm stumped.

Who to call?

My first impulse is to ring Miriam. She's my only real friend, the person I go to when I need to talk. But Miriam didn't know Philip—we didn't meet until after he'd gone missing. It seems wrong to call her first.

Family, I think. I should call his family first. But Philip's father, from whom he inherited the company, died years ago, and his mother has Alzheimer's and barely knows what's going on around her. Like me, my husband has no brothers and sisters—I had no family at all until I met Philip and we had Leo.

My finger is still hovering over the telephone keys. I hesitate. I suddenly feel a strong urge to ring Johann. Johann Kerber is an old family friend of the Petersens, someone Philip looked up to and went to for advice, and whose shrewdness, level-headedness and fatherly counsel I relied on when Philip went missing. It was Johann who saw to all the financial and administrative details that needed dealing with, and there was a lot to sort out—Philip was, after all, the most important stakeholder in the business. Nothing will please Johann more than to hear that he's been found alive and is on his way home. But the second I enter his number, I feel guilty. Of course Philip's mother should hear the news before anyone else. Alzheimer's or no, it would be wrong not to tell her first. So I leaf through my little black address book and find the number of the nursing home.

The phone rings only once before a resolute female voice answers.

'Hello, this is Sarah Petersen,' I say. 'Could I speak to my mother-in-law, please?'

'Oh, Mrs Petersen,' the voice replies. 'I'm sorry, but your mother-in-law isn't in a good way today. I'm not sure it would be wise to speak to her on the phone—it's likely to confuse her. But you could drop in if you liked. You can come and see your mother-in-law any time—there's no need to call first.'

I feel another stab of guilt. I haven't been to see Constanze for ages. I've been too wrapped up in myself and my own troubles.

'Thank you,' I say. 'I'll drop in as soon as I can.'

I hang up and call Johann's mobile. It rings and rings, but no one picks up. I curse under my breath and then look up Johann's office number, which he gave me for emergencies and which I have never used.

A woman answers almost at once, friendly but businesslike.

'Hello, this is Sarah Petersen,' I say. 'Is Mr Kerber there, please?'

'Mr Kerber is away on a business trip,' the woman replies.

'Oh yes, of course,' I say, remembering. He had been going to Beijing for a few days. 'When will he be back?'

'He'll be back in three days. Would you like to leave a message?'

'No, thanks,' I say. 'Do you know how I can get hold of him while he's away?'

'I can't give you Mr Kerber's private mobile number, I'm sorry. Perhaps you'd like to ring again when—'

'It's all right,' I say. 'I already have his mobile number. I'll try it again later. Thank you.'

I hang up without waiting for a reply and immediately enter Johann's mobile number again in the absurd hope that he might have switched on his phone in the few minutes I've spent talking to the woman at his office.

'Come on, come on, come on,' I mutter, but this time I get a recording of a bored voice telling me Johann is currently unavailable, and I hang up. By now I'm in a kind of frenzy. I have to speak to Johann. I curse again, think for a moment, but there's nobody else I can ring. I decide to try Miriam's number after all. Once more I wait impatiently for the call to go through, almost expecting it to be engaged or ring out, but then I hear a familiar voice.

'Martin Becker speaking.'

'Martin! Hello! It's Sarah.'

'Super Sarah!' cries Martin.

He likes calling me that, as if I were some kind of superhero. For once I ignore it.

'Can I talk to Miriam?'

'I don't know. Can you?' Martin replies, and I can almost hear his crooked grin down the phone.

I usually have a lot of patience for his jokes, but today is different. I have to talk to somebody right now.

'Is she in or not?' I ask, making an effort to control my voice.

Martin notices that I'm not in the mood for jokes.

'No, she's out shopping while I keep an eye on the kids. Everything all right with you?'

'Everything's great,' I say. 'There's something I wanted to tell her, but it will have to wait.'

'Suit yourself,' Martin replies.

42

I say goodbye and hang up. I can't get my breath. I try Johann's mobile one last time, but it's engaged. I go back into the garden.

It's even hotter than it was. A few fair-weather clouds are moving lazily across the sky and I can make out some of the animals I saw at the zoo today: a baby elephant, a tiger, a polar bear. Only seconds after stepping out of the house, I can feel the sun beating down on my head. Nothing is stirring in the neighbourhood—everyone is holed up indoors, trying to escape the sweltering heat. No screeching teenagers in the neighbours' pools, no juddering lawnmowers, no children swinging in the cherry trees. All I hear is the gentle hum of the bees as they go about their day's work, hovering from flower to flower, oblivious to heat and holidays.

Once again I have the sudden feeling I'm about to burst. My stomach lurches like it did at the zoo, and I lean forward, pressing my palms against my thighs. I close my eyes, count my breaths, and the nausea vanishes, leaving only a faint dizziness. I feel a strange sensation somewhere beneath my breastbone, a bubbling, hiccuping feeling in my chest, which rises higher and higher and then breaks out. I'm giggling—softly at first, but then I roar with laughter, on and on for who knows how long.

Suddenly I start, hearing a voice to my right, behind the fence that separates our garden from that of old Mrs Theis, our neighbour. Mrs Theis is well into her eighties, sprightly, outspoken and something of an eccentric. She doesn't like children (apart from Leo) and says she's been a great deal happier since being widowed. Nothing against her husband, she says, but some people are made for solitude and she happens to be one of them. She always has cat food in the house, although she has no cats of her own—in case a hungry stray should drop in, she says. She regularly bakes cakes, although she doesn't like cake, simply because she likes it when the house smells of baking. I adore her.

'Sorry to startle you, my dear,' she says.

'Hello, Mrs Theis,' I say. 'Are you well?'

'Mustn't complain,' she says. She holds aloft a little basket of raspberries she has clearly just picked. 'The gardening keeps me as right as rain!'

She hands the basket over the fence, and I take a berry and pop it in my mouth.

'They're as sweet as sugar!' I say. 'Thank you!' I try to hand the basket back to her, but she refuses.

'They're for you and Leo,' she says. 'I know how much you both like them.'

'That's so kind of you,' I say. 'Leo will be very happy.'

Mrs Theis gives a dismissive wave and turns back to her gardening. I watch her in silence for a while. She's like a sort of surrogate grandma to Leo—and, indeed, to me—but she doesn't have much to do with the other neighbours. They think she's crazy, and she is, but she's harmless.

'My husband's coming back,' I burst out. 'Philip's alive. They've found him!'

I couldn't hold it in any longer—I had to tell someone. Why not dotty old Mrs Theis?

She looks up at me and frowns, as if wondering whether she's heard right. Apparently she decides she *can* believe her ears.

'How extraordinary!' she says. 'After all this time!' She looks shocked at first, but then seems to decide it's good news, and beams at me. 'That's lovely, my dear. I'm so pleased for you, really I am.'

'I've only just heard,' I say. 'He's alive. He's coming home.'

It occurs to me that it's the first time I've said it out loud. I begin to sob and soon I can't stop. Mrs Theis only stands and

44

stares. Maybe she doesn't know what to say.

Finally I collect myself. 'Excuse me,' I say, 'I'd better be going back in. Got a lot to do. Thanks again for the delicious raspberries.'

Inside it is cool. In the kitchen I tip half the raspberries into a little bowl, which I put in the fridge for Leo. Then I sit down on the kitchen floor and thrust the rest of the berries into my mouth, one by one.

Leo looks at me wide-eyed. The words I have just spoken are still reverberating in the air. I thought long and hard about how to tell him—where to tell him and what words to use: 'Your father' or 'Dad'? 'He's coming home' or 'He's alive'?

I tried to remember what it's like to be eight. To climb the highest tree without fear because you don't yet know that you're mortal. To fiddle around with your wobbly milk teeth until they fall out, and think nothing of it. To dig tiny graves for dead birds you've found in the grass, make them little gravestones and hold funerals for them, serious and giggly by turns because you've never been to a real one. To run everywhere, all the time, just because you can.

'Dad's coming home,' my son repeats, as if turning the words over and over, trying to see them from all sides and work out what to do with them.

For Leo, Philip is no more than an idea. His father is just one of the many heroes in the stories Mum tells him, sitting on the edge of his bed every evening, a fairytale prince, lost in a faraway foreign land.

Now he's confused and I can't blame him. I wish there were more time—time to explain everything, to let him to get used to the idea gradually. But there is no time, neither for him nor for me.

Philip is coming home.

Not sometime—tomorrow.

Leo wraps his arms round me in silence. We sit there like that for a while. Poor Leo, it must all be a bit much for him. I'm about to ask him what he makes of it all and how he's feeling when I notice that he's breathing very slowly and steadily. I realise in astonishment that my son has fallen asleep.

stand naked in front of the mirror, trying to see myself objectively.

The woman in the mirror is neither tall nor short. She is slim, with close-cropped hair that gives her a boyish look and makes her appear younger than she is. Her skin is tanned, her breasts small. On her left hip she has a tiny, faded-looking tattoo: a small butterfly. She looks slightly unsure of herself.

I try to work out how I've changed in seven years.

Am I still the woman Philip remembers?

Have I aged?

How much have I aged?

I come up with no answers. And anyway—what's the point in worrying myself over it?

Once, not long before he went missing, Philip told me that he didn't believe in love—that there was no way love could exist. I have no idea what we'd been talking about before that, but I remember frowning at him.

'When we think we love someone, do we really love that person?' Philip asked. 'Or do we just love the feeling that person gives us?'

I rolled my eyes.

'Of course love exists,' I said.

He smirked, as if I'd fallen into a carefully laid trap. 'But if love exists, how could we ever *stop* loving? If it's not the feeling we love, but the actual person, how could we ever stop loving them?'

I didn't have an answer then, but it's a riddle I've often come back to since.

I tear my eyes away from the mirror and get dressed. It's another hot day, so I slip on a loose, airy dress and a pair of light sandals with a low heel. I glance in the mirror again. In my white summery dress I look a little like a bride, only without a veil. I feel a little like a bride too—as excited as a timid young woman on the threshold of a new life, wondering what is waiting for her on the other side.

I go into the next room to see how Leo's getting on. He's reading a comic and seems more or less unfazed by the situation. Perhaps he hasn't yet realised that his life is going to change dramatically today—that it won't just be the two of us any longer.

The doorbell rings and I flinch, startled.

'Let's go,' I say.

We're gliding through town in a mercilessly air-conditioned four-wheel drive. I'm cold in my white summer dress, my teeth softly chattering. Mr Hansen from the Foreign Ministry looks just the way I imagined him: tall, slim, elegant, fifty-ish, small glasses. The driver, in his dark suit and mirrored sunglasses, is straight out of Hollywood.

We drive in silence. I had another brief talk with Hansen yesterday but gleaned little new information. Yes, Philip had been kidnapped in Colombia. No, they didn't yet know why there hadn't been a ransom note—maybe there was a communication failure, or the kidnapper got cold feet. Yes, of course it was being looked into—the local authorities were on the case. Yes, those responsible would be called to account. Yes, Philip was now safe. Yes, his health was satisfactory, although the experience had, of course, left its mark on him, physically and psychologically. He didn't go into detail about the abuse Philip suffered in the remote jungle camp, perhaps because it made him uncomfortable, but it was clear that the last seven years of my husband's life had been even worse than I'd always feared. Mr Hansen said Philip had asked about me, about our son. Had I remarried? Did Leo even remember him? Was his mother still alive?

Hansen also warned me that there were bound to be a lot of journalists and photographers at the airport. Poor Philip, I think. He always did his best to avoid the media, never liked having his photo taken or answering questions, and let the company's publicity department handle media events and press conferences. When he disappeared, the police asked me for a photo of him, and I had trouble finding one. If my mother-in-law is to be believed, he was camera-shy even as a child. I was always glad that Philip refused to be a public figure—that there were no photos of him shaking hands with politicians and investors with a fake smile on his face, that ultimately he belonged only to me and Leo and to his work. Will that change now? Will we be besieged, taken apart, dissected?

I feel Leo's hand seeking mine. He is staring out the window. Just the two of us. I've almost forgotten anything else. Maybe I should make the most of the last moments.

And then Hamburg airport suddenly rises before us like a mirage. We are there.

sometimes have the feeling that the world is a stage set. We step onto the tarmac—goodness only knows how Hansen managed to get permission. The small private plane, carrying Philip and the team accompanying him, is going to land a short distance from the major airlines. Everyone is sweating in the sun, but I still feel cold. I run my hand through my short hair. Leo is jumping up and down excitedly at my side—he loves planes so much I think he's forgotten why we're actually here—and I have to smile in spite of the strain. I am grateful that we've been permitted to watch the plane land here, and I try to ignore the dozen or so reporters who have taken up position behind us.

In my head, I go over the words I've prepared, but suddenly, now that I'm here, they feel somehow wrong—fake and stilted, like lines from a monologue. But what else can I say to him? I think of my talk with Leo this morning and decide to follow my own advice and simply say what I feel.

It's so good to have you back, I think.

Yes, that feels right.

It's so good to have you back.

I repeat the words in my head, like a mantra.

'Are you all right?' Hansen asks and I nod.

I don't know why everyone keeps asking me that—Mrs Theis, Miriam and Martin when I called with my news, even Leo. My husband is alive. Of course I'm all right!

We stand around in silence, not really knowing what to say.

'There,' says Hansen pointing up in the air.

I follow his gaze and see a plane approaching.

I take my son's hand and we look up at the plane together.

It's so good to have you back, I think, as the plane begins its descent.

It touches down on the airfield, shoots past us and almost stops. Then it starts to roll again, turning and moving slowly—unbearably slowly—towards us, until it comes to a standstill. I scan the little windows, looking for Philip, for his familiar face, though I know it's silly of me. Philip's somewhere in there and that's all I need to know.

It's so good to have you back, I think. *It's so good to have you back.*

We stand there for what feels like forever, but even Leo doesn't pester me or complain. He too only stares tensely.

Then the door of the aeroplane begins to open—this too happens unbearably slowly—and my heart lurches. There are people. It's them. Philip—where's Philip? I smooth a non-existent strand of hair behind my ear. Then there is movement at the door. I freeze completely, while around me all hell breaks loose: a storm of flashes, pushing and shoving, shouts, cameras pointing at me, photographers calling my name. I ignore it all, my hand clutching Leo's, my eyes on the door of the plane. I'm not going to miss this—I'm not going to miss the moment when Philip steps through that door, back into my life. Nothing is happening, though, and I'm beginning to think it's all a mistake—that something's gone dreadfully wrong, that Philip isn't on the plane at all, that the plane is empty, no pilots, no crew, no passengers, a ghost flight—when a small group of people suddenly emerge, one at a time, and climb down the steps to the airfield: a tall blond woman in a black tailored suit, a dark-haired man in jeans and a jacket, a man of about sixty in a grey suit, another woman, this one with short, snow-white hair, a flight attendant (and another, and another) and then a man and woman, both in pilot's uniforms. My nerves aren't going to last much longer. Where is Philip? I try to breathe steadily as the little group steps onto the airfield. I tell myself that I have waited seven years and can hang on for a few seconds longer, hardly noticing that the photographers and journalists' shouts are getting louder and louder. In the eye of the storm, I am calm. I ignore the people around me and the people trooping towards us, my eyes fixed on the cabin door.

And then it happens. It is such an ordinary, everyday sight that at first I don't realise what it means: the cabin door is closed and the steps are wheeled away.

I frown. This is all wrong. That's the plane that was supposed to bring Philip home, but Philip hasn't appeared yet and someone has wheeled the steps away—how is he supposed to get off the plane? I stare at the shut door: no Philip. No Philip.

Somebody grabs my elbow. I barely register the physical contact, but I start slightly all the same. The little group has reached us; reluctantly, I turn away from the cabin door to face them.

Where is Philip?

Why wasn't he on board?

What's the matter with him?

Has something happened to him?

Nothing can have happened to him; it can't have done, not after all he's been through.

The dark-haired man and the tall blonde woman are almost upon us. Mr Hansen says something to me, but I don't understand.

I'm only just beginning to register the noise and chaos around me. 'There he is,' Mr Hansen repeats.

I don't understand and follow his gaze, helpless, distraught. The photographers' shouts grow louder: 'Mr Petersen! Mr Petersen!' And in that instant, the stranger with the dark hair raises his arm in greeting, gives a brief wave in the direction of the press photographers—and then turns his attention to me. I feel his gaze weighing on me and can only stand there. I still don't understand, but I feel that something is expected of me, a few words, some reaction—anything. But I can only stand there, my head buzzing. Something is going dreadfully wrong here. Massively wrong. I stand there, my shoulders hunched, as if to protect myself from a gale that only I can feel. The Somebody at my side fills my silence, saying: 'Mr Petersen, I am Wilhelm Hansen. On behalf of all the team I would like to say: Welcome back.'

And the man says: 'Thank you, Mr Hansen.'

His voice is low and rasping. It is the voice of a stranger.

The world stands still. The laws of time and space no longer apply. Weightlessness. I look down and notice that my feet are no longer touching the ground; I stretch my toes, feeling for a foothold, but find nothing. I am floundering. I try to cling to something but everything else is floating too: objects, people. At first I am only a few centimetres above the ground, then suddenly a whole metre, two metres, ten. I flail my arms and legs, but there is nothing I can get hold of—no resistance; only emptiness. I am rising, higher and higher, as high as treetops, as high as skyscrapers, slowly and inexorably, while beneath me the world grows smaller and smaller.

Then, all of a sudden, gravity is back and I fall. The world hurtles towards me; I come down hard.

And here I am again, back on the airfield, my feet on the ground.

The stranger is standing in front of me. He looks at me expectantly. Then, when I make no sign of reacting, he approaches me in silence, his movements jerky and robotic—he's not like a person, I think, he's like an automaton—and presses me to him. I give a gasp of alarm and try to back away, but can't. It's as if I'm paralysed. The stranger doesn't let go.

I stare at the man before me—stare into his face, looking for a sign of recognition, but find nothing. It isn't that Philip was tall and strong, while this man is hardly bigger than me—nor is it the beard which covers his cheeks so that I have no way of knowing whether the stranger has dimples like Philip. It isn't even the strange way in which this man moves.

It is his eyes, which lack all warmth. The hair on my neck stands on end. However exhausted the stranger may look, there is a disturbing energy emanating from him.

THAT. IS. NOT. PHILIP.

am caught in a nightmare so grotesque that my brain can't make sense of it.

Who is this man?

Why is he holding me so tight?

Why is everyone calling him Mr Petersen?

I shake my head like a shying horse.

Do they really think it's Philip?

I can't get my breath.

They really think it's Philip. What's going on here? I don't understand. Why is he doing this? Who is this man? I've never seen him before in my life. Why is he here? Why is he pretending to be Philip? How can he have the impertinence to touch me, and where— where the hell is my husband?

I can't get my breath, panicking, suddenly afraid that the stranger is going to squeeze the breath out of me, right here, in full view of everyone.

But then the man loosens his grip. I gasp for breath as bright spots spread at the edge of my field of vision, the first signs of a blackout. But no, I'm not going to black out now—I have to say something. It's important, very important—but I can't think straight, can't speak, can't find the words to express all my horror and shock, all the questions in my head. Feeling dazed, I try to choke out a protest, but the words that come out are the ones I've rehearsed.

'It's so good to have you back.'

The stranger smiles. It seems I have said exactly what he wanted to hear. Then he crouches down beside me and only now do I remember that I'm still holding on to Leo, whose little hand is glowing warm and damp in mine. He holds on tight, shooting me a worried glance when he realises that the stranger is trying to greet him. Misinterpreting my stern look, he lets go of my hand reluctantly and lets the stranger pick him up. My son in his arms, the stranger turns to the photographers. The flurry of flashes intensifies. I'm in a kind of trance. As if from far away, I hear the stranger saying he's happy to be home. He'd like to thank everyone for coming, but he hopes they will grant him and his family the privacy they need to get back to their everyday lives.

I look around me. Is this a joke? It can't be a joke—no one would be so cruel. Even so, I look around again, waiting for an explanation. A cold shudder runs down my back, from the nape of my neck to the base of my spine.

The people around me are looking at the stranger and smiling. The stranger is looking at me.

He isn't smiling.

I look about me in desperation. I can't be the only one who notices that this isn't Philip! But then I examine the faces around me—the reporters, the officials—and I realise that I'm the only one here who actually knew Philip and knows what he looked like. There aren't even any official photos of him, so these people don't have a clue.

My legs give way. I stumble and only just manage to catch myself. I can't collapse here—not in front of all these people, in front of my son, in front of the stranger.

'Everything all right, Mrs Petersen?' The tall blond woman from the plane sounds concerned.

I nod, but of course I'm not all right. Philip is still missing, and that man—the man holding my son and smiling, exhausted but satisfied, into the cameras, while the photographers go wild—that man is not my husband.

I shake my head again and step towards the stranger to take Leo away from him. Leo's too big to be picked up in any case—it's ridiculous, he's eight years old—but at that moment the stranger sets him down. I pull Leo close, a little too abruptly, and he opens his eyes wide in surprise, but no one notices except him and me. All eyes are on the stranger. It makes me wild to hear them all calling him Philip. I'm still trying to gather my wits when the Foreign Ministry officials set off across the airfield towards the airport building, sweeping us along with them. The journalists throng behind us, and a few photographers overtake us at a run, to get a clear shot as we enter the building.

The stranger walks in front of me, talking to the white-haired woman who got off the plane with him. I look around frantically and find myself staring into a sea of unfamiliar faces. Where is Hansen? I have to speak to Hansen!

We're surrounded by a crowd of reporters and I'm struggling to keep my panic in check, almost hyperventilating, at the same time trying to keep an eye on Leo, who has let go of my hand. A small gap opens up between the two men behind me and I see Hansen's calm, dignified face. I cast a glance in Leo's direction. The friendly blond woman who spoke to me earlier is walking with him. She bends down to him and says something, but in the way you speak to an adult, not a small child, and Leo replies, smiling proudly. He likes being treated like a big boy. There's too much yelling going on around us and I can't hear what they're talking about, but Leo seems okay—that's good. I turn and elbow my way through the crowd to talk to Hansen. Two men give me annoyed glances as I push past them, but they say nothing. Hansen looks at me with slightly raised eyebrows. I'm having so much trouble breathing that I can hardly speak.

'That's not my husband!' I blurt.

Hansen frowns, and for a moment I'm filled with the childish thought that everything is going to be all right now—that Hansen will take care of things, that he'll say he too had his doubts, and he'll sort out this mistake.

Hansen shakes his head slightly. 'Sorry?' he shouts, to make himself heard above the screaming photographers. He puts his hand to his ear to signal that he hasn't understood.

I take a deep breath and am just about to shout at him that the man isn't my husband—that it's all a terrible misunderstanding—when the crowd around us suddenly slows and stops. We've reached the entrance to the airport, but it's blocked by photographers. Hansen raises an index finger, as if to signal that he'd better go and sort things out but will be right back.

'Wait!' I yell as he turns away, instinctively clutching at his arm, but he looks at me in such horror that I let it go again. 'That's not Philip!' I say.

'I'll be right back,' Hansen replies, as if I'd said something utterly banal that could be taken care of later. Then he disappears from view. Panicking, I look around again and see that Leo is still talking to the nice blond woman. My gaze wanders—and meets the stranger's. His look goes right through me.

I turn quickly away. I see that Hansen is talking to the photographers at the entrance to the airport—that he has been successful—that the way is clear. We set off again. Once more I fight through the crowd to Hansen. I come level with him and enter the terminal at his side.

'Mrs Petersen,' he says, 'everything all right?'

'No,' I say. 'That's not my husband!'

Hansen peers at me through his expensive glasses, and I have the feeling he's suppressing a sigh.

'I appreciate that this isn't easy for you,' he says. 'But your husband has been through a lot. I'm sorry I wasn't able to prepare you better for the reunion.'

I'm speechless. Is it that he doesn't understand or that he doesn't want to?

I take a deep breath. 'No, please listen!' I say. 'That's not—'

'You'll have to excuse me,' Hansen says, interrupting me. 'My colleague over there is calling me.'

Is he running away from me?

'Mr Hansen!' I call after him. 'Mr Hansen, please listen to me!'

But he's already halfway across the terminal. I look about me and see that we've crossed the arrivals hall and are coming to the exit.

A snatch of conversation reaches my ear: 'How does it feel to set foot on German soil again?'

I spin around to see where the voice is coming from. The white-haired woman from the plane is still talking to the stranger who claims to be Philip.

No, I think. *No, this is all wrong.*

Someone takes my elbow. I see the friendly face of the blond woman who was so nice to Leo.

'Mrs Petersen, what's wrong?' she asks.

'The man—'

She frowns. 'What man?'

'The man,' I say. 'That man there. I don't know him.'

The woman gives me a sympathetic look. 'It must be a lot to take in,' she says, as the crowd sweeps us to the exit and spits us out of the terminal. 'It's almost as though your husband has come back from the dead—it must seem completely unreal.' Then she turns and begins to rummage in her handbag. 'Here's my card,' she says, holding it out to me, and I take it mechanically. 'If there's anything you need, just give me a ring, all right? But first you must have a rest.'

'Don't you understand?' I say—no, shout. I know I need to keep calm if I want to be taken seriously, but I am angry and my anger wins out. 'Don't you understand? That's not my husband. That's not Philip.'

My voice is drowned out by the pandemonium around us. The photographers have realised that we're going to be gone any second and are determined not to pass up the chance of a last photo. If the woman did understand what I said, she clearly didn't consider it necessary to take action.

I'm seized with panic again, and instinctively turn to search for my son, but I can't see him. I turn round and look back at the airport, all the time being propelled forward by the people around me, onto the pavement, on and on. Where is Leo? Where is my son?

I suddenly can't see the stranger anymore, either, and for a few hideous seconds I think that my worst nightmare has come true—that a monster has come and carried off Leo.

'Where's my son?' I ask, addressing the question to no one in particular and receiving no reply, but then, between the broad backs of the two men in front of me, I catch a glimpse of him. I push my way through to him and take his hand. There are so many people around us, elbowing and jostling—but where is the stranger? I don't want him popping up at my side all of a sudden with his frightening eyes, don't want him touching my son again. The crush is getting worse until suddenly I feel a hand in my hair, gently but firmly pushing my head down. At first I don't understand what's going on, and I try to shake the hand off, but then the man in front of me steps to one side and I see that I'm standing at the kerb, that there's a car parked there, that people are trying to bundle us into it, and I let them, because all I want is to get away from here, far away—the din around us is deafening and the press of bodies is suffocating. I feel Leo squeezing my hand, tighter and tighter—it's all getting a bit much for him, and no wonder, we're being crushed!

'Mummy,' says Leo.

I don't hear the word—I lip-read it.

'It's all right, sweetie,' I say, managing to manoeuvre him onto the back seat. I'm about to get into the car myself, desperate to get away, when I feel someone gripping my arm. I turn around. The stranger. He lets go of my arm before I can jerk it away, leans in. His voice is just a whisper.

'I know what you did, Sarah. I know all about it, and you're not going to get away with it.'

He draws back, smiling at me, as if he had just told me how happy he was to see me. I stand there, unable to move. Frozen.

'Mummy?'

It is Leo's voice that brings me back to life, and somehow I get into the car. I've only just sat down when first the stranger and then Hansen get in the car, too. The door slams shut behind us and the screams of the photographers are suddenly muffled. Within seconds the car is moving. I can't breathe.

Next to me is the stranger.

burst into the bathroom, only just making it in time. I lift the toilet lid and lean over the bowl. My stomach seizes up a few times and I retch heavily, feeling the tears rise to my eyes. I vomit in spasms, cold sweat on my forehead, and as always when I have to throw up, I think I'm going to die—that it's never going to stop—that I won't just spew out the contents of my stomach, but all my inner organs and eventually my soul, until I'm no more than an empty husk, slumped on the tiles like a deflated rubber doll.

Then it's over at last. I heave myself up and flush the toilet, shivering all over and bitterly cold, my clothes clinging damply to me. I can hardly stand. This is how it must feel to be poisoned.

That Leo is safe with my best friend and her family is my sole consolation now. He proclaimed in the car that he wasn't coming home with us, throwing a tantrum when I tried to soothe him, crying and sobbing and pummelling me with his fists. I knew he could be like that, but I hadn't been expecting it. He'd been so calm and collected this morning, bordering on indifferent. He must have picked up on my own fear and panic, must have smelt it in the air. I was trying to seem calm, but Leo saw through it, and it freaked him out. Mummy is never scared—but right now she is terrified.

The stranger gazed out of the window as if it were none of his concern, while Wilhelm Hansen stared at us, a look on his face that I couldn't read. Concern? Mild disgust? It was his suggestion that we drop Leo off at a friend's house, and I immediately agreed. My mind was racing. Miriam. Maybe this was an opportunity. Should I let Miriam know what had just happened? Would she be able to help? Or would that make matters worse?

The stranger turned his head, looking at me as if he'd read my thoughts.

When the driver stopped at Miriam's house, Leo flung open the door and jumped out of the car as if he were fleeing the scene. I wanted to get out, too, but the stranger held me back.

'Mr Hansen, would you be so kind as to escort my son to the door, please?' he said. 'I'd like to talk to my wife in private for a moment.'

Hansen hesitated, then nodded and got out of the car. I watched him catch up with Leo.

'I don't know what you were planning at the airport,' the stranger said, his voice low. 'But if you think you can get rid of me that easily, you're mistaken.'

What was I supposed to say?

'What did you tell Leo?' he asked.

I watched my son vanish into Miriam's house. Hansen was speaking to Miriam, explaining, gesturing back towards the car.

'Nothing,' I said.

And then Wilhelm Hansen was back, and the driver took us home.

In the bright light from the window, the stark white of the bathroom suddenly reminds me of an operating theatre. I sit down shakily on the side of the bath, knocking a slim phial of bubble bath, which falls into the tub with a clatter. The noise strikes me as unnaturally high and loud. I watch the little bottle roll to and fro until it comes to rest. Bright spots swell in my field of vision and for a moment nothing makes any sense. Everything is smooth and white: cold, white tiles; the smooth, white surface of the bathtub; a white basin, a white orchid, white towels, white soap dispenser, white shower curtain. Only a few dabs of colour: the narrow bottle in the bath, filled with liquid—sapphire blue; a small diving mask with a snorkel—fluorescent green; a tiny plastic Darth Vader figure—black; a squeaky duck—shocking pink. And me. I look down at myself—at my tanned legs, sticking out from under my white dress—at my cherry-red toenails. I blink. I feel the cool, smooth surface beneath me. I feel my arms breaking out in gooseflesh and stare at the tiles in front of me. The white flickers before my eyes. A tap drips—*plink, plink, plink*—getting louder and louder—*plink, plink, plink, plink*—but I can't get up and turn it off; I have to sit here and wait for the numbness to pass—the trembling, the dizziness. The faint smell of a scented candle on the edge of the bath rises to my nose. I've forgotten what it is that smells like that—vanilla? lemon? amber?

My heartbeat is only slowly steadying.

I am so angry at myself. How could I have failed to make myself heard at the airport? Why didn't I insist on speaking to Philip on the phone before he arrived? Since when have you been such a pathetic little mouse, eh, Sarah? Pull yourself together, I think. Get up! Do something!

I get up and go over to the basin. I rinse my mouth and splash cold water over my face.

Good. Now think!

I think, although the gears in my brain are grinding slowly and my teeth are chattering. Today my husband, my darling Philip, should have come home, and instead there was a stranger on the plane. I was in shock, and allowed myself to be bundled into a car with him and driven home. But now I'm here, in my own home. I've got a grip on myself. I have a moment to think before I go back outside.

I have no idea what the stranger's plans are.

What could he possibly want from me?

I have to ring the police.

Immediately.

I turn round. My hand is on the doorhandle when I hear it. Footsteps.

I feel my heart grow small and hard with fear.

When I left the stranger and Wilhelm Hansen sitting in the car and burst into the house, fighting back the vomit, my hand to my mouth—did I make sure the door clicked shut behind me?

I swallow heavily.

The stranger is in the house.

The twittering of birds comes in at the bathroom window; my gaze shifts to the garden. The rich green of the horse chestnuts gleams in the sun, against the dark blue of the sky. Soon the trees will throw down their conkers onto the heads of passers-by like tiny bombs. Mothers like me, who still make things with their children, will fashion little people out of them, with matchsticks for arms and legs, before sending their sons and daughters off to football practice or the games console. It is almost as if the idyllic summer's day were mocking me.

The stranger and I are alone in the house. Instinctively I feel for my phone, which I always keep in my pocket—but my white dress doesn't have pockets, so my phone must be in my handbag, which I dropped somewhere in the hall. I curse under my breath. If I want to ring anyone—if I want to call for help—I'll have to leave the bathroom. I'll have to go out into the house. I sit down on the toilet lid and bury my face in my hands. I wish I hadn't gone to the airport alone; I wish I'd had somebody at my side. Why does Johann have to be away just when I need him, for Christ's sake? A few minutes pass. Outside the bathroom door it's quiet, but I know the stranger is there. I run my hand through my hair, my fingers trembling. I can't stay in here for ever.

Get up! I think—and I get up. I count to three under my breath.

Open the door, I think.

I open the bathroom door—and the stranger is standing right in front of me.

He smiles.

My anger gets the better of my fear and I take a step towards him. 'This is *my* house,' I say.

He bows his head and turns away. His short beard is uneven—beneath it I can see his jaw muscles working—and he's taken off the jacket he had on at the airport, revealing tanned arms. There is something peculiar about the way he holds himself.

'Who are you?' I ask.

'Who are *you*?' the stranger says.

I stare at him, perplexed.

'What do you want from me?' I ask.

'What do *you* want from *me*?' the stranger says.

For a moment I'm thrown.

'What are you doing in my house?'

'What are *you* doing in *my* house?' he says.

Shaken, I take a step backwards. He's crazy!

'Who the hell are you?' I ask, almost whispering the question.

The stranger raises his eyebrows. 'I'm Philip,' he says. 'Your husband.' The corners of his mouth twitch. He seems to find this amusing.

My body feels utterly numb. Is this a dream?

'You're not my Philip. I've never seen you before in my life.'

He laughs openly at me, making no effort to hide his derision. 'You're right,' he says. 'I'm not your Philip.'

Almost without knowing what I'm doing, I raise my right arm and give the stranger a resounding slap on the face.

'Where's my husband?' I hear myself scream. 'Where's Philip? What have you done to him?'

Quick as a flash, he grabs my arm. I try to pull back, but I don't have a chance. He draws me up close to him and stares into my face. 'I'm your husband,' he hisses. 'You *love* me—remember?'

'Get out of my house!' I yell, pushing him away with a shove to the chest that momentarily throws him off balance. 'Get out!'

I grab him by the arm and try with all my strength to drag him towards the door, gasping for breath, tears of hatred in my eyes. He resists and pulls himself free.

'Get out of here!' I shout. 'You can't seriously think you'll get away with this.'

He just stares at me, all calmness and composure. Suddenly he no longer seems crazy at all; he looks as if he knows exactly what he's doing. He spreads out his arms in silence, as if to say: *I already have done*.

I think of the airport—all the people, the photographers. I think of tomorrow's papers. There will be a photo of the stranger holding my son—and beneath the photo, Philip's name. I think of myself, surrounded by journalists, letting the stranger hug me, speaking that fateful sentence: '*It's so good to have you back*.'

'I'm calling the police,' I say.

'You need to calm down,' he says.

I push past him towards the living room, the phone. I expect him to block my way, try to stop me, attack me physically. He does nothing of the sort, but as I pick up the phone, I realise he's followed me.

'You're being ridiculous,' he says calmly.

I press the receiver so tightly to my ear that it hurts, but I hear nothing—no dialling tone. I look up. The stranger is holding the telephone cable in his hand. He has unplugged the phone.

Panic seizes me when the stranger suddenly takes a step towards me; we are alone in this big empty house and I know nothing about this man, nothing. My eyes flit around the sitting room in search of something I could use in self-defence and come to rest on the big windows looking out onto the garden. One of the windows is ajar; I can hear lawnmowers and laughing children. It all seems so surreal: I'm in here with a strange man and outside it's a beautiful summer's day.

'I warn you,' I say, 'if you come any closer, I'll scream the house down. The neighbours will call the police.'

My voice shakes; I don't know whether from anger or fear or both. That was a lie; there's no one out there except perhaps old Mrs Theis and a few children. The neighbours on the left are away. And Mrs Theis's lawnmower is roaring.

'Is that really what you want?' he asks, coming a step closer. 'You want to talk to the police?'

'I warn you,' I repeat, more to bolster myself up than because I have any real hope of rescue.

The man stares at me. He shakes his head for a long time, over and over, reminding me a little of the depressed elephant at the zoo—except that the elephant looked sad, not dangerous. I look around for an escape route; I have to get out of here, that much is clear.

He takes another step towards me. I retreat, and he steps forward again.

'If you were my husband,' I say, desperately, 'you'd have no reason to be afraid of the police.'

He laughs. Our eyes meet; again there is an amused glint in his.

'I'm not the one who should be afraid of the police,' he says.

Slowly, very slowly, as if in pain, he crouches down. Then there is a soft click and I realise that he has plugged the phone in again. The stranger pulls himself up to his full height and looks at me, quiet, self-confident, almost as if he's challenging me.

'Would you like to call the police?' he asks.

A second passes, two seconds, an eternity.

'I didn't think so,' he says.

The stranger

Keep going.

Do what has to be done.

I clench myself like a fist, keeping everything I can't use right now on the inside.

That way, no one stands a chance against me.

Keep going, just keep going.

Don't stop.

Sarah

It is now late afternoon. I have been frantically making phone calls, deciding to ignore the stranger's threat, and my horror at the situation has only grown.

When I picked up the phone again, the stranger shot me a mocking glance.

'I'm not calling the police. I'm calling your good friend Wilhelm Hansen,' I retorted, realising I wasn't making any sense, that this would not make any difference to him whatsoever. But to my surprise he just smiled, and I'm beginning to realise why.

It won't be so easy to get rid of the phoney Philip, especially now that I've as good as acknowledged him as my husband in front of rolling cameras. Mr Bernardy of the crisis management team, to whom I'd spoken briefly yesterday, simply shook me off—of course Philip's identity had been thoroughly vetted—although I could, of course, make an appointment to see a member of the team in the coming week if I still had reservations.

'Reservations'—he actually said 'reservations', as if this were a completely innocuous concern rather than a matter of life or death.

Hansen had his secretary tell me he wasn't around—or else he really wasn't.

The stranger looked on calmly, as if amused.

And now we are standing here, facing each other in silence, while I wonder what to do next. It is another hot summer's afternoon, but I have gooseflesh. I clench my teeth to stop them chattering. Sunbeam falls lazily through the window onto the parquet. I see little motes of dust dancing in the light like elves in a fairy ring and prefer to look at them than at the stranger. His face with its cold, hard eyes is strangely beautiful. Who knows what is going on in his head? I am so glad Leo isn't in the house.

'I have to sit down,' says the man.

I watch in anger as he makes his way slowly and cautiously across the living room towards the sofa. He looks at me as if I were a terrified child he doesn't want to scare any worse. Then he lowers himself onto the sofa. I don't like that; the sofa is where I lie with Leo to watch cartoons, or documentaries about meteorites and dinosaurs. Next to it is the stranger's luggage: a medium-sized dark brown leather holdall, not big enough for anything but the bare essentials.

I had made up my mind not to talk to him again, but I can't help myself.

'What is it you want from me? Come on, tell me,' I blurt out. 'Is this some kind of sick joke?'

He blinks.

'Oh, it's no joke, Sarah, believe me,' he replies.

It infuriates me, the way he says my name—as if he could somehow bring us closer by persistently calling me by my first name. It's sickening. Besides, Philip almost never called me by my actual name, but of course the stranger can't know that. We stare at each other. I don't know why he's keeping up this charade; it must be clear to him that he can't fool me. Perhaps he's afraid I might somehow unmask him if he steps out of his role for even a second. Maybe he's scared that I'm secretly recording him, or that someone might overhear him.

Silence sets in again while I try to come up with a plan. The stranger's gaze weighs heavy on me.

Before long he gets up again.

'All right then,' he says. 'Enjoy your telephone pranks.'

He takes his bag and disappears towards the kitchen.

I stand quite still, listening out. I hear his footsteps recede, a door click shut. I ought to follow him, but my body won't obey me. I am simply glad not to be in the same room as him anymore. I stand there in the living room, blinking, looking around me. There is the cream sofa where I often sit with Leo in the evening, its cream cushion covering a cocoa stain. There is the armchair I read in and beside it the little orange tree, which has just started to blossom and gives off a heady scent. There is the television, the stereo, Philip's shelves of records and next to them my bookshelves. There is the windowsill, the framed family photos: Leo, Philip, me. I pinch myself, which makes me feel stupid, but I feel the pain in my arm—as if through an anaesthetic, it's true, but I feel it, just as I feel the floor beneath my feet. All this is real—it's really happening. It's not one of my nightmares—there's no door with horrors lurking on the other side, no rumbling sound, no incubus sitting on my chest, sucking the breath from my lungs.

I'm not about to wake up sweaty and crusty-eyed but relieved. No one is going to wake me.

I can think now, though, without the stranger watching my every move. I can't expect any help from Bernardy and Hansen—I know that now—but what about the tall blond woman who gave me her card at the airport? I dig the card out of my handbag. It has nothing on it but her name, Barbara Petry, and a telephone number—both in straight black writing.

I dial the number and hold my breath. She picks up after the second ring.

'Barbara Petry?'

'Hello, this is Sarah Petersen.'

'Mrs Petersen—what can I do for you?' she asks.

I have to swallow. 'I urgently need your help,' I say. 'Could you come round briefly?'

'Has anything happened?'

How can I put it to make her take me seriously?

'I know it sounds crazy,' I say, 'but the man you and everyone else think is Philip Petersen is not Philip Petersen. I don't know who he is, but he's not my husband.'

There's a pause before she replies. I expect her to ask what's going on.

'I'll set off right away,' she says instead.

I thank her, tears of relief pricking my eyes. I blink them away.

'But of course,' Petry says. 'That's what I'm here for.'

I sit down on the sofa and stare at the framed sailing ship on the wall. Constanze gave it to Philip and me years ago and I've never liked it, but it's a consolation to me now in an utterly unreal situation. I almost have the feeling that the ship is moving on the waves. Out of the window I can see the neighbour's lawn, where four ravens are hopping about on the grass. I remember my grandmother telling me she couldn't stand ravens; they were birds of death. Nonsense, my mother had replied, but she didn't like them either because they frightened off the songbirds. Soon, she said, there would be no blue tits or robins left, no nut hatches or sparrows—only ravens and crows. I was as old as Leo is now and I loved robins and blue tits; in the winter I was allowed to feed them. After that, I threw stones at the ravens to scare them away—until my mother put a stop to it.

The ravens outside make throaty noises. Where have they come from all of a sudden? Disturbed, I avert my eyes. Close them for a moment.

Immediately, the photographers' shouts sound in my ears: 'Mr Petersen! Mrs Petersen!' And then Hansen's voice: 'Mrs Petersen? Everything all right?'

My thoughts wander and I remember that Philip used to call me 'Mrs Petersen' whenever I annoyed him, whenever he thought me too severe or too serious. It used to make me wild. I didn't like my surname—could never really get used to having Philip's parents' name instead of my parents'. It hadn't been an easy decision, and we'd argued for nights on end, weighing up the pros and cons over red wine and takeaway pizza. In the end Philip suggested playing rock, paper, scissors, which was what we always did when we couldn't come to an agreement—we were going to do it too, we had decided, when choosing names for our children, because Philip was adamant on Arthur for a boy and Linda for a girl, while I preferred Leo and Amélie. At any rate, we played for my maiden name and I lost. I was never a good loser.

I recall one of our trips to the North Sea. I was heavily pregnant. We were sitting on a towel on the sand, breathing in the smell of suncream and the sea and arguing about some nonsense or other.

In the end, Philip raised his hand and said, 'Okay, you're right, Mrs Petersen. Let's stop arguing.'

'You see?' I said, more argumentative than ever. 'That's what I mean—it was the same with that name.'

Philip groaned.

'Really, Sarah? I can't believe you still hold that against me. We bet—you lost. Do we have to keep coming back to it?'

'You tricked me,' I said.

'Okay, now you really are being ridiculous. You can't cheat at that game—that's the whole point.'

'I don't know how you did it,' I said. 'But I'm sure you cheated.'

'You think I'd do a thing like that?' he asked, honestly indignant.

'The thing is, you're used to getting your own way, whatever happens. It probably isn't even your fault.'

'What do you mean by that?'

I didn't reply.

I just told myself that my son would definitely be called Leo.

Fight or no fight, I wish I could stay forever in my memory of that day on the North Sea. But I have to face up to reality.

Maybe I shouldn't be sitting here—maybe I should get up and go in search of the strange man wandering around my house.

No, I think. No rushing into things.

I have no idea what the stranger wants from me, but it's not going to be my problem for much longer. I only have to hang on a little while—only until Barbara Petry gets here. It's best if I stay exactly where I am until then.

I don't know how long I stare at the wall like that, waiting. The stranger doesn't reappear. In the end my whole body is quivering with impatience. I can stand it no longer.

Where has he gone?

The stranger

She's in the next room.

She's on the phone. I'll wait for the moment.

The boy isn't here. That's a good thing.

I'm in the kitchen.

I drink a glass of water.

I take food out of the fridge.

I don't feel hungry, but I eat anyway.

Chew, swallow, keep going.

It was a long journey. But now I'm here. I can find out the truth.

I feel strong.

Whatever she does, I'm not going to be put off my plan.

Sarah

I find him in the kitchen. The place where I read the paper and drink coffee, where I make jam, cut sandwiches for Leo and sit at the table with him in the evenings while he tells me about school—that a certain teacher is stupid, that the new boy in his class seems all right, who's been in a fight on the playground, which of the children in his class have smartphones, how many goals he's shot.

When I enter the room, the stranger looks at me, completely relaxed. He has obviously had a shower and got changed—his hair is wet and shining, and he's dressed in black jeans and a black T-shirt. He's leaning back in the chair, feet on the table, hands behind his head. I know that male pose—take up space, flaunt your dominance. He has a bottle of cold beer in front of him and is eating ham from a packet that Miriam brought when she came for breakfast the other day. I feel sick at the smell of it, and now that I'm standing in front of the stranger, I've forgotten what it is I wanted to say.

'Sarah,' he says, playing the host, 'come and sit down.' He takes his feet off the table and pushes the ham across to me, then folds his arms behind his head again. 'Hungry?'

I shouldn't answer, but instead I say, 'I don't eat meat. Neither does my husband.'

The stranger laughs. 'A vegetarian with ham in her fridge,' he says.

Before I can reply, the doorbell rings. The stranger starts and his eyes narrow to slits.

Hugely relieved, I head for the front door to let in Barbara Petry, almost tripping over my handbag in the hall. I gather it up, hang it on a coat hook, smooth my clothes and open the door.

In spite of the searing heat, Barbara Petry looks as if she's stepped out of a fashion magazine. She seems to be one of those people who never sweat.

'Mrs Petry,' I say, giving her my hand, 'thank you for coming so quickly. Come on in.'

I lead her into the kitchen, trying to put my thoughts in order. She got off the plane with the stranger, so she must have accompanied him on the flight, and presumably met him some days before that. She will have read reams of information to familiarise herself with his history, with the details of his case, and then, in an emotionally charged moment of high drama, met the spurious Philip, never once doubting that she was dealing with a hostage who had been through terrible things and needed protecting. I am curious to see how they greet one another.

'He's in here,' I say as we reach the kitchen—and then stop in disbelief.

At the kitchen table is an exhausted-looking man who bears the marks of a long journey. He seems weak, almost fragile, sitting slumped in his chair, smiling wanly but warmly at Barbara Petry. The beer and ham have vanished—only a faint whiff of smoked meat lingers.

'Barbara,' he says, so charmingly that I almost retch again.

He gets up, carefully, as if in pain. Crows' feet appear at the corners of his eyes as he gives Petry his hand, and she smiles back, obviously bowled over by his charisma, his warmth, his charm. She too is dressed in black, I notice—two black figures, and me in my white frock. Chessmen.

'Have a seat,' I say, in an effort to take control of the situation.

'Thank you,' says Barbara Petry. She sits down, hanging her elegant black handbag over one of the kitchen chairs and momentarily turning her back to the stranger. His glare then is like ice, but as soon as Petry turns to face him again, he resumes his friendly mask and busies himself fetching her a glass of water—playing the host again—before he sits down.

And so here we are at the kitchen table—Barbara Petry at the head, and the stranger and I facing each other on either side of her. It is warm in the kitchen—sunlight streams in at the big window that overlooks the garden, and glancing out I see a beautiful summer day, its calm, heavy quiet broken only by the buzz of a bumblebee. The ravens, I am glad to see, have gone.

I force myself to focus on the present. This should really be quick and straightforward. This isn't my husband, so what's he doing in my house? I don't need a mediator—I need someone who'll take the stranger away so that I never have to see him again and can finally get on with my life.

'All right then,' Petry says. 'How exactly can I help?'

Her gaze rests on me, and all at once I feel as if I'm facing an examination panel—the racing heart, the red ears, the terror of saying the wrong thing, although I've learnt all the vocabulary, all the formulae, all the dates.

I've already told her what the problem is, but she seems reluctant to believe me. Still, she is here—she must have taken me seriously. I pull myself together to make sure I don't say anything that sounds crazy.

'First of all, thank you very much for coming,' I say. 'And at such short notice, too.'

The woman gives me a smile that does not reach her eyes. What can she be thinking? I hesitate, knowing how important it is to find the right words. I look down at my hands on the table, and my eyes fall on my wedding ring. I noticed in the car that the stranger wasn't wearing one. I take a deep breath.

'I realise that what I'm saying must sound completely insane. And I also realise that you don't know me and have no reason to trust me. But I assure you that this man here is not Philip Petersen. I've never seen this man in my life. He looks like Philip, yes—but not so much so that you could mix them up. Anyone who knew Philip personally will confirm that for you.'

The stranger sits there motionless, staring down at the table, only once shaking his head briefly as if hardly able to believe my foolishness. Barbara Petry opens her mouth, but I don't let her speak. I know what she's going to say—that 'my husband' was of course vetted, but that it's no wonder I feel overwhelmed by the situation. It's nothing unusual, not the first time she's witnessed this kind of thing.

'I'm sure I don't have to tell you, Mrs Petry, that my husband is an extremely wealthy man. As I'm sure you can imagine, that makes someone in my circumstances a target for frauds. It doesn't seem unreasonable to expect to be taken seriously when I say that this man is *not* my husband—he's an impostor!'

For a second, Barbara Petry seems thrown off balance.

'What reason would I have for lying?' I ask.

The stranger gives an almost imperceptible snort, but neither Barbara Petry nor I fail to notice.

'Okay,' says Barbara Petry, without answering my question. 'Can you give me some slightly more precise grounds for your doubts?'

Out of the corner of my eye I see that the stranger is no longer studying the grain of the kitchen table, but looking straight at me.

'I don't have *doubts*,' I say, finding it hard not to shout. 'I'm certain. And I don't need to give grounds. That is not my husband! This isn't a matter for discussion!'

Barbara Petry puts her fingertips to her temples as if to massage away a headache, but quickly replaces her manicured hands on the table when she realises.

I have disappointed her. She was prepared to believe me, I think, or at least willing to give me the benefit of the doubt, but she assumed I'd have some kind of evidence.

Suddenly the stranger speaks, and I start.

'You just said that everyone who knows me will know at once that I'm not Philip,' he says, his gaze shifting between me and Petry. 'Why don't we ask someone? Someone who knows me? Would you be convinced then, Sarah?'

It infuriates me that he calls me Sarah like that, as if we knew each other. I've had enough of this madness.

'Nothing—nothing at all—could convince me that you are Philip Petersen.'

He knows all about me, of course—he knows, the bastard, that I have no family, that Leo and I are alone. But no sooner have I spat these words out than I realise what he's done. His suggestion

85

can only sound constructive to Barbara Petry—and I've rejected it out of hand. If I refuse to get anybody else involved, it will look as if I'm afraid to be proved wrong.

'But I'm not the one who needs proof,' I say, turning to Petry. 'If it would help to convince you, of course I'd agree. Ask whoever you like—anyone will confirm that he's not my husband.'

'All right then,' Petry says after a pause. 'Who would you suggest?'

I think for a moment. Philip's father is dead, and his mother, Constanze, is out of the question—no doubt the stranger already knows that already. But there is Johann, of course. A smile steals onto my face. Why didn't I think to suggest this myself? He's played right into my hands.

'How about Johann?' the stranger asks.

I look at him in alarm. He knows Johann? How does he know Johann? Where has he heard about him?

'Who's Johann?' asks Barbara Petry.

'Johann Kerber is an old friend of my family who took me under his wing when my father died,' says the impostor. 'And I know he's someone Sarah trusts too—at least, she used to.'

Inside, I fall apart, but I don't let it show.

'Johann's abroad,' I manage to say eventually. 'He's on a business trip in China. I've tried to get in touch with him several times to tell him that Philip had been found, but he hasn't been available.'

'When does he get back?' Philip asks.

'In three days, according to his secretary,' I reply. 'But I can't wait that long.'

'No, of course not,' Petry says. 'But I'm sure this Johann isn't the only person who could confirm your husband's identity.'

'He's not my husband,' I insist.

Petry briefly closes her eyes.

I am not going to let anyone say that man is my husband, no matter how much it annoys Barbara Petry. That is not my problem—it's hers.

'Now,' she says, 'there must be someone who could help us clear up this...' She hesitates. 'This business.'

I think of Constanze, unable now to recognise her own reflection, and Philip's only remaining relative except for Leo and me. I can't think of anyone else—no other family, no one at work he was particularly close to. He'd been the boss—he'd always tried to keep a bit of distance. He still saw a couple of friends from university, too, before he disappeared, but no one I'd know how to find now. I lost touch with them a long time ago. What was all this nonsense, though? Shouldn't my word be enough?

Barbara Petry sighs when I don't reply. She seems to regret coming. I feel a sudden rush of saliva in my mouth.

'Excuse me for a moment,' I say hoarsely.

Barbara Petry and the impostor are silent.

I leave the kitchen with head held high, but break into a run as soon as I'm out of sight. I slam the bathroom door behind me, kneel down at the toilet bowl for the second time and vomit in hard painful spasms. Then I rinse my mouth and prop myself up on the basin to stare at my reflection. My eyes are black with anger.

Not with me, you don't, I think. I've been through much worse than this. Much worse. Not with me.

The stranger

Getting other people to like you is easy. I sit hunched up. That makes me smaller, less menacing—it emphasises my physical exhaustion. I run my hand over my eyes as if I can hardly keep them open. I blink a few times. Then I look up and smile bravely.

Keep going. Get rid of Barbara Petry, then we'll see.

'What's going on here?' she asks, her voice lowered.

'My wife's not in a good way,' I say vaguely. 'I think it was all a bit much for her today. She just needs some rest.'

Petry frowns.

'Your wife's behaviour doesn't seem to surprise you,' she says.

'No,' I say, with a faint sigh. 'I'm afraid it doesn't surprise me in the least.'

'You've seen this before?'

I nod. 'Yes,' I lie, 'more than once, I'm afraid. But don't worry. I know how to handle it.'

Barbara Petry's expression is inscrutable. 'I don't want you to overdo it,' she says. 'You're in dire need of rest yourself.'

'I'm all right,' I say. 'But please promise not to mention this to anyone. It would be embarrassing for Sarah, once she's herself again.'

Barbara Petry holds my pleading gaze for a moment—then her expression softens. 'Of course not,' she says with a little smile. 'Of course not.'

Sarah

M y eyes fall on the lotus-white bathtub and a picture flashes
through my mind. I see Philip and me in the bath together,
a beer on the edge of the tub for him, apple juice for me. My bump
is sticking up out of the bubbles. Philip is relaxed and happy; I see
his dark eyes, his dimples, and as he takes a gulp of beer, billions of
tiny iridescent bubbles run down his chest and—

Why didn't I think of it before?

I leave the bathroom and head back to the kitchen.

'What did you miss most, apart from your family?' I hear
Petry ask.

'Schnitzel and schnapps,' the stranger replies, and Barbara
Petry laughs.

I haven't been gone five minutes and he already has her

wrapped around his little finger. They really are acting as if they were having a cosy chat over coffee. I feel the gall rising again.

'I'd like to ask him a few questions,' I say.

A steep line appears on Barbara Petry's forehead. She glances questioningly at the phoney Philip.

He hesitates. 'Maybe it's not a bad idea,' he says, and the feigned compassion in his voice makes me feel more nauseous than ever. 'Maybe it would help Sarah if I answered a few questions.' He runs his hand over his face. 'I'm just so ridiculously tired,' he says. 'The stress, the long flight, the jetlag…' He trails off.

'You don't have to do this,' says Petry feelingly. 'We'd understand if you'd rather be left in peace for the moment. After all you've been through.'

There's no missing the reproach in her voice. I'm going to have to persuade her—but the stranger knows about Johann, what else does he know about Philip? And, indeed, about me?

'It's all right,' says the stranger. 'Whatever helps.'

'Okay then,' says Petry. She looks at me expectantly.

I take a gulp of coffee, but it's no use playing for time. I'll never come up with a surefire way to persuade her that quickly. I decide to plunge straight in.

'When's Philip's birthday?' I ask.

'Twenty-seventh of January,' the stranger replies like a shot. 'Same as Mozart's,' he adds smugly.

That was easy, of course. Anyone could have googled that. I'm just warming up.

'When's Leo's birthday?'

The stranger smiles—this question too he answers with confidence. 'I can't believe I'll be here for his next birthday,' he adds. 'I thought of him every year…'

'When did Philip and I get married?' I ask, interrupting him.

I'm not going to let him talk about my son.

The man looks at me. He seems confused.

'Early summer,' he says after a while.

'I want a date,' I say.

'Oh God,' he says, and his eyes dart to and fro between Barbara Petry and me. 'Oh God, I've forgotten. I…oh, yes, I do know…I just can't remember. I—'

'What did I wear at our wedding?' I ask. I'm not giving up now.

Barbara Petry sighs. 'I think that'll do for now,' she says.

'No!' I shout.

Petry gets up, evidently fed up with the whole business. 'Mrs Petersen, I have the impression that there's no convincing you, no matter how many questions your husband answers.'

'That's not my husband,' I retort, getting up too. I can hear how stubborn I sound, but what am I supposed to say? 'You have to help me!' I implore her.

Petry considers me, then turns to the stranger, who has got up now too. 'Mr Petersen,' she says, 'I would suggest you come with me for the time being. We'll put you up in a hotel until everything's been sorted out, and then you—'

'No,' says the stranger.

Petry raises astonished eyebrows.

'This house has belonged to my family for generations,' says the phoney Philip. 'I returned home today after seven years. I am not sleeping in a hotel.'

Barbara Petry lets this sink in, then she nods.

'Mrs Petersen,' she says, with an apologetic undertone, 'would you sleep somewhere else tonight?'

I stare at her in disbelief. Has she gone crazy? Does she really think I'd be prepared to leave my house to this stranger?

'No,' I say.

Again she suppresses a sigh. 'The way things are, I don't think it's a good idea for you to stay here together.'

'Then take this man with you,' I say.

'Please be sensible—' Barbara Petry begins, but I interrupt her.

'I want to see his birthmark,' I say.

Petry's head swings round. 'What birthmark?'

'My husband has a very prominent birthmark on his chest,' I say. Now I've got him.

Barbara Petry seems uneasy. I see her exchange a glance with the stranger.

'I can't,' he whispers.

'Of course not,' Petry replies softly.

'Have you gone crazy?' I shout. I see anger flash in Petry's eyes. 'You have no idea what this man has been through! This madness ends right now. This has gone on for far too long, anyway.'

I am shocked by this outburst. For a while, nobody says anything.

'I'll see you to the door,' the stranger says finally, getting up.

Barbara Petry gets up too.

'I'm sorry,' she tells him.

As she turns to leave, I jump up, almost knocking over a chair. 'I request a DNA test,' I say. I see with triumph that the impostor is staring at me open-mouthed.

'DNA tests can only be undergone voluntarily,' Barbara Petry replies.

I look at the stranger. He looks back—for an eternity, for two eternities, three.

'All right,' he says.

The stranger

Philip Petersen was born in Hamburg on 27 January 1976.

Sarah Petersen, née Wagner, first saw the light in Cologne on 4 April 1978.

Leo Petersen, the couple's only child, came into the world on 28 August 2006.

Philip's mother, Constanze, has her birthday on 18 May. His father, also Philip, was born on 11 November and died on Christmas Eve 2002.

Sarah Wagner and Philip Petersen met on 2 August.

Philip's birthday is not only Mozart's birthday; it is also the day of the liberation of Auschwitz.

On 4 April 1968—ten years to the day, that is, before Sarah Petersen was born—Martin Luther King was shot in Memphis.

Leo Petersen shares a birthday with Goethe.

I have always had a good head for dates. Of course I know the date of the wedding—it was 11 April.

I'm just a bit tired. That's all.

Sarah

The light coming in at the window has changed—it is warmer and less glaring, a reminder that it will soon be evening.

I can't possibly spend the night under the same roof as that man.

I sit curled up in the reading chair, trying to calm down. I was completely thrown when the stranger agreed to a DNA test—had no idea how to react, lost all control of my face, must have looked horrified. The stranger gave me a superior grin. Barbara Petry raised her eyebrows and looked at me with undisguised mistrust. If, to begin with, she had at least entertained the possibility that I might be right, the stranger's consent to this request changed everything. I could have knocked over the kitchen table out of sheer frustration, but I got a grip on myself, of course, and somehow managed to say something—I don't know what. My brain kept circling back to the same question: how could he possibly agree to that?

As if they had come to some arrangement, Barbara Petry and the stranger set off for the front door together. I wasn't quick enough; for a moment my body refused to obey me, and then I had no choice but to hurry after the two of them—in my own house. It was then that I heard him say it, his voice sunk to a confidential whisper.

'I'm sorry, Barbara, my wife really isn't in a good way. Can I trust you not to…'

And Petry, her voice suddenly full of warmth, as if I wasn't there at all: 'Don't you worry, Mr Petersen, I won't mention it to anyone, if you don't want me to.'

He's done it, I thought. He's got her now.

And very calmly, very sincerely, very softly, he replied, 'Thank you.'

I was stunned. And I thought, God, he's good.

When Barbara Petry had gone, I told the stranger one last time to get out of my house, but he simply said, 'No,' and left the room.

He is like one of those animals that invade an alien ecosystem and destroy it from within.

I look down at my lap, at the book I have pulled down from one of my shelves without really looking. It's a game I used to like playing—taking down a book with my eyes closed and then opening them to see what chance had placed in my hands, and puzzling over the message sent to me from the universe or my subconscious. My literary horoscope. If I took down Jack Kerouac's *On the Road*, it meant I would be going on a journey. Goethe's *Faust* heralded an important decision, and Chuck Palahniuk's *Fight Club*, of course, a fight. Some books—*The*

Catcher in the Rye, for example, or *The Master and Margarita*—carried a more equivocal message, while others, such as Kundera's *The Unbearable Lightness of Being*, seemed perennially apt. My bookshelves take up an entire wall of the living room. I love books. I need them, those self-contained little worlds between two covers where I can travel whenever I have the feeling I'm living in the wrong world—or when my own world is hemming me in or eluding me or hurting me.

In my lap is Dostoevsky's *Crime and Punishment*. I give a snort, get up and put the book back. Then I reach up to one of the higher shelves, run my finger along the spines without looking at the titles and eventually grab one and pull it out: Kafka's *Trial*. I reach up again, take down the book next to it and look at the cover: Kafka's *Judgment*.

I put the books back where they belong. I have to stop playing games and face up to reality.

My eyes fall on the grand piano. When we first moved in, Philip used to play a lot. But the more he worked, the less time he had to play and his favourite bands on vinyl began to replace the organic sound of the piano. I remember the first time he played to me, something pretty and light—Mozart, I think. It was lovely, listening to him. After a while, he had moved over on the piano stool and patted the empty space beside him. I sat down and Philip began to explain the instrument to me, and I was happy because he was happy—and because of his dimples, which appeared whenever he was having fun. His dimples and that contented little laugh of his. He taught me a piece, a very easy one that we could play together and that only required me to play a single key at a specified time. We giggled. I got it wrong a few times—it was great fun. I had, of course, had piano lessons in my childhood for a few years and was quite capable of playing the

Flea Waltz, but I didn't tell Philip—he was enjoying teaching me far too much. Philip liked being the expert. I often pretended I couldn't do something or didn't know something because it gave him such pleasure to show me things and explain them to me. How to change a tyre. How to use a drill. Classical music, modern art. I would sometimes make myself a little smaller, because I liked it when he was big. Looking back, that was stupid of me.

A sudden thought spurs me to my feet. The piano! It annoys me that I didn't think of it when Barbara Petry was here. The piano will blow his cover! What are the chances he can play as well as Philip?

At present all my hopes are pinned on the DNA test. But it will take time. Barbara Petry is going to 'see to it'—her words as she was leaving—and I shall have to 'be patient for a few days'. It is, I think, probably wise to keep out of the stranger's way until then, but remembering him sitting in my kitchen with his feet up, drinking beer, I am flooded with energy. I don't want him thinking he can park himself here as easily as that.

I gallop up to the first floor, taking the stairs two at a time.

At the top I pause. Where is he? Instinctively I head for the spare room. I always feel a little uneasy coming in here to air it or do the dusting—unused rooms with their strange smell freak me out, like anything absolved of its function. If there are ghosts anywhere in the house, then it's here. The spare room is small, with a window overlooking the garden. A bed, a bedside cupboard, a little wardrobe and a tiny occasional table are the only furniture. I never have guests anyway.

I fling open the door. I had expected the stranger to be here, but all the same I get a fright when I find myself face to face with him.

His leather holdall is on the bed. I'm just in time to see him slip something in and pull the zip shut with a jerk.

'What have you got there?' I ask, instantly on the alert.

'What?'

'What did you put in your bag just now?'

'Nothing,' says the stranger, without looking at me.

'A weapon?' I ask.

He snorts.

'Of course not! Sarah, please!'

'May I see?' I ask, making a grab for the bag. But the stranger intervenes.

'Is that what you've come for?' he asks. 'To search my bag?'

'No,' I say. 'I came to ask if you wouldn't like to play me something on the piano.' I find it hard to conceal the note of triumph in my voice.

'I don't understand,' the stranger says.

'What don't you understand?' I ask. 'Philip always loved playing the piano for me. And since you're claiming to be Philip, I thought it would be nice if you played me something.'

The stranger turns pale. There is a pause. The silence swells and throbs between us.

'Well?' I ask. 'How about it?'

The stranger stands there like a monolith. The way that everything I say bounces off him drives me mad. The way he thinks he can make himself at home in my spare room drives me mad. I step past him, make another grab for his bag and yank at the zip.

What happens next goes very fast. Only split seconds.

The stranger lunges at me. He tears the bag out of my hands and it slides to the floor.

'Stay away from my things!' he shouts—so near that I feel his hot breath on my face. 'Stay away from my things!' He swoops into the middle of the room, grabs hold of the little solid wood table and hurls it at the wall. It falls to the floor with a crash, lies there like a wounded animal, wood splintered like bones.

I stare at the stranger. He is breathing heavily. There is something primeval in his gaze, his pupils so large that his eyes look completely black. Never have I seen such fury.

'You'd better go now,' he says into the silence.

'If you think you can drive me away, you're wrong,' I spit at him. 'You have no idea who you're dealing with.'

'You're hysterical,' says the stranger with relish. 'If you could see yourself! Carry on like this and you'll end up in the psychiatric ward! Do you realise that?'

I steady myself and stick out my chin. Inside, I may be shaken, but I'm not going to let anyone terrorise me in my own house.

'Don't you threaten me,' I say. 'I know exactly what you're thinking. You look at me and you see a small, delicate woman. The perfect victim. But you have no idea who you're dealing with. You're talking to a woman who went six months without sleeping for even an hour at a stretch when her husband disappeared, but still didn't miss a single day of work. You're talking to a woman who has done five triathlons over the last year. You're talking to a woman who intervenes when there's a fight on the underground while everyone else just looks on. You're talking to a woman who would give her right arm for her child—and I don't mean that as a figure of speech. That's the woman you're dealing with. That's me. And let me tell you one thing: I'm not afraid of you. I've been through worse than this.'

The stranger looks at me and says nothing.

'I don't know who's sent you,' I say. 'I don't know why you're doing what you're doing. But believe me, you're going to regret that you ever came. And now,' I say, sarcastic, 'what about that damn piano?'

The stranger doesn't reply. He doesn't move a muscle. I'm not going anywhere, he seems to say.

I storm out of the room, run down the stairs, sit at the piano, lift the lid and bash the keys as hard as I can. The noise is awful and dissonant and beautiful—it sounds like my anger, like my despair, and I bash and bash the piano until I'm out of breath, until my ears are buzzing, until my arms are numb, until I can't anymore.

Then I get up. The piano strings reverberate for a while longer. That's it. I've had enough. I don't care what happens. I don't want to have to see this man anymore.

'Either you leave my house this second,' I call up the stairs, 'or I'm ringing the police.'

Without waiting for a reply, I return to the living room and take the phone from the charging station. The stranger appears. I almost expect him to attack me, to wrest the phone from me, but he just stands in the doorway, an impenetrable look on his face.

'Go on,' he says, 'go ahead!'

He looks at me challengingly.

'But if you ring the police now, you'll lose everything—your house, your job, your son, your whole beautiful life.'

For a second I'm thrown.

What does he know? What does he think he knows?

I stare at his face. For an eternity, for two eternities. He withstands my gaze.

No.

He's bluffing.

I begin to dial.

'Perhaps you weren't responsible after all,' the stranger says. 'You should tell that to the police—they might even believe you.'

I stare at him. Something inside me shifts; something is

released and floats slowly to the surface—something bad. I am standing outside a door. Behind it there is a rumbling sound. For a split second everything goes black and I see nothing. Only darkness, blackness, night, the door, the rumbling, Philip. And blood. Blood on my hands.

I tear open my eyes.

What was that?

A noise leaves my throat such as I have never heard before.

I swallow.

The stranger looks at me.

What does he want?

I notice that I am holding the phone in my hand.

I notice that I am lowering it.

Slowly.

Putting it down.

Carefully.

The stranger looks at me a moment longer, then disappears.

The stranger

I am alone. That's good. I breathe. Get my bearings. Remind myself I have every reason to be here.

I simply walked out and left her, and she didn't follow me. I take the necessary equipment out of my bag. Without making a sound I open the door, go to the bathroom at the end of the passage and lock myself in. I look at my face in the mirror above the basin.

'Philip Petersen,' I say and have to laugh. I almost scare myself—I never laugh, or only for a particular purpose: to reassure someone, express agreement, signal social belonging, dispel tension. Things like that.

I set everything out and shake the can of shaving cream. I prepare to shave off the beard I have grown, but then I think better of it, and put the razor down on the side of the basin.

Back in the room, I take the mobile phone out of my bag. I switch it on, dial, let it ring for a long time, hang up. I dial again— nothing. I fight back my disappointment. Keep going. I switch the phone off and put it back in my bag. I sit down and look about me. A spare room. Bright. Bare.

I don't really need the information I'm waiting for. She has guilt written all over her face, and her fear of the police leaves me in no doubt.

But before I act, I need to know the details.

Sarah

feel like the main character in Leo's favourite fairytale. It's as if I'm living in the Snow Queen's palace, where everything is made of ice: the walls, the furniture, the rugs, the pictures—even the people. I crawl under the quilt to warm myself, shaking with cold although it's the middle of summer. I think of Leo, wonder how he's feeling, what he must make of this situation. He's safe with Miriam and Martin, and I'm glad, but I've never felt so alone.

I hadn't realised how desperately I needed to sleep until I almost passed out.

Night has fallen—and whatever tomorrow may bring, I must face it halfway rested, at least. I feel uneasy letting the stranger out of my sight, but I can't watch him 24/7—that's something I've had to face up to. He can't get in my bedroom—I've barricaded myself in, locking the door and wedging a chair under the doorhandle so that nothing can happen to me—or at least that's the idea.

Who knows what he's doing. Is he asleep? Plotting? Making phone calls? Thinking? Laughing at the clueless Barbara Petry and the helpless Sarah Petersen? What does he know? How deep down into our past has he dug? Does he know things I don't know? How well did I know my husband? How well do I know myself? And always the nagging question: why is he doing this? Why is he pretending to be my husband?

The whole thing is absurd. There must be some way of unmasking him—here, now, not in a few days or weeks. The birthmark, I think. I'm too upset to stay in bed. I get up, grab my phone and open the camera app. No, that's idiotic—but it makes me think of my conversation with Hansen, who implied when I first spoke to him that the man they found in the jungle camp had suffered some form of abuse. Is that why Barbara Petry protected him so fiercely?

I have another idea and activate the dictation app instead. At first the stranger seemed in complete control, but since he freaked out earlier today, I know there are cracks in the facade. Maybe I can get him to say something rash if I provoke him again. I take the chair from under the doorhandle and turn the key in the lock, carefully, without making a sound. Still, I hesitate before opening the door. What if he's lying in wait for me?

I count to three in my head, then fling open the door. It wouldn't surprise me to see the stranger standing there, but the dark corridor outside my room is empty. I give a sigh of relief and realise that I've been holding my breath without meaning to. I wait until my breathing is steadier, until my eyes have grown accustomed to the darkness, then I glance left and right down the passage to make sure that I really am alone, and make my way to the stairs. A glimmer of light shines up from the ground floor.

Soundlessly I creep downstairs, skipping the fourth step from the top because it creaks—I know this house like my own body. The light is coming from the living room. How could I let it come to this? How could I let him spend the night here with me?

I breathe as quietly as I can and tiptoe into the living room. Cautiously, I peer around the corner. The little reading lamp next to my armchair is on, but the chair is empty, and so is the sofa. The television is on mute. One of the commercial channels I never watch is on. An advert shows a good-looking young family of four, the boy brown-haired like the father, the girl blond like the mother. They are eating yoghurt on a day out in the country in their big dark family car with their big good-natured family dog.

Three beautiful teenage girls chat about boys as they wash their faces with a foamy cleanser; drops of water spray, the girls giggle. An attractive middle-aged couple look at each other amorously over a deep-freeze pizza; a housewife thrills at her clean washing; a model preens over her long lush lashes; a sportsman over his dandruff-free hair. I wish I could just lie down on the sofa and watch the yoghurt families being normal and happy. I switch the television off.

A faint creak makes me jump. I spin round and stare into the darkness of the dining room behind me. But there is nobody there. Nobody. It was just one of those noises this old house sometimes makes to remind its occupants that it is still alive.

Where is he? What is he doing?

I suddenly can't bear the thought that I don't know where the stranger is. Enough of this creeping about. I walk from room to room, turning on the lights. Then I go upstairs. Here too I fling open doors, flick switches. The bedrooms, the bathrooms—all empty.

In Leo's room I pause. My gaze falls on the pencil marks and dates charting Leo's growth on the doorframe. One of his shirts is lying on the bed—the blue checked one. He couldn't make up his mind what to wear to his first meeting with his father and had changed more than once. I'd watched him rub gel into his hair and inspect his outfit in the mirror, making an effort to conceal my emotion.

'Time to go,' I said eventually. 'Are you ready?'

Leo nodded. Then paused.

'Nearly ready.'

He'd pulled the blue checked shirt over his head—mussing up his painstakingly gelled hair. Then he'd thrown the shirt on the bed and grabbed the olive green one instead. I watched him do up the buttons, resisting the temptation to help him, to try to speed things up. I waited as patiently as I could while Leo carefully smoothed his shirt.

'Come on, let's go and fetch Dad,' I said.

I could hardly get the words out.

It all seems so long ago now.

The phone rings and I tear my eyes off Leo's blue checked shirt. I dash down the stairs and into the living room and pick up.

'Hello?'

Nothing.

No, not nothing—breathing.

'Hello?' I say again, feeling my pulse shoot up.

Then the breather hangs up.

Frowning, I put the phone down. I'm only a few metres away when it begins to ring again. I pick up.

'Hello?'

No answer.

'Who is it?'

A click. Hung up again.

Bewildered, I hang up too and go into the kitchen. I put bread and peanut butter on the table and get myself plate and knife. I know that, like everything I've eaten lately, the food won't taste of anything, but I have to get something inside me. I take a slice of bread and put it on the plate, doing my best to ignore the phone, which has started to ring again. I take the knife, spread some peanut butter on the bread and take a bite. The telephone stops. No taste in my mouth—only texture. Wallpaper paste on cardboard. The phone starts up again. I feel sick. I try to swallow the pap in my mouth, but it's an effort. The phone stops, then starts again. I throw the bread and peanut butter in the bin. Quickly I put plate and knife in the dishwasher and go back to my bedroom. I block out the ringing phone and collapse onto my bed. As I wait for the nausea to subside, I think things over.

It ought to come as a relief, but it only makes me more nervous than ever—the stranger has vanished.

This place is full of spiders. My shady old house, whose myriad hidden corners provide them with such excellent shelter, is crawling with the things. Nowadays I get along all right with the timid creatures I sometimes see scuttling across my floorboards, but this wasn't always the case. I used to call Philip to get rid of them. The key at such moments is not to take your eyes off them. Spiders are quicker than you think and there is nothing worse than seeing one and then letting your attention wander for a moment and realising it has given you the slip. Not knowing the whereabouts of the thing I'm so afraid of—that's the worst. An enormous spider in full view on the wall may be horrible, but at least you know it's not suddenly going to walk over your bare legs. An enormous spider you can't see, but which you know is somewhere about—that really is unbearable. It's the same with the stranger—that's why I feel so jittery not knowing where he is, or what his plans are. Even his bag is gone.

My head is so full of questions. What does he want from me? What are his plans? Why is he doing what he's doing? And most important of all, how did he manage to hoodwink the authorities? How does he know so much about Philip? Once again I wonder why the stranger agreed to the DNA test. It can't all—

I fight back my anger and confusion, and force myself to calm down and think logically—to consider the problem objectively.

The stranger agreed to a DNA test.

Firstly—at least from the point of view of Barbara Petry—that gives him an air of credibility.

Secondly, it presumably takes a few days for the results of such a test to come through.

Thirdly, whatever the stranger's plans are, he can't be expecting to keep this up for long, because however good a job he may be doing at present, it's only a matter of time before he's unmasked— at the latest, when a DNA test is carried out.

Fourthly, if the stranger doesn't mind undergoing a DNA test, which would unmask him within three or four days, that must mean he needs at most a few days to implement his plan.

But what, for God's sake, is his plan? And where do I fit in? And what's the idea behind the telephone terror? Is someone trying to wear me down?

When I climb the ladder and open the hatch to the loft, I'm met by waves of stuffy air, baked by the hot sun of the previous days. It's like crossing an invisible boundary. Dust tickles my nose. I don't know when I was last up here—I avoid the loft with its boxes full of the past. I'm not one of those people who keep a diary, wallow in old photo albums or dissect the first years of their life with expensive therapists. I've never understood people like that. The old diaries I kept as a teenager are lost, and I'm sure I wouldn't recognise myself in the thoughts of the person I was then. When I look at old photos of myself, I see a ghost, a being who no longer exists.

The loft is strewn with old boxes and all the stuff I haven't needed these last years but haven't been able to bring myself to get rid of either—mostly because it isn't connected to my own memories, but to Philip's. Heirlooms his father left him. A surfboard. Other sports equipment. An acoustic guitar. I sneeze, sniff and open a box at random. Leo's old baby things. Philip's old Nikon, which he had with him in hospital when Leo was born. I swallow hard and force myself to close the box back up.

I find the case where I keep Philip's pistol without having to hunt for it. The code that opens the combination lock is his date of birth. Reluctant to take the gun in my hand, I stare at it. I remember Philip convincing me to learn at least the basics: I know how to hold the pistol, how to load and unload it. I hesitate all the same. A gun should never be taken out unless it's absolutely necessary.

I haven't touched the thing for years. My aversion to guns is so strong it's almost physical. It shouldn't be possible to kill like that, I think, whenever I see the pistol—not animals and certainly not humans. If you can help it, you shouldn't kill other human beings at all, but if you're absolutely set on it, then it should at least be difficult—it should require exertion and determination. Anyone who really wants to kill another person should have to strangle them, to squeeze the life out of their body, using nothing more than their own bare hands, very close, face to face. Hardly anyone can do that—our inhibition against killing is far too strong, our physical strength too weak. But what if you only have to crook a finger? It's so easy. So terrifyingly easy.

I come down from the loft, the gun in my hands. I listen out for a long time. All is quiet.

Back in my bedroom I lock the door behind me and then open the safe where I keep an emergency supply of cash and a small box of ammunition Philip stashed away years ago that I have never touched. Again I hesitate. Then I load the gun, put it

113

back in its case, close the case, scramble the numbers on the lock, open my wardrobe, push the case to the back of the top shelf and arrange some T-shirts in front of it. I feel better, but at the same time worse. I slip off my sandals and collapse onto the bed. Then I think again, and get up to open the door. If there's a strange man moving around in my house in the night, I want to be able to hear him. I sit down on the bed, knowing I won't be able to stay awake if I permit myself to lie down, but sleep overtakes me almost instantly, and I succumb to it, letting myself drift down into the darkness.

I am walking along a passage. Bare walls. All around me it is silent, and I am scared—very scared. I don't know what I'm so scared of, but the fear is driving me almost out of my mind. Then I hear it and stop in terror. A rumbling. The noise terrifies me, but I walk towards it all the same. There is a door. I stop a short way off and listen. There it is again! It's coming from the other side of the door. I walk towards it, steeling myself for whatever is lying in wait for me on the other side. Then I push down the doorhandle and fling open the door. I see what is lying there on the other side. I blink in confusion and—

I wake up, struggling to free myself from sweat-drenched sheets. My heart is fluttering in my ribcage like a frightened bird. I blink. It must be the middle of the night, because it's pitch black, not a glimmer of light coming through the slats of the blinds. I'm groping for my phone to see what the time is when it hits me. I fell asleep with the light on! The lamp on my bedside table was on!

He has been in my room.

I gasp for breath and reach for the light switch, feeling blindly for it in the dark. I am terrified of brushing up against something—or someone—in the darkness, but I try to calm down, telling myself I must have turned the light out when I was half asleep and forgotten about it. How many times had I done that—fallen asleep with the light on and turned it out when I was half asleep? Must be hundreds. I give myself a reassuring nod. Then I find the switch. The room is bathed in warm light—and I catch my breath.

A nightmare within a nightmare.

I hadn't sensed his presence. I cannot at first process what I see.

My bedroom. The light of my little bedside lamp. And in the glow of the light, the stranger, staring me in the face.

The room begins to spin and my heart beats faster and faster and faster.

He is like a ghost—no sound of breathing, no smell, nothing. Only a slim figure, dressed in black. Pale skin, dark eyes. He is standing at my bed, looking at me.

Instinctively I crawl as far away from him as I can, until I feel the bedhead against my back. The stranger blinks, as if I had torn him out of a kind of trance. He screws up his eyes. Who knows how long he has been standing like that in the darkness, watching me. Like a shadow.

For a few moments I'm too shocked to react, but then I'm on my feet and at the door, the stranger behind me. I feel dizzy—I'm not thinking straight yet, still doped with sleep. I trip over the chair I used to barricade the door earlier in the night, stumble and bang my ankle. The sharp pain jolts me into alertness and I bolt through the door. I run barefoot along the passage, feeling the coolness of the floorboards beneath my feet. Behind me, the stranger, the stranger's footsteps. I pick up speed, fly down the stairs, almost fall, don't fall, reach the bottom. It's only now I remember the gun I've left in my room, but it's too late.

Then I hear the stranger.

'Sarah,' he calls.

Nothing else.

And then again.

'Sarah!'

Everything in me resists his voice.

I run through the dark towards the front door, his footsteps behind me. I daren't look back—I can feel him behind me, quicker than me, behind me. He'll get me at the front door, I think. I'll have to stop and open it, and I'll lose a few seconds—I'll be almost out and he'll get me. I run as fast as I can. I see the front door, almost skid towards it in a raging panic, tear it open—and just as I'm about to burst through it as if through some magic portal, he gets me. Grabs me by the waist and drags me away from the door. I struggle to free myself from his grasp—out of here, let me out, through the door, down the dark street, let me run and run and never stop. But I can't get free. He pushes the door shut, spins me round by the shoulders to face him, and then twirls me round, as if we were dancing, interposing himself between me and the front door. Again I try to tear myself free and am amazed when I succeed. I run for dear life, not thinking about where I'm going, dodging past the television, round the sofa, towards the back of the house. I'm going to make it, I think. This time I'm going to make it.

I push open the back door and set off at a run, the almost full moon shining coldly and wanly on the lawn. I feel cool dew under my feet, slip in the high damp grass, run past the fruit trees.

The garden shed comes into view. I hear nothing behind me, no footsteps, no breathing, but when I glance back he's only a few metres away. I don't even have enough air in my lungs to scream. I have to get out of here, get out. I tread on something slippery, maybe a slug, but I don't get as far as feeling disgust. Run, run. The idea of barricading myself in the shed flashes through my mind—into the shed, shut the door, drive the bolt home. He's so close now, so close, it's my only chance. I struggle with myself for a moment—for two, three—but I can't make up my mind to it— no, then I really would be trapped. I race past it and make for the fence. There's an access road on the other side and I know that somewhere in the fence there's a hole Leo sometimes wriggles through, although I've asked him not to so many times because he's always tearing his clothes. I run towards the spot where I think the hole is, the stranger behind me. I get down on my knees and grope about frantically, but I find it, I actually find it, and I push my way through. A sharp pain shoots through my left leg, but I ignore it, keep crawling, struggle up, limp off. I'm on the road. A street lamp shines dimly. I race barefoot over the asphalt towards the main road. There's not a soul about at this hour of the night, not a soul, but the main road can't be deserted, it can't. I hear him behind me again—he's discovered the hole in the fence and is coming after me. What is he hoping for? What does he want from me? I run on, over the asphalt, which is strewn with sharp gravel so that I'm soon running on sore feet—and reach the main road just as a car goes speeding past. I wave frantically. Spinning round, I see the stranger approaching. I look left and right—no other car in sight, only the dark sedan that just shot past me and whose driver watched my desperate waving in the rear-view mirror, if at all. I turn round—turn to face the stranger, who is only a few metres behind me now—and prepare to fight. Then I hear it.

The car. The driver of the estate has stopped and gone into reverse. The car comes hurtling towards me, whirring and whining. Without a moment's hesitation, I run to meet it, and it stops in front of me. I sense the stranger behind me. Sweat is streaming down my face, a few strands of hair clinging to my forehead. I push them away as the driver lowers the passenger window with a hum. He is in his early sixties maybe—Johann's age—burly, dark-haired, bearded. A strong, kindly man, who looks as if he works in a DIY centre.

'Everything all right?' he asks.

'Please,' I gasp, 'help me. This man's chasing—'

That's as far as I get, because the stranger has come up to me.

'God, Sarah, what on earth are you doing?'

I spin round again and see the concerned face he has put on for the driver.

'You're not my husband!' I hiss at him.

It's all that comes into my head. I try to open the car door to get in, but it's locked.

'Let me in,' I shout, my voice shrill with panic. 'For God's sake, let me in!'

'Please excuse us,' the stranger says, turning to the driver, 'my wife's in rather a bad way.'

I lose all self-control and rattle the handle of the passenger door.

'Let me in! Can't you see what's going on?'

The driver's gaze shifts between the stranger and me. I am suddenly aware of the picture we must present—me barefoot and distraught, the stranger composed and serene, neatly dressed, that benevolent mask on his face, the one he put on for Barbara Petry.

'I know you,' the driver suddenly says. 'You're that hostage. I saw you on television.'

His gaze wanders to me and travels over my face.

'I know you too!'

The stranger smiles winningly at the man, with just the degree of exhaustion you'd expect from someone who's returned home after a long odyssey.

'My wife's in rather a bad way,' the stranger repeats.

The driver nods deliberately and glances at me.

'Don't believe a word of it,' I say. 'That's not my husband.'

The driver looks at me for a moment. Then he averts his eyes. The window goes up and the man puts the car into first gear.

'That's not my husband,' I shout again.

Then the driver of the sedan puts his foot on the accelerator and drives off. For a second I watch him go, then I turn back to face the stranger. Again I feel the impulse to run away. He notices. Almost imperceptibly, he shakes his head.

'Look at you,' he says after a while. 'Look at the state you're in. Where were you thinking of going?'

He hesitates, then turns and heads back to the house. When he notices that I'm not following him, he stops again.

'Come on,' he says.

I stand and stare at him.

Run away, I think. Away from here.

'I'm warning you,' the stranger says, as if he's read my mind.

The words he spoke earlier flash through my head.

You'll lose everything. Your son. Your whole beautiful life.

I swallow.

'I don't know what you think you know about me,' I say. 'But you're wrong! I'm only a mother! A teacher! I wouldn't hurt a fly!'

The stranger laughs. Mirthlessly.

He takes a few more steps towards the house, and again he

120

stops when he notices that I'm not following him.

'Come on!' he says.

It's as if I'm rooted to the spot. I don't know what to do.

'If I wanted to hurt you, I've already had ample opportunity tonight,' he says. Then he says it again—'Come on!'—but more gently this time, as if he were trying to coax a timid cat.

There's a storm raging in my head, but then, slowly, gradually, one thought detaches itself from all the others and crystallises, growing louder and louder until it fills my head: *There's no point running away.*

And then: *If I leave now, I am ceding the house to him. If I run away, he has won.*

I breathe deeply, in and out. Then I get a grip on myself and follow the stranger back into my house.

The stranger

Estoy cansado. I am tired. Not only because I haven't slept for three days. No, more than anything because of the constant stress.

No organ consumes as much energy as the brain. It is a strain having to stay a hundred per cent focused and alert. Not being allowed to make the slightest mistake saps your strength.

The situation is proving more difficult than I had expected.

She is more difficult.

I hadn't imagined her like this.

I open my holdall, take the phone out of the little compartment inside and switch it on. Grimm hasn't got back to me yet. I try to check my impatience. Nothing that happens is good or bad. Events as such have no meaning. It is we who give them meaning.

I lie down on the bed and stretch out.

As so often in the last few days, my thoughts stray to the past. And as always, I force them back to the present as soon as I realise.

I can't let myself be distracted.

I close my eyes for a second.

I am ready.

I go to the window and wait for dawn.

Sarah

It is growing light—dawn is near. I'm sitting in my reading chair in the living room—I didn't have the strength to drag myself up to my bedroom. My lungs are on fire, I have a bloody graze on my calf where I scraped it on the fence last night, and my feet, now in trainers, are still sore. A tune pops into my head, goodness only knows where it's come from. 'Karma Police', Radiohead. And of course the tune makes me think of Philip, of how it all began. I let my thoughts drift.

'The night Sarah and I met, lightning struck—and that's not a figure of speech.'

Philip always began the story like that. I can't tell it as well as my husband, but I remember everything. It was the hottest day of the year and Radiohead were giving an open-air concert. I had gone along by myself, not yet knowing anyone who might have gone with me. I'd only just moved to Hamburg to study and was a little lonely, but thought it all right to be a little lonely. The concert was sold out. People as far as the eye could see. Bodies—all around me, sweating bodies. I was in the middle of the crowd and it felt as if I'd fallen into a snake pit. So many people. Body heat, sticky skin, sweat-soaked T-shirts. We were like pilgrims who ignore hunger and thirst and any other physical need because they know they will soon receive something more nourishing than food or drink. For one hot evening, music was our religion. When the band came on stage, they were greeted by a noise that seemed to come from a single, parched throat. A surge went through the crowd. Then the music began and with it the lights—it was like looking in at the gates of heaven, it was so beautiful, so dazzlingly bright. The lights flickered across my retina and the music throbbed. I didn't just hear it with my ears—I heard it with my stomach, my fingertips, the down on my cheeks. Every cell in my body was vibrating. I closed my eyes to hear better and the people around me vanished and nothing hurt anymore, nothing mattered anymore—I let myself be swallowed up, carried away. I was drunk on rock music and a lack of oxygen—a heady mix. The crowd burst into cheers every time the band started a new song. I looked about me. The pupils of the people around me reflected the stage lights, tears were rolling down their cheeks. It was so loud and so quiet, so unbearably and unfathomably beautiful. The sun went down behind the stage, bathing everything in a light that was not of this world. The music boomed; the speakers bulged towards us. Fifteen songs were played that night, eleven litres of tears were shed, eight hundred and fifty-one people fell in love—so much energy. The grass under our feet would never grow back; a thousand moths singed themselves on the floodlights and died happy. Then came the rain. As if from nowhere, storm clouds appeared. It was so sudden. Within seconds, single drops had given way to a downpour. And with the rain came the wind, and the wind whipped up into a gale. Lightning sliced the sky into left and right, up and down. The dreamy gazes and the teary faces vanished—suddenly the crowd was all elbows and shoulders, pushing and shoving. The lightning flickered, the thunder followed almost immediately, the gale shook the steel structure of the stage, the band stopped playing, the crowd around me poured towards the exit. For a few metres I was dragged along, then I stumbled and almost went down. Struggling to stay on my feet, I was jostled along by the crowd towards the exit until I stumbled again, an elbow in my back—or a knee. I caught my breath and almost fell, but then somebody grabbed my arm and held me up, and I clutched the hand that was stretched out to me and didn't let it go. I had regained my footing. I glanced up, looking for the face that belonged to the hand, and caught a glimpse of a tall, dark-haired boy, but there was such a crush and I was still being pushed towards the exit, my face in somebody's back, bodies everywhere, no room to turn your head even. Then suddenly I was through the bottleneck at the exit and could breathe again. The grass was sodden with rain. I was soaked, water dripping down my face, my dress clinging to me. Everywhere there were people running, everywhere thunder and lightning. I could only stand and watch. Noise. Chaos. Pushing and shoving. Dazzling flashes. I looked at it all as if it were a picture you could step into. I was in the eye of the storm, wrapped in a cocoon that kept the thunder at bay. Where I was, it was calm. And then I felt a hand on my lower arm. Turning, I saw the dark-haired boy, and I pulled him to me, into my cocoon, where it was quiet and still and where we could at last look at each other in peace. The dark-haired boy smiled and

I saw that he had dimples. I lowered my eyes, and then the spell broke and the bubble around us burst and the wind lashed rain into our faces and the thunder was deafening and the boy took me by the hand and we ran, while above us the sky flickered and somewhere far, far away, people stopped to look at the summer lightning over the distant concert grounds. Music and thunder, electricity and pounding hearts. That's how it was with us. That's the kind of night it was.

I return to the present, Philip's face still on my retina like a blurred photograph of a ghost. I close my sore eyes and try to retrieve the image, but I can't. Out of the window I see the night sky slowly fade to morning.

I think of Leo.

And then I think of Philip again who, if Constanze is to be believed, looked just like Leo when he was little. Even now, when she sees Leo, she sometimes says, 'Just like my Green. The spitting image.'

I often asked my husband why he was called Green when he was a boy, but he never told me, always dismissing the question with a breezy 'I'll tell you some other time'. I assumed the story must have been in some way embarrassing to him and didn't insist. I myself am not a fan of nicknames—Philip's insistence on only ever calling me 'Princess' drove me mad after a while.

My thoughts circle back to Leo, who doesn't have a funny nickname and who is now asleep somewhere in Miriam's cosy house. I wonder whether he let Miriam read him a bedtime story. Probably not—stories are probably uncool and he'd rather his best friend didn't know that he still likes being read to. I think of a conversation we had, one evening in bed, long before we'd heard that Philip had been found. Leo asked me whether his father was dead, and then wanted to know all about death and dying. I reassured him as well as I could, of course. No, his father wasn't dead—one day he'd come back. And he didn't need to worry about dying—he was far too young for that. I sat on the edge of his bed and told him a real whopper of a fairy story—the tale of a safe and ordered world where the sun keeps rising and winter never fails to follow spring. I lie to my son because I want him to feel secure, but in fact all kinds of things, even the most atrocious things, can happen at any moment. How am I to know when I go to bed at night that Leo will still be breathing the next time I see him?

When I found out that I was expecting a baby, I was stiff with fear. Philip was delighted, but I wasn't. Of course, I told everyone I was thrilled, but it was a lie. I was afraid—not afraid that I wouldn't be able to take care of the child properly—no, it wasn't that. I was afraid that the child might resent me for bringing him into the world unasked, into a world I couldn't explain to him, a world so full of wonders and atrocities, so unfathomable and inexplicable. I was afraid because I had no answers to the most elementary questions. It preoccupied me a great deal at the time. The other mothers-to-be I got to know at the antenatal classes fed their unborn babies Mozart and macrobiotic fare. I read philosophy. I'm not the brooding type—more pragmatic. I like order and clarity and purposefulness. But all through my pregnancy I read philosophical texts. It didn't get me anywhere, of course—the more I thought and the more I read, the clearer it became to me that there are no answers to the big questions. Where do we come from? Where are we going? Why are some of us healthy when others are sick? Why are some of us rich when others are poor? Why am I the person I am rather than anyone else? What does it all mean? There are no answers to these questions, that much I know now. It is of no significance why things are the way they are. All that matters is what we make of them. That's what I'll tell my son when he asks me—and it's what I tell myself today, at the end of this nightmarish night. It's up to me.

The stranger is in the spare room. After my humiliating encounter with the driver of the sedan, we returned to the house without a word, then he turned to me and said that he was going to bed and would advise me to get some sleep too. He withdrew to his room and hasn't emerged since. But he isn't asleep—I can hear his footsteps making the floorboards creak overhead. To and fro he goes, to and fro. He can't get to sleep any more than I can.

What on earth does he want of me? How am I to understand the hatred that flashes in his eyes when he looks at me? I run my hand over my face. Am I still thinking straight?

Is the stranger after Philip's money? I asked that question myself when Barbara Petry was here, without pursuing the thought: Philip was—*is*—a very wealthy man. Of course that attracts con men.

A recent conversation I had with Johann flashes across my mind. He had wanted to discuss money with me again, and again I had refused. I earn more than enough to make ends meet, and I live in this enormous house with its wonderful garden—a house which is really far too big for Leo and me—with no rent, no mortgage to pay. I have all I need. I can do without Philip's money. And I wouldn't dream of having him declared dead or doing anything else to be able to access my husband's funds.

'Whether you like it or not,' Johann had said, 'it's your money. You're not only Philip's wife, you're his heir. Whether you're comfortable with the idea or not, you are a very, very rich woman.

129

We have to protect you and your money, if not for your sake, then at least for Leo's. Have your husband declared dead.'

Whenever it cropped up, I tried to change the subject, but Johann wouldn't let it drop.

'I don't know why you're so keen to avoid the issue,' he said. 'You could do good things with Philip's money. You could help people if you wanted.'

'Philip isn't dead,' I replied every time. 'So I'm not his heir.'

Philip isn't dead, I tell myself even now. He's only missing. I try the thought for size like a tailor-made jacket I haven't had on for a while—see if it still fits. For seven years I've been repeating the words like a mantra. Philip isn't dead. Philip is alive. But now this stranger is going about pretending to be my husband—and once again I don't know what to think.

I recall something else Johann said, after I'd told him that I wasn't interested in money—that I'd never been bothered about money and never would be. Johann had smiled his quiet smile and put his head a little to one side.

'But Sarah, please. You say that because you want for nothing. But believe me, when the going gets tough, it always comes down to money.'

I nod deliberately.

There is only one reason for the stranger to pass himself off as Philip and worm his way into my house.

I don't know how he came up with the idea. I don't know how he did it. But I do at least know why now. For the money—my money, Philip's money.

So let's begin at the beginning.

Firstly, the stranger's in it for the money.

Secondly, he will be expecting me to use all available means to unmask him.

Thirdly, he will have taken the necessary precautions.

Fourthly, it seems likely he had help. How else could he know so much about me, details he could never find online? That means I have to be careful whom I speak to. And above all, I can't act the way he expects me to act.

A hideous thought flashes across my mind. If the authorities believe the stranger is my husband, does that mean he can have me locked up? And if he can do that, what other discretionary power does he have over me? If I were to have an accident and fall into a coma, could he have the life-support machines switched off? And what about Leo? My throat tightens.

I run over my encounters with Barbara Petry and the driver of the sedan. The stranger is clever, and so far he's been able to rely on me to act like a raving lunatic. Maybe—no, definitely—that was part of his plan.

If it's part of the stranger's plan that I act like a madwoman, I've so far been playing into his hands. My breakdown at the airport, my manic calls to Mr Bernardy, Wilhelm Hansen and Johann, the talk with Barbara Petry, and most recently—I shudder when I recall the scene from this point of view—my carry-on by the side of the road. There I was, in a kind of frenzy, barefoot, soaked in sweat, shouting at the driver, rattling at his car door. I wonder whether any of the neighbours witnessed the scene.

Maybe it really is as simple as that. Maybe the stranger is trying to drive me mad—or at least make it look as if I were mad. It would get me out of the way and leave him free to help himself to Philip's money.

I realise how absurd that sounds and have to shake my head. Who would do such a thing? But when I think of all the crazy things people do for money, it doesn't seem quite so improbable after all.

I close my sore eyes, relax my muscles and try to get into a more comfortable position. I don't expect to be able to sleep—not, I think to myself, after all I've been through today. But then I feel my body growing light and my consciousness dissolving like a tablet in water.

I'm walking along a passage. Bare walls. All around me it is silent, and I am scared—very scared. I don't know what I'm so scared of, but the fear is driving me almost out of my mind. Then I hear it and stop in terror. A rumbling. The noise terrifies me, but I walk towards it all the same. There is a door. I stop a short way off and listen out. There it is again! It's coming from the other side of the door. I walk towards it, steeling myself for whatever is lying in wait for me on the other side. Then I push down the doorhandle and fling open the door. I see what is lying there on the other side. I blink in confusion. The door doesn't open onto a room.

The door opens onto a dark road.

I start, instantly wide awake. It was a noise that woke me. What was that? A door? I catch my breath.

I heard the stranger in the spare room until late into the night. To and fro, he went, to and fro, his footsteps making the floorboards creak. Did he get to sleep in the end after all? No, there it is again—footsteps. My guts signal danger, my pulse quickens and I realise that it's not the footsteps themselves setting off alarm bells—it is the cautious, tentative nature of the footsteps. Someone is creeping along the hall upstairs. I prick my ears. Without making a sound, I sink back into my armchair, close my eyes and breathe more slowly, as if, worn out by the night's exertions, I have dropped off again. I strain my ears, but hear nothing. Sitting here with my eyes shut, I lose all sense of time and don't know whether

I've been waiting for two minutes or twenty. Was I imagining things? No, I can hear something, barely audible. The stranger is coming. He moves terrifyingly quietly, but the fourth stair from the top betrays him with a gentle creak. That wouldn't have happened to Philip. He grew up in this house, lived in it nearly all his life. I squint cautiously through my eyelashes. It's hard work breathing calmly and evenly when the man is gliding down the stairs towards me, getting slowly and steadily nearer. The wan light shining in at the living-room window has transformed the room into the set of a black-and-white film, and in the middle of this grey world stands the stranger, only a few metres away. He stands there in the middle of the room and looks across at me. My instinct is to hold my breath, but I force myself to keep breathing, nice and steady, nice and calm, in and out. My eyes are only open a slit—I see his trouser legs, but nothing else. If I were to raise my head and look him in the face, he'd know at once that I'm awake. He stands motionless for a while and it feels like forever. I wonder what he can be thinking. He's not going to attack me physically—I feel sure of it. What he said last night seems plausible to me: if he wanted to harm me, he's already had ample opportunity. Then a jolt goes through him and he leaves the living room as quietly as he entered it.

It's not until I hear the back door that I realise he's going out. I now have two possibilities: I can run upstairs and search his luggage in the hope of finding something that incriminates him—or at least gives me some clue to who he is, what exactly he wants and where he's come from.

Or else I can go after him. I follow my gut. I count to thirty, grab my handbag and set off after the stranger.

The stranger

I am wandering around the city like a remote-control robot. It is utterly unfamiliar, yet I know exactly where to take a left and where to turn right. My body feels light: the cumulative effect of the sleep deprivation of the last days and weeks.

In other circumstances I would have collapsed long ago. But our bodies obey our will—it's astonishing how much they can put up with in the pursuit of a fundamental goal. As long as our brains say, 'Walk!' our bodies will walk.

I am walking.

The early morning is pleasantly cool. Empty streets. Horse chestnut trees. Cars parked at the kerbside. A boy of maybe sixteen on a black bike, headphones over his ears. A woman in her mid-fifties with short, jet-black hair, and a dalmatian on a lead.

Two policemen in navy blue uniform. A homeless man asleep in a doorway, a big pink fluffy rabbit beside him.

I set one foot in front of the other.

I register everything, but none of it touches me.

I draw myself up, inhale deeply. I've been waiting for this moment for a long time. For years.

Now it has come.

Here goes.

Sarah

As I squeeze my way through the hole in the fence—more carefully this time—and step out onto the same road that I was careering down like a lunatic only a few hours ago, I glimpse him turning the corner. I follow him cautiously but do not, of course, have a clue how you go about following someone without being noticed. He would only have to turn round to see me. But he doesn't. He walks serenely, as if guided by a built-in compass. I follow him down the avenue and along the main road, vaguely aware that the sun is rising. The pavements are empty, the joggers and dog owners who will soon fill them not yet out. But there are cars on the roads.

The road from my dream flashes across my mind. Not now, I think. Not now.

He walks on, neither particularly fast and purposefully, like someone with a specific goal, nor slowly and indulgently, like he's out for a stroll. He simply walks. The morning world through which we are moving is black, white and green. White houses, wrought-iron railings, green lawns. Lime trees. Horse chestnuts. An old copper beech here and there. Rosebushes. Orchids or model ships in bay windows. Tasteful. Everything in this part of town is tasteful. As I walk beneath the lime trees I glance down and quickly step aside to avoid treading on a bumblebee lying on the ground—and then realise I've trodden on another. I scan the pavement under the trees and see that it's littered with the bodies of dead bumblebees. At first I see three, then ten and soon dozens of plump little bodies. I look up into the treetops, but do not, of course, find any explanation. There must be an explanation, I know, but still the dead furry creatures seem to me like a bad omen.

I turn my attention back to the stranger, making sure that the distance between us remains more or less constant.

It's as if he were pulling me along behind him on an invisible rope. I contemplate the back of his head and wonder who this man can be. I remind myself that he too was once an innocent baby, weighing no more than a few pounds, and that billions of major and minor decisions have brought him to this particular place, at this particular moment. How did he end up here? What course can his life have taken to bring him to this point?

Suddenly something occurs to me. What if I'm not the first who's been put through this? What if he's done this before? Maybe the stranger has no identity of his own. Maybe his identity is precisely that—he's a con man, an impostor. Maybe it works so well because it's so audacious. Maybe this is his business model, and the project with Philip his next big coup.

I jump when the stranger comes to a sudden halt, and stop too, to be on the safe side, concealing myself behind one of the old trees that line the avenue. Old houses, old trees, old money. The stranger seems to be looking at something I can't make out from where I am. What on earth is he doing? But even as I'm wondering, he sets off again and I follow him, frowning as I pass the place where he stopped. There is a bin, a perfectly normal red litter bin, like all the others in our town.

I can't see anything out of the ordinary—no hidden message, nothing. The unpleasant feeling of having overlooked something steals over me, but I have no time and quicken my pace, so as not to lose sight of the stranger. He is making for the centre of town.

Songbirds lustily greet the new day as it dawns, and the sounds of the city swell. The further we get from the smart area where I live—and where I still feel out of place, even after so many years—the more people there are out on the street: the first workers on their way to early shift, the last of the late-night revellers making their way home. I'm scared that the stranger might hail a taxi and give me the slip, but first one taxi and then another drives past him and he doesn't raise his arm.

The pulse of the city quickens as we move further and further away from home and the sun climbs higher and higher. I don't know how long we've been walking—I don't wear a watch and don't want to stop to dig my phone out of my bag. But we've been going for a while and the stranger still shows no sign of wanting to take a taxi or even the underground. We keep walking, and suddenly the city is awake, like an ogre jumping up from sleep with stertorous breath—people, traffic and bustle coursing through his veins.

The stranger walks on and on. He walks into a part of town I hardly ever set foot in anymore, although I used to love it. Here nothing is refined or tasteful—everything is colourful. We walk past record shops and wine bars, bookshops and tattoo parlours. Past pavement cafes whose red umbrellas are just being put up, and people hurrying to work, eating cinnamon buns and drinking caffe latte from paper cups. As the stranger carries on towards his mystery destination, occasionally dodging particularly hectic briefcase carriers or particularly thoughtless skateboarders, I see a cafe with homemade benches outside. I'm so tired, I'd like to sit down on one of the benches and not get up for a very, very long time. I don't know where the stranger is heading, and I'm beginning to doubt that he has any goal at all when he stops again, on a busy street. Across the road is a large church. The stranger throws back his head and looks up at the spire.

When the pedestrian lights change to green, he crosses the road and steps through the door of the church. I'm still wondering whether to follow him in when he reappears, glances about him, walks another five hundred metres and then stops again. I too come to a halt and watch him as he scans the houses on the other side of the road, the stream of people washing past him as if he were an island in the middle of a river. I too look across at the houses, perfectly normal houses, some of them with graffitied facades and bikes outside. I see the stranger cross the road and stop in front of the house directly opposite. He glances in my direction and I dodge behind a news kiosk just in time. The stranger digs a slip of paper out of his trouser pocket, unfolds it, studies it, looks up at the house again, which has a number forty-one so large you can't miss it, and puts the paper back in his pocket. For a few moments the stranger just stands there. Then he climbs the steps to the front door and rings the bell. Soon afterwards the door is opened. I can't see who has opened it—whoever is in the doorway is hidden from view by the stranger. A few seconds later, the impostor disappears into the house and the door closes behind him.

I'd give a lot to be able to turn myself into a mouse like one of the wizards in the fairytales I read Leo, so that I could slip into the house unnoticed and eavesdrop on the conversation. I need to find out whose house this is and what is being discussed. I memorise the address and resolve to find out who lives there.

I wait for a long time. I'm beginning to think the stranger isn't going to re-emerge, when he suddenly appears at the door. He looks left and right, without noticing me in the now bustling street, then goes down the steps and on his way. I step briskly towards the house from which the stranger has just emerged, desperate for a glimpse of the person he's been talking to.

Before the door closes, I see him.

It's a man. I start when I see his face. Adrenaline shoots through me.

I know him.

The stranger

She's been following me ever since I left the house. I see her dart across the edge of my field of vision and sense her presence behind me. It isn't easy to act as if I hadn't noticed her. My first impulse was to turn round and confront her. But that would have been unwise. Only one thing is certain: she is absolutely unpredictable. Who knows what she is capable of? But as long as she's following me, I know where she is and what she's doing. I have to concentrate on what lies before me. I can do without distractions.

I've almost reached my target. I go through my plan once more and look at the clock. Just six. Good.

Sarah

My synapses click and a dull, unpleasant sensation spreads through my stomach. I know that man. I've seen him before, although I have no idea where. Something tells me it's crucial that I remember who he is, but I can't. He had a soft face, almost youthful, although he must have been about forty. Jeans, polo shirt, a bit of a belly—nice enough looking at first sight, but at the same time somehow threatening. Strange.

Cyclists and pedestrians weave past. The sun dazzles me as it climbs higher and higher in the sky, but my thoughts are still with the man who just disappeared behind that door. I briefly consider ringing the bell to find out who he is and what he knows, but I tell myself I can do that another time if I think it wise, and decide instead to continue following the stranger, who has already turned the corner and vanished out of sight.

When I turn the corner myself, I'm momentarily afraid that I've lost him, and cursing under my breath, I hurry on. I look left and right, stand on tiptoes, spin round in a circle, but he's nowhere to be seen. Then, just as I'm on the point of giving up and turning back, a small knot of people disperse in front of me and I spot him disappearing into an underground station. Is he suddenly in a hurry? Has he noticed me? I make a dash for the station and try to guess which way he's headed. Trains to the city centre stop at the platform on the left, and trains travelling in the opposite direction stop at the platform on the right. The place is teeming with people now—it's the middle of the rush hour.

I've lost sight of him again and decide on the city centre, letting the current of people carry me down the stairs to the platform and hoping that my gut feeling won't let me down. I fight my way through the sweaty, surging mass of coffee-swilling, smartphone-swiping bodies blocking the platform—and almost run into the stranger. He is suddenly right in front of me, although his back is turned to me. I come to an abrupt halt and step to one side, almost crashing into an elderly gentleman whom I dodge without taking my eyes off the stranger. I take up position a few metres behind him. It is so full here that he probably wouldn't see me even if he turned round. He doesn't seem to sense that he's being watched at all, but stands calmly in the middle of the crowd, not drinking coffee, not using a smartphone, just standing there, a faint, dreamy smile on his lips as if listening to a beautiful tune that only he can hear. I don't like his expression at all. He looks incredibly contented—no, he actually looks *happy*.

The train pulls in. I wait for the stranger to get on, then I walk to another door further down the carriage and get on too. I remain standing, so I can keep an eye on the stranger and react quickly.

He is also standing, just a few metres away, with his back to me. The doors close slowly, and I almost expect him to slip out at the last moment and throw me a look of triumph from the platform as the train carries me away. But nothing of the sort happens. The train moves off, bearing us into the dark, hurtling with us through the city's entrails. We move, we stop. Passengers get on and off. I keep a close eye on the stranger, but he doesn't make any move. We stop again—twice, three times, four times—before we arrive at the main railway station. This time he gets off.

I almost get stuck on the train—I've chosen a bad spot, too far from the doors, and the train is already filling with passengers who are pouring in towards me. I fight my way past them, making good use of my elbows—no time to be polite—then scrabble through the bottleneck and at last make it onto the platform before the doors close and the train sets off again. I look frantically up and down the platform. Radiant sunshine streams in through the windows high above me—you can feel that a hot day lies ahead. The stranger is on the escalator, going up, and I scurry after him. He saunters across the station concourse, past commuters and homeless people, fast-food temples and coffee shops, past passport photo booths and florists and newsagents, past couples in tears, parting or reuniting. I hardly glance at any of that—my eyes are fixed on the retreating head of this stranger who claims to be my husband. He stops at a vending machine, and I see him dig change out of his trouser pocket, studying the array of multicoloured products on display behind the glass. I wonder whether the vending machine is a meeting place—whether the stranger is waiting for someone.

Nonsense, I tell myself. No one's going to come—this isn't a spy film. But even as I'm thinking that, someone appears and approaches the stranger—a small wiry man with short brown hair, dressed in dark jeans and an FC St. Pauli shirt. I'm too far away to hear what they're saying, but I can see their mouths moving. They are momentarily concealed from view by a group of noisy teenagers, and by the time I have a clear view again, the small wiry man has vanished. I just have time to see the stranger slipping something I can't make out into his pocket with an exaggerated display of nonchalance. Then he puts money in the slot, fiddles around with the buttons, waits for something to fall into the opening at the bottom, bends over to take it out—and heads towards the exit. I wonder what I have witnessed. Was the stranger given information? Or did an exchange take place between the two men?

The stranger leaves the station. As before, he looks as if he's just out for a walk, as if he has no clear goal, but I now know that isn't the case. He does nothing without good reason—everything is part of an elaborate plan, but I can only guess at what that plan might be. I think again of the man the stranger called on earlier, picture his face, so strangely familiar, and I rack my brains trying to remember how I know him, but it doesn't come to me.

Outside the station, wasps are buzzing around a group of tourists sitting in the sun, as they drain their paper coffee cups and catch a last blast of ultraviolet light before hurrying off to their trains. Smokers stand around here and there, hastily finishing their cigarettes before the next train leaves. The only people not contributing to the hectic atmosphere are the homeless, who stand around in clusters, chatting and smoking or listening to the bald, bull-necked preacher who has planted himself in front of them and is declaiming loudly from the Bible, telling them insistently that Jesus came down to save them. The stranger stops for a moment as if to listen to the preacher, and I expect someone else to approach and slip him something on the sly, but instead he walks towards the homeless men. I can't hear what is said, but I see him pull a bundle of banknotes out of his jeans pocket and distribute them among the men. I can't believe my eyes. What in heaven's name is he doing—and why? He's not giving this money away out of the goodness of his heart—that much is clear to me. Is he paying the men? But what for? Then it hits me: they could be extremely useful to him. Keeping a discreet eye on anyone arriving at the station. Watching, gathering information, reporting back to him. Testifying, if necessary.

I reach no clear-cut conclusion and have to move on, because the stranger has crossed the road and is disappearing into a side street, calmly munching on his chocolate bar. My forehead is beaded with sweat, and now my phone's ringing too—I fish it out, cursing. Mirko. Now of all times. Still, I take the call.

'Mirko, not now, please,' I hear myself say like a broken record. I hang up.

Not long after, the phone rings again.

This time I refuse the call.

When I look up, the stranger has disappeared into the crowd.

On my way to fetch Leo, I drive as if on autopilot, still trying to remember who that man was at number 41 and where I've seen him before. I beat my brains until they ache, but get nowhere. I realise I'm driving too fast, racing over the asphalt, and I try to concentrate, but it's impossible—my thoughts are a maelstrom.

I can't bring Leo home, can't have him in the house with the stranger, but I don't know what to do—what to tell him, how to explain, what reason I can give Miriam. When she texted to check I'd be there soon, I just got in the car and set out, hoping some plan would come to me on the way. I overtake a convertible, get back into the right lane and try to force my brain back on track.

I'm turning into Miriam's street when I realise I can't do it—if I go through her front door, if I let myself be enveloped by my friend's warmth, the cheerful chaos of her house, I'll break down. If I see Leo, see my beautiful son, I'll fall apart.

I take my foot off the accelerator, flick on the right indicator and park at the kerb.

Yes, I decide. I take out my phone, ring Miriam and ask her to keep Leo a little longer—just for this afternoon, or possibly this evening, too. I'm not sure yet, I tell her.

'Of course,' she says. 'You know how much we love to have him here. But is everything okay, hon?'

'Tell him I love him,' I say, keeping my voice as steady as I can. 'And that I'll see him very soon. How's he doing?'

'Honestly, hon, he's fine. I'm sure the scene at the airport must have been completely overwhelming, but you know what kids are like—one minute they're having a full-on tantrum, and the next they're fine. Three seconds after he came in the front door he was right as rain. I'm sure he'll be thrilled to stay a little longer, too, so no need to worry. You know what those boys are like when they're together—they're out in the backyard, playing in the treehouse Martin built for them. I practically had to climb up there myself and drag them down last night when it was time for bed.'

I force a laugh. 'Thanks, Miri,' I say, 'I owe you one,' and then, before she can ask me about Philip, I hang up.

Then I turn the car around and set off again.

The nursing home where Philip's mother lives is in one of the nicest parts of town. The park surrounding the buildings, lush and green in spite of the heat, is deserted—no dutiful children or grandchildren strolling beneath the old trees with their fragile relatives, no carers ferrying residents about in wheelchairs. It must just be too hot. I haven't been here for a long time, and I'm sorry about that now—although Constanze and I were never close, even before the wedding. She had wanted something more for her son than a humble teacher—maybe one of the beautiful daughters of her wealthy friends. The kind of woman who can wear white without messing it up and organise charity events— the kind who looks good in pearl necklaces and tailored suits.

The wedding was the final straw for her, though. Philip and I had been married in Las Vegas, without family, without anyone. Just him, me, the registrar, the fat Elvis, a hired witness and the neon signs, flashing in our eyes. It had been Philip's suggestion, a spur-of-the-moment thing, while were on holiday in California. Tasteless, Constanze had pronounced it. Utterly tasteless. I wondered then what my own mother would have said. I think she'd have been pleased. Philip told me not to worry—Constanze was annoyed, but she'd get over it. She wasn't annoyed, though— she was furious. He was her only child, and she hadn't been invited to his wedding. We had our American marriage officialised as soon as we got back to Germany—Philip insisted on doing everything properly—but Constanze refused to accompany us to the registry office.

He'd been thinking of me, I know it—trying to protect me. I had no family, and if we'd had the big society wedding Constanze wanted for her son, it would have been painfully obvious—but she couldn't see that, or didn't want to.

I sit in the car, the air-conditioner humming, my thoughts shooting about like ball bearings in an old-fashioned pinball machine, lighting up now this part of my memories, now that one. I think of Las Vegas, the fat Elvis impersonator, my ring from the bubble-gum machine, our friends' cheers when we returned from the States a married couple. I think of Philip, so handsome in his rented tuxedo, and what it felt like when he took me in his arms and kissed me. My body responds to the memory of it, even after all this time, a delicious warmth spreading from the pit of my stomach. When Philip held me I was astonished every time at how perfectly my body fitted into his, my cheek pressed into the hollow between his shoulder and neck. I think of Leo's birth, of Philip cradling him in his arms for the first time and not crying, but laughing. I think of the night we met. Being young.

Thunder and lightning. Summer skies. I would so much rather think of the first time we saw each other than the last. I don't remember what Philip was wearing when he left for the airport. I don't remember whether he kissed me on the forehead or the mouth. I only remember the banality of the last things we said.

'Give me a ring when you get there.'

'Of course.'

'And don't forget to get in touch with your mother. You know what she's like.'

'Will do.'

Then the phone rang inside the house. I usually waved to Philip until he was out of sight, but this time I didn't watch him leave—he never looked back anyway. I went back into the house and shut the door. I can't even remember who was on the phone.

Yes, I much prefer to think of the first time we saw each other than the last.

I shake my head, turn off the engine and step out into the heat.

Yesterday, when Barbara Petry asked me who could confirm my husband's identity, I immediately thought of Johann and was perhaps too quick to reject the idea of involving my mother-in-law. Constanze has, I'm afraid, gone rapidly downhill mentally in the past few years. It was only when she could no longer cope at home even with professional help that we could persuade her to move into a home, but she still has her lucid moments—and right now, she's all I have.

I march resolutely into the reception area. White, pastel tones, orchids—but these attempts to make the place more homely with soft colours and flowers have only made it more clinical. I breathe deeply, ignoring the pungent smell of PVC flooring and disinfectant. If I want to pull this off, I have to seem confident. No nervousness. That's another thing I learnt from Philip.

To my astonishment, there is no humming and hawing from the nursing-home staff when I announce that I'd like to borrow my mother-in-law for coffee. Instead, I am greeted with congratulations. Mrs Kawatzki, the director of the home, a spindly little woman with kindly pale blue eyes and short hennaed hair, tells me they've been expecting me. Her fat blond colleague, whom I don't know, gives a friendly nod, and I understand: they have heard about Philip's homecoming. I have no time to be thrown off my guard.

'We thought your husband might be dropping in,' says Kawatzki, 'to see his mother again after all these years. But this is nice too, of course—that you've come to pick her up. You can all have a lovely cosy chat with each other at home.'

I nod, only just managing to keep my impatience in check.

'We tried to tell Mrs Petersen about her son yesterday, when we heard the good news, but she didn't understand,' the blond nurse says. 'But she's having a good day today, so you'll be able to tell her yourself, which is even nicer.'

I nod politely, smile and promise to bring Constanze back in time for supper. But the two women, I realise, aren't remotely worried about that. The return of the long-lost son, the newspaper and TV reports—it's just like seven years ago. They all want their share of the drama. I swallow heavily and brace myself to meet Philip's mother. It's been so long since I last saw her that I don't know what 'a good day' means nowadays. I hold my breath as Mrs Kawatzki knocks at the door of her room.

'Come in,' Constanze calls. She is sitting in an armchair, knitting. She looks up and sees me in the doorway behind Mrs Kawatzki. She hesitates, then her face brightens. 'Sarah,' she says, 'what a surprise!'

We are hurtling over the asphalt, which is so hot that the air above it is shimmering. It took a while to bundle Constanze into my car. She insisted on walking rather than letting me push her in a wheelchair. I could appreciate that—I wouldn't be too keen on having anyone push me either, certainly not someone I didn't particularly like.

Constanze sits beside me in silence, looking out at the summer-green landscape flashing past.

I glance across at her. How fragile she is, with her translucent, parchment-like skin, her fine white hair. A little plucked bird. She stares dreamily out of the window, a faint smile on her thin lips. I don't like to think about how small her world has grown in the past few years. I should have visited her more often. I shake the thought off and focus on the road, glad that she is as taciturn as ever.

I suppose what I'm doing is wrong—I ought to tell her what's going on. But I want a genuine reaction from her and I want it in front of witnesses. It is crucial that I get back before the stranger does. I'm racing along the road, ignoring the speed limit, ignoring Constanze's occasional disapproving comments on my driving style. I brake abruptly at a zebra crossing, and then, almost eaten up by impatience, decide not to drive the usual way, but to take a short cut through town—it's still early, and the roads are reasonably clear, so I should save myself a few minutes. The staid part of town where I live gives way to a hipper neighbourhood and I realise I've made a mistake—the traffic is heavy here, in spite of the weekend. Too many zebra crossings, too many prams and pushchairs, too many double-parked cars, too many red lights. At one set of lights, I watch, irate, as an old woman ambles across the road with a small shaggy dog. Then my attention is caught by something else. A movement. A man. He's walking down the street, away from me—I see him only from behind. His back. The back of his head. I know the back of that head. I know that gait. I would recognise it among thousands.

My heart lurches. I watch him walking down the street until he vanishes amid all the other people waltzing along the pavement. Then, at last, I react. I cut the engine, pull out the key and fling open the door. I leave the car where it is with my mother-in-law sitting in it. She calls out after me, a surprised 'Sarah, what on earth are you doing?' I ignore the angry hoots behind me. Nothing matters anymore, nothing. I sprint down the street after the man. When I reach the spot where I lost sight of him, I pause for a moment, look left, look right. Where is he? Where's he gone? I set off at a run, striking out at random, straight ahead—he can't have disappeared—I saw him—he must be somewhere about. But I can't see him. He's not in front of me. I'm standing on a street corner; he must have turned left or right; if he'd carried on straight ahead I'd have seen him. So left or right, left or right, don't waste time thinking—left or right, all or nothing? I pull myself together and turn left. I run, but the crowds hamper my progress, I dodge, I weave, I fight my way through, I push and shove, I don't apologise. Where is he? Then I see him. The back of his head, his white T-shirt, only a few metres away. I yell. At the top of my voice.

'Philip!'

A few people turn and stare, wondering what's going on. I ignore them and fight my way through to the man. I'm almost level with him when he turns his head slightly, revealing his profile. It's not him. It is not him. I followed the wrong man. I stop, devastated. I made the wrong decision—I should have turned right. I hurry back the other way, against the current of people and come to the corner again. I take the other street this time, scanning the crowd for the back of his head, the white T-shirt—but I don't find him. He has vanished.

The world around me suddenly seems frenzied, like a video that's been artificially speeded up. I close my eyes for a second. What have I done? I've left Constanze in the car. What if she's gone when I get back? What was I thinking, for Christ's sake?

Worst-case scenarios run through my head all the way back to the street where I left the car, but when I arrive it's still parked there at the pedestrian crossing, angry drivers swerving around it. I breathe a sigh of relief. Constanze, too, is still there. She gives me a look that is part anger, part confusion.

'What on earth's going on?' she asks.

I get in, ignoring the horns blaring at me.

'Nothing,' I say, my mouth dry. 'I thought I saw someone.'

I drive off. Constanze is silent.

I tell myself that I didn't see Philip—it wasn't him. I tell myself I am very tired. I tell myself that I must focus on the task at hand.

At home, I offer Constanze a seat on the living-room sofa, help her to sit down, give her a glass of water and withdraw to my bedroom to make a phone call. I don't bother to check whether the stranger has got back. He has no keys, so he can't be in the house, but he's bound to turn up sooner or later. If he wants to carry on playing the part of Philip Petersen, he'll have to come back. This time I'll be ready for him. He's going to like the little surprise I've planned for him, I'm sure.

I dial Miriam's number and invite her to an impromptu coffee party. She's delighted—partly, I suppose, because she thinks she's going to meet Philip at last.

'I'll go get Leo down from the tree house,' she says. 'We'll be right over.'

'No!' I say. 'No, don't bring Leo. Let him stay and play a little longer.'

Miriam hesitates. 'Is everything okay, Sarah?'

'Everything's fine,' I say, but I know that won't convince her. 'I'll explain later. You don't mind him staying a little longer, though, do you? Martin won't mind having both boys and the baby to look after on his own?'

'God no,' Miri says. 'Martin loves having Leo here too—the more the merrier, as far as he's concerned.'

She tells me that everything will be all right, that she's coming right round, and if there's anything—anything at all—that she and Martin can do to make things easier for me, all I have to do is ask.

After talking to Miriam, I go and check up on Constanze, who is leafing through one of the poetry books on the coffee table. She looks up when I enter.

'I do like that print,' she says, pointing at the framed picture on the wall opposite.

Either she has forgotten she gave it to us herself—or else it's her strange sense of humour, which I never understood. Constanze looks at me, a thin smile playing on her hard lips, her eyes sparkling. A joke, then.

'Hasn't changed much here,' she says, looking about her.

Any minute now she'll get up and run her finger over the furniture to check for dust. I sigh inwardly. I know exactly why I visited her so rarely.

'The bookshelves are new,' she says, pointing at the wall. 'And my rug's gone.'

Patience, Sarah.

'Personally,' Constanze says brusquely, 'I find bare boards rather vulgar, but tastes differ.'

I try not to roll my eyes.

'Sarah? Are you even listening?'

'Yes,' I say. 'Yes, of course.'

Constanze looks at me with a frown and returns to her poetry book.

I decide it's all right to leave her by herself for a few minutes longer, and then, feeling a little giddy, I go and call on my neighbour, Mrs Theis.

When I get back to the house, I notice that I'm still wearing the white summer dress I put on for Philip's homecoming. I hurry upstairs, jump in and out of the shower, dash into my bedroom and put on jeans, T-shirt and trainers.

Then I fetch my handbag and take out my phone. I don't even bother to work out what time it is in China—I just try Johann again straight off. Who cares if I wake him? What matters is that I get hold of him. It's a long time since we had a proper chat—it was from the papers, not from him, that I found out about his company's financial difficulties. Is that why he's so hard to get hold of?

Once again, he doesn't take the call. Frustrated, I give up.

The broken table in the spare room is still lying there in pieces. The stranger's holdall is also on the floor. I quickly open the zip and rummage through the things inside. Clothes, mainly clothes. Also a razor, shaving foam, deodorant, a book, a phone, a charger. I stop short. I haven't yet seen the stranger with a phone. Was that what he tried to hide from me? I swipe the screen, but it's switched off. I curse under my breath. Then I pick up the book and open it at random. It's in Spanish, a language I don't read.

156

I leaf through the pages. There are no underlinings, no notes. There doesn't seem to be anything special about this book at all. I'm on the point of putting it away when something occurs to me. Unlikely, but still. I open it at the first page and can hardly believe it. Handwriting. Blue biro. *For Vincent. From Dad. May 2005.*

Vincent.

I suddenly hear Constanze calling.

Quickly, I stuff everything back in the bag.

Before long, we're sitting round the kitchen table, which is laid with tea and coffee, milk, sugar and lemon, cake and biscuits. Mrs Theis has brought brightly coloured dahlias from her garden.

Constanze is sitting in state opposite me. On my right is Mrs Theis, and opposite her, Miriam. It was a good idea to invite Miriam and Mrs Theis, not just because they'll be witness to the meeting between Philip's mother and the stranger, but also because their pleasant chatter fills the kitchen and soothes my nerves.

Mrs Theis, as always, talks about her garden. Miriam, as always, talks about her children. To my amazement, Constanze regales us with anecdotes from Philip's childhood. I ought to listen, but it's not easy.

The party can begin.

The stranger

My discovery of a spare key under a flowerpot has made things rather easier. I was surprised that she should be so negligent, but then some people think they can get away with murder.

I unlock the door and go in, satisfied with the day so far. The conversation I had was disagreeable but helpful. I've taken a significant step forward. Now I know exactly what I have to do. All I'm waiting for is Grimm's call—the last piece in the puzzle. Patience. No giving up. No mistakes, now that the end's in sight. It did me good to get out of the house and stretch my legs. My body is refreshed, my thoughts in order. I see more clearly than I did. I slam the door shut behind me—I want her to know I'm back. I cross the hall with a firm tread. She put me slightly off my stride, but that's over now. I just have to keep going.

I hear low voices and stop, puzzled. I'm wondering whether she's on the phone when she suddenly appears before me. I quickly slip the key into my trouser pocket. She notices, but astonishingly enough says nothing.

What's she up to?

Sarah

My assumption that the stranger will instinctively follow me into the kitchen proves right. Now is not the time to get annoyed that he has found my—admittedly very badly concealed—spare key, which I'm afraid I didn't think of in time. I can see to that later.

As if it were the most natural thing in the world, I sit back down on my chair while Miriam and Mrs Theis peer expectantly towards the door. Only Constanze continues to sip her tea calmly.

The stranger enters the room and stops in stunned shock when he realises we're not alone. He immediately covers up his surprise, conjuring that look on his face again—that mixture of charm, strength and exhaustion that was so irresistible to the journalists—and Barbara Petry, too. He smiles at Mrs Theis. He smiles at

Miriam. Then Constanze turns in her chair to face him. I watch him closely. The stranger is put off his stride for a moment—his expression slips. Maybe he knows or can guess who she is. It shouldn't be that hard to put two and two together. He gives her a strange look—bewilderment? suspicion?—then collects himself and readjusts his mask. Before he can say anything, before he can come up with a strategy, before Miriam or even Mrs Theis can get up and introduce themselves, I rush in.

'Constanze?' I say, getting up. 'I have a surprise for you. Philip's here. Your son.'

She stares at the stranger. He can't withstand her gaze even a second, and guiltily averts his eyes.

'Constanze,' I say, 'aren't you pleased to see him?'

Miriam frowns. Is it because of my chilly manner? Or because there's a certain tension in the air? Mrs Theis seems to catch her breath too. Constanze still hasn't spoken.

The stranger hesitates a moment longer, then seems to come to a decision. He raises his arms and takes a step towards Constanze, who sits there as if turned to stone. As he reaches out to hug her, she shrinks back, waving an indignant hand at him, then leans on the table, frail arms shaking, and pushes herself up. The table jerks beneath her hands, knocking over the milk jug, and the chair she was sitting on only a moment before falls over sideways with a clatter. Out of the corner of my eye, I see Miriam leap to her feet.

'That's not my son!' Constanze says, her voice faltering. 'That's not my son! I've never seen that man in my life!' She gasps for breath, as if these words have cost her all her strength.

Miriam is the first to react: frowning at me, she goes round the table to the old woman, steadies her, speaks soothingly to her. She's wondering how I could inflict a shock like this on such a fragile soul.

The stranger hasn't moved. As if in slow motion, he lets his arms sink back to his sides.

I triumph secretly. Good that Miriam and Mrs Theis heard that. Good that they've been talking to Constanze all afternoon and can testify that she was lucid and compos mentis when she spoke those words.

Miriam helps Constanze to sit down, and I'm just about to tell the stranger that he's upsetting Constanze and had better leave, so that I can explain everything to Mrs Theis and Miriam, when Constanze starts to speak again.

'My son is dead,' she says. 'My greedy, deceitful daughter-in-law killed him. Everyone in Hamburg knows that. Everyone.'

I feel all the colour drain from my face.

Mrs Theis and Miriam look at the floor in embarrassment.

Constanze gives a bitter laugh. 'My son's probably at the bottom of the Elbe.'

The milk from the overturned jug drips onto the wooden floorboards. I grip the back of a chair and watch, transfixed, as the milk forms a little white pool. Bigger and bigger it grows— plink, plink. I block out everything else until I see only its smooth white surface. I can feel my mouth hanging open, but I can't close it. I am paralysed—and I'm not the only one. The entire room is frozen. No movement, no sound, no word. Horror and a hint of vanilla hang in the air.

Then Miriam breaks the spell. She makes reassuring noises, soft murmuring sounds, until gradually Constanze calms down. When the old woman begins to ask for her long-dead husband, I feel suddenly dizzy and drop into a chair.

Mrs Theis gets up then and excuses herself. 'I think it's time I was on my way,' she says. 'Got ever so much to do today.' Within seconds she has vanished. I hadn't realised she could be so nimble.

Miriam offers to take Constanze home, but I wave the offer aside. I can do that myself.

'Are you sure?' she asks.

I nod.

Miriam throws me a glance I can't interpret.

'We'll wait outside,' she says and begins to steer my mother-in-law out, stopping by the door to tell the spurious Philip that she's delighted to have met him at last and is sure they'll see each other under more auspicious circumstances next time.

He goes to shake her hand, the perfect gentleman, then lingers at the door, blocking my way as I try to get past.

'What was all that about?' he snaps.

'Your mother wasn't exactly overjoyed to have you back,' I say.

'Do you want to talk about *your* mother, perhaps?'

That winds me, like a physical blow.

'You'll regret this,' he whispers.

The stranger

Over the past years, I've learnt to cope with extreme stress—pain, hunger, fear. I was permanently exposed to the elements—to the wet, to the cold, to unbearable heat and humidity. Then there were all those creatures. My habit of shaking out my shoes and boots before putting them on, the way my fellow prisoners in camp taught me, will probably stay with me all my life. I remember sitting on my plank bed one morning and pulling my boots over to me, shaking the left one, shaking the right one—and then looking on in horror as an enormous bird-eating spider fell out and scuttled away.

Here in Hamburg there are no dangerous creatures. Only dangerous people.

But I know how to deal with those too.

I open the fridge and take out ham and cheese. I eat both straight from the packet. Once again, I run over the scene she staged. What was it all about? What did she hope to achieve?

I put the food back in the fridge, pour myself a glass of water and drain it in one draught.

Then I remember. I am suddenly wide awake. How could I forget? That is just the kind of negligence that could be my undoing.

I set to work at once.

Sarah

The sun is beating down. It's the kind of day when children are taken to hospital with sunstroke and the elderly die of dehydration. The scene in the kitchen runs round and round in my head as I speed over the hot shimmering asphalt, Constanze beside me in the passenger seat. She is humming quietly to herself and seems positively cheerful. Spraying her poison has given her a kick, as it always does.

I flick on the right indicator, let a cyclist past and turn onto the main road. The street ahead is unusually empty. Anyone who can has left town, gone to the pool or at least stayed inside out of the sun. I glance at Constanze and see that she has closed her eyes and is smiling.

'Everything all right?' I ask.

'Yes, thank you, Monika,' she says. 'I'm fine.'

I have no idea who Monika is—one of the nursing-home staff, perhaps, or somebody from the past. It occurs to me how little I know about my husband's mother.

Once out of my quiet area, the traffic is slow-moving. Constanze and I sit in silence for a while. When I've had enough of that, I put the radio on. Summery pop comes from the speakers, and I turn it off again.

'I dreamt of my Green today,' Constanze says. 'My Philip.'

At once my heart begins to beat faster.

Her eyes are still closed, as if she can recall the dream images better that way.

'Really?' I ask, cautiously.

'Yes.'

I shift into gear, then come to a standstill again at the next set of lights. I'm beginning to think that Constanze isn't going to say any more when suddenly she goes on.

'We were in a kitchen. Everything—the people, the place—seemed so familiar to me, and at the same time not at all, as so often in dreams. It was strange. We were eating cake, I think, and drinking tea. My son was there, my Philip, and my daughter-in-law too. Then I was somewhere quite different, back in my room, I think. Do you have dreams like that, Monika, when you change place from one moment to the next and just carry on dreaming about somewhere quite different?'

Constanze opens her eyes and looks at me. Only she doesn't see me—she sees Monika.

I nod. 'Yes,' I say. 'I do.'

'I have far too many dreams about my room,' Constanze says. 'If I had my say, I'd never dream about my room—it seems such a waste. Who knows how many dreams I have left? If I could choose, I'd dream I was flying a helicopter or going for a walk on the beach with my husband or playing with my little boy again, the way I used to.'

She relapses into silence.

The low sun is dazzling me. I don't have my sunglasses with me and have to squint, concentrating on the road to make sure I don't overlook any cyclists—but I'm still wondering how I can find out why Constanze said earlier that I killed her son. She can't seriously think that.

'You dreamt about your daughter-in-law?' I prompt.

Constanze sniffs.

'What did you dream?'

She doesn't reply.

'Constanze?'

No reply.

No sooner have we set foot in the reception area than Mrs Kawatzki comes hurrying to greet us. 'The two Mrs Petersens,' she says. 'There you are again.'

In businesslike fashion she sets Constanze in a wheelchair. My mother-in-law suffers it without protest and Kawatzki accompanies us to Constanze's room, perhaps hoping for some exciting snippets about Philip. As she manoeuvres the wheelchair into the lift, she comments on the sweltering heat and tells Constanze what's for supper. 'Have a nice afternoon did you, Mrs Petersen?' she asks eventually.

Her tone gets me down—she always sounds as if she's talking to a child. Constanze doesn't reply and I'm glad. The lift doors close and an awkward silence descends. Mrs Kawatzki and I stare at the illuminated buttons telling us which floor we're on. Constanze stares into space.

When we've dropped Constanze off in her room, I heave a sigh of relief, ready to say a quick goodbye and get away as fast as I can—away from this depressing place, and away from this woman, too, who was forever trying to poison my marriage, and whose venom is still deadly now, though she has grown so old and decrepit. I give Mrs Kawatzki my hand, thank her and turn to leave.

'I had a strange dream,' Constanze suddenly says. 'About my daughter-in-law.'

I let go of the doorhandle and turn round.

Mrs Kawatzki smiles mildly. 'What nice things did you dream about your daughter-in-law then?' she asks.

'I remember the first time my son brought her to see me—such a mousy little thing,' says Constanze. 'She was a student teacher—a dull-witted girl, no family, no ambitions, thoroughly common. And there was something in her look…' She pauses to reflect on it. 'Deceitful is probably nearest the mark,' she says. 'It was a mystery to me what Philip saw in her.'

Mrs Kawatzki looks awkwardly at the floor, but I'm sure she's enjoying herself.

'She looked as if butter wouldn't melt in her mouth, but she didn't take me in for a second. I can sense it when somebody's hiding something. My mother always said I had it from my father, and he was a judge, you know.'

'Your father was a judge?' Mrs Kawatzki asks, evidently embarrassed after all and keen to change the subject.

Constanze nods. 'I've been hearing my mother's voice a lot lately,' she goes on. 'All kinds of things she used to say when I was a child have been coming back to me—it's strange. So many things, all flying back to me—who knows where they've been all this time. Funny words we used when I was a child, for example. Tea was made in a treckpott, and the woman next door who helped bring little babies into the world was called the stork auntie. And do you know those big buzzing May bugs that come in the spring? We used to collect them, because they were lucky, but our word for them was *eckelteev*. I had such a happy childhood, you know. My mother was a beautiful woman. And my father was a fine man, only…'

Her voice trails off. I look across at her and see that she is frowning.

'Where was I?' She makes it sound more like a statement than a question.

'The mousy little thing,' I say. 'Your daughter-in-law.'

Mrs Kawatzki clears her throat loudly, but doesn't intervene. She is not, however, discreet enough to leave the room.

I don't care.

'Oh, her,' says Constanze. 'The first time he brought her to see me I had a good look at her, of course. I asked her things any mother would have asked, although Philip claimed it was more like an interrogation.'

I swallow heavily. I remember that meeting with a painful clarity.

'When Philip told me he wanted to marry her—this was much later, I don't know exactly when—I was flabbergasted. Horrified. I did what my husband would have done if he'd still been with us. I hired someone to make enquiries about her. And my gut instinct proved right. That drab little mouse wasn't right in the head. I collected all the evidence and then presented it to Philip— the report about her spell in a psychiatric hospital, for example.'

Oh my God.

'And all the rest.'

She knows.

'He could see then what kind of a woman he was thinking of marrying. Or rather, he didn't see. He wouldn't listen to me. He swept the papers off the table and said he didn't want to hear it, that he was a grown man, he trusted the woman and I'd have to get used to the idea. He didn't even want to draw up a prenuptial agreement, the stupid boy. Then one day I got a card from abroad. Sarah and Philip Petersen. That wedding was a disgrace. They didn't even have the decency…'

She lets the sentence fizzle out.

'Did you have enough to drink this afternoon? You dehydrate so fast in this heat,' says Mrs Kawatzki, but I interrupt before she can go on.

'You said earlier that your daughter-in-law murdered your son.' I try to strike a chatty tone, but Constanze doesn't reply, apparently more interested in her knitting, which she tries, unsuccessfully, to fish off the table.

Mrs Kawatzki hands it to her and turns to me. 'Maybe you'd like to come back some other time,' she says, turning to me. 'Your mother-in-law obviously isn't in a good way.'

'I always warned Philip about falling for women who were only out for his money,' Constanze says. 'And then he went and did just that, the stupid boy.'

Mrs Kawatzki inhales sharply.

'How do you know your daughter-in-law was only after the money?' I ask.

'Because I put her to the test,' says Constanze. 'I offered her money to leave Philip.

What is she on about?

'A great deal of money,' says Constanze.

That isn't true.

'And how did she react?' I ask.

'It wasn't enough for her,' says Constanze. 'She wanted more. She haggled.'

I shake my head. 'Constanze?' I say.

She turns her head and looks me in the eye.

'That's a lie,' I say. 'You've made that up. Maybe because you had such a grim marriage yourself and begrudged your son his happiness. Maybe because you didn't know any better. Maybe because you're just a bad person.'

Constanze blinks a few times.

'Good Lord,' she says eventually, her voice friendly. 'None of that matters anymore anyway.'

I don't know what to say.

'Now for a cup of tea,' says Constanze.

I leave the room without looking back, but her words are still with me when I'm in the car again and the nursing home is growing smaller and smaller in the rear-view mirror.

The stranger

The pain in my head is so intense it's almost blinding. I'm having trouble reining in my anger. I've searched all over the house but found nothing, and it's gnawing at me. Grimm still hasn't been in touch. But I'm okay. I'll soon have a grip on myself.

Time for a change of tactics: I take a walk around the house, making a conscious effort not to look for hiding places, but to see everything with the eyes of a first-time visitor. I start upstairs, in the guestroom, already so familiar that it's hard to see it with fresh eyes. The next room has *Star Wars* posters on the wall, a half-built Lego castle on the floor, a book of fairytales and a few comics in the bookcase. I try to imagine the life of the boy who lives here, but it eludes me. I take a comic from the bookcase and sit down on the bed with it, careful to avoid the blue checked shirt lying there. I leaf through the comic without really looking at it. I put it back, leave the room, resume my search.

I soon find myself in the main bedroom. Bed and wardrobe, bedside table, chest of drawers. Pink bed linen, cream carpet. A reading lamp on the bedside table, hand cream, a packet of tissues, a pair of earplugs, a pack of aspirin, a book, a phone charger. I turn the book over—Dostoevsky—then pop an aspirin out of the blister pack and swallow it without water.

I open the wardrobe. It is tidy and scrupulously organised. On the inside of the door, where no one can see it, an ancient poster announces a Radiohead concert.

I close the wardrobe and open the chest of drawers, which I have so far rejected as too obvious a hiding place. I rummage around a bit, but, as expected, find nothing. No old letters, no diary, nothing like that.

I feel a brief pang of guilt. Yes, you could feel sympathy for the woman who lives here, bringing up a small boy on her own. You might even mistake her for a perfectly normal person—respect her, maybe even admire her.

But she is not a good person—not the nice, rather reserved teacher and mother she makes herself out to be. I can't let myself forget that. I'm probably the only person alive who knows what she is capable of.

I close the chest of drawers and leave the bedroom, none the wiser. I shall resume my search elsewhere.

Sarah

I'm sitting on a bench looking out over the Outer Alster Lake, snatching a few minutes to myself. The sun beats down on my head, warms my face, my bare arms. I watch the people out for a walk, children playing football on the grass, boats on the water, and I relish the normality of it. I've been sitting here for ages. Soon it will be dark and I'll have to make my way home. But I'm not ready yet.

Then, as a cloud scuds past the sun, I think of the eclipse. It was only a few days ago, but it feels like an eternity.

*

The world is black. The sun above me is black.

I stand, head thrown back, eyes wide open. I try to drink in the moment, to commit it to memory, to block out any other thought. I made a promise to myself many years ago, and now the time has come to make good that promise. I nod, as if to seal the bond with myself. The trees are rustling softly, almost ceremonially. Only the birds high in the branches seem unimpressed: they sing as if to spite the darkness, as if singing is all that matters. The sun is black and I stand and bask in the sight. There is no more warmth. No light.

Soon afterwards, I leave the woods. I return to my car and get in, braving the stifling heat. I take my phone out of my bag and see that Mirko has called—he'll be wondering where I've got to. I think of Mirko, of the two of us together, and it feels like betrayal. I think of the first time I saw him—the new, good-looking young colleague Claudia and the others had been raving about. I think of our first kiss, at my front door after a school party one evening. I look at my phone and reluctantly read the text that arrived while I was in the woods, saying my last goodbyes to the love of my life. It's from Mirko, only three words. I stare at them.

Life must go on, I tell myself. I've made my decision.

I invite Claudia and her husband to dinner. I ring Mirko and ask him to join us, telling him that it's time he got to know my son—time to put an end to the secrecy.

I go to the local hair salon, walk past it once, twice, three times before I have the courage to go in. Before I have time to change my mind, I'm sitting in a swivel chair, pulling the page I tore from the magazine out of my bag. Less than an hour later, I'm back out on the street, my head strangely light, almost as if I can breathe again, for the first time in years. I buy vegetables. I buy lemons and herbs and a chicken. I clean and cook. I open the doors and windows, sweep out the ghosts of the past and watch them swirl away. I pick up my son, give him his dinner, lay the table for my guests. I am alive. My husband is dead, but I am still here. I have people in the house—company. Mirko throws me blatant looks which I ignore and take pleasure in. I am an attentive hostess. I laugh. This is how life can be.

I lead the way to the front door, say goodbye to Claudia and her husband, thank them for coming, tell them how lovely it was to see them, realise as I say it that I mean it—and watch them disappear into the darkness. I thank Mirko for the lovely evening and the flowers. Mirko looks me in the eye and gives me an awkward pat on the shoulder.

He was the only one who knew it was the first time in seven years I'd had guests in my house. You can tell Mirko that kind of thing.

We're silent for a moment.

'It was about time,' he says, and I nod.

'Seven years,' I say. 'Seven years is a long time.'

He shakes his head. 'Time the two men in your life got to know each other, I mean.'

'Oh.'

'I like Leo,' he says.

'I think Leo likes you,' I reply. 'But now I should say goodnight and go in and check on him.'

Mirko smiles and gives me a kiss on the forehead. 'Can't I stay here tonight?'

I stare at him in surprise.

'I've been very patient,' he says.

I can't. I can't sleep with him in Philip's house, in Philip's bed.

'Please, Sarah. I've been very patient,' he says again.

I wrestle with myself, but eventually I give in. As we go into the house, I signal to Mirko to be quiet. Whatever happens, I don't want Leo to hear him.

And all the time I'm reading Leo his bedtime story, I'm thinking that my husband is dead and that Mirko is waiting for me in my bedroom.

We go on like that for a few nights. Somehow it feels wrong, but Mirko insists and I'm tired of arguing with him. I know it's time I started a new life, and I do my best, my absolute best.

Mirko says he's tired of the secrecy, that he wants our colleagues to know about us, wants Leo to know about us. I know he's right, but I'm afraid of how Leo will react. I begin to prepare myself, trying to decide the best way to tell him.

Leo must realise something's up, because I suddenly say yes to everything—suddenly Mum lets him do whatever he wants, even promising to take him to the zoo, when he knows she hates zoos.

The night before our trip to the zoo I lie awake, asking myself the same old questions.

Only the answers are new.

Philip has died. Philip is dead. Philip will never come back to us.

In the middle of the night I get up and pull on some clothes. After a moment's thought, I take a clean cotton handkerchief out of the chest of drawers. I leave the bedroom, creep downstairs and go out into the garden. It is quite a bit cooler, despite the day's heat, and the air smells clean and fresh. There isn't a sound. I feel like the loneliest person in the universe, but that's a good thing—I need to be alone for this.

I love our garden. In the first few years after Philip disappeared, I tried to keep it the way it had been before he left, just as I tried to keep everything in the house the way Philip had known it. But in recent years I've let nature have its way. I only occasionally mow the lawn under the apple and cherry trees, and here and there I've let the wildflowers seed themselves and run riot. The result is an enchanted place where Leo and his friends like to play and where I sit and watch the little spiders spinning their tiny webs in the branches of the currant bushes.

Now the garden lies silent, the only light coming from the kitchen window. No moon, no stars. I step out onto the grass, moving out of the light and deeper into the little wilderness sown by nature these last few years. My eyes grow accustomed to the dark and I make for the small shed behind the apple trees. I open the door and grope around until I find the spade. I close the shed again and let my eyes wander, then decide on a spot beneath one of the trees.

I plunge the spade into the earth, lever out a square sod of grass and lay it aside. I dig deeper, piling up the soil until the hole seems big enough. The air of a clear summer's night mingles with the pungent smell of earth. I put the spade down and stare into the hole I have dug.

I think of my husband. I see him by the water, in the place on the Elbe Beach where we first kissed and where we decided to get married—our place. I think of the way he used to be— the way *we* used to be—before that night, young and easygoing and free. I think of the smell of his hair, the curve of his upper lip, his dimples. I think of the ease with which he could pick me up—something no one has done since. I think of his insistence on always continuing a discussion to its bitter end and his frequent complaints about my silence. I think of his sense of humour. I think of all the arguments we got into when we first moved in together. We argued about the pettiest and most ridiculous things. About his craze for listening to Nick Cave's 'Do You Love Me?' umpteen times a day, which used to drive me mad. About the way he left everything standing around without a lid because he was too lazy to put the tops back on bottles of water, jars of jam, tubes of toothpaste. About my refusal to pay bills until the first reminder came, although we had more than enough money, and about my habit of leaving a spare key under the big flowerpot at the front door because I was always locking myself out.

'How can anyone be so stupid?' he would ask. 'How can you leave the key under a flowerpot? Where do you think we are? In some crazy utopian dream world?'

'Calm down,' I would say. 'No one would ever look for a key in such an obvious place.'

They were ridiculous, trivial arguments—arguments that inevitably ended in laughter or sex.

For the first few years, at any rate.

I know what I have to do now—I just don't know if I can. But I take a deep breath and do it. Seven years are suddenly enough. I pull the wedding ring off my finger. My flesh resists, but I pull the ring as hard as I can, wrenching it over the creases at my knuckles until at last I'm holding it in my hand. I take the old-fashioned handkerchief that once belonged to my adored grandmother and wrap the ring in it. With the slow, ceremonial movements of a funeral-goer, I sink to my knees, and then carefully, very carefully, I lay my wedding ring in the hole I have dug. When I stand up again, I have the feeling I ought to say something, but I don't know what. During all the lonely nights I've lain awake, I've said all there was to say, felt all there was to feel.

I think to myself that love is not a state, not a feeling—it is an organism that hungers and thirsts, a living being that can grow and atrophy, fall sick and convalesce, go to sleep and die.

A single tear rolls over my cheek and down my neck, soaking into the collar of my T-shirt as I take up the spade and cover my wedding ring with earth.

'Goodbye, Philip,' I say.

I put the spade down, and for a moment I stand there, my bare ring finger throbbing, before I pull myself together and go back into the house.

Not long after, I take Leo to the zoo. We look at the tired lion and the bright-eyed meerkats. I had expected to grieve, but instead I feel light. I have cut all ties to the past. A new beginning. A clean slate. I am so grateful. I smile cautiously and suddenly feel that everything is going to come right, that I can find new happiness.

I am looking at my son, searching for words, when my phone starts to ring. When I pick up, a man tells me that Philip is alive and coming back tomorrow.

I feel like laughing and crying, and at the same time I have the urge to take one of Philip's old golf clubs and trash the entire contents of my house.

I don't know what to feel, what to do. Can't eat, can't sleep, drift about aimlessly. I call my best friend but can't get hold of her. I call Johann but can't get hold of *him*. Distraught, I yell down the phone, but there's no one there. My head feels strange, my body peculiarly light. The whole world seems to have slipped, somehow. All the colours are different—red no longer looks red, green no longer looks green. I eat the raspberries my neighbour gives me and puke them up in little bright red puddles on the parquet. That's when Leo starts to worry, and I know I have to pull myself together. I'm like a robot that walks and talks and does things but is hollow inside. I talk to Leo, tell him everything will be okay. I call Mirko and tell him it's over between us and he's not to call me anymore. When he calls back, I don't pick up.

I rearrange the house, trying to put everything back the way it was when Philip last saw it.

Before the car arrives to take us to the airport, I go out into the garden, fetch the spade from the shed and dig up my wedding ring.

I remember how it felt, beginning afresh after seven years' gloom: no Philip, no fireworks, no brimming emotions. But a new chance of happiness.

Poor Mirko. It's over between us, that much is clear.

I was ready to drop him the moment I heard Philip was coming back. We can't be together anymore. He'll understand, in the end. And perhaps one day I'll manage to forgive myself for so pointlessly destroying everything I'd gone to such trouble to build up—for rejecting Mirko for the sake of a stranger.

I get up from the bench by the lake with a sigh. My life has become too complicated. I don't know where things go from here.

The stranger

I must have nodded off, in spite of everything. I sit up in a daze. I shouldn't have lain down. Haven't I learnt anything over the past months and years?

My pulse steadies. All is well. The situation is under control. If she'd come back, I would have noticed. I never sleep deeply—I'm on my guard even when I'm not awake. Still, I ought to make sure.

My gaze falls on the framed photos on the wall. So far I've avoided looking at them—what would be the point? Now I step closer. Most of the pictures are of her with the boy, but there is one photo that shows her laughing and happy in her husband's arms. There's no indication of when or where the photo was taken, but they both look very young and very happy. I tear myself away from her radiant smile and take a nearer look at the man. He is wearing a blue polo shirt and a self-confident grin. I feel faint repugnance welling up inside me—he looks like one of those people who have everything fall into their laps and don't realise their luck. I used to be like that. He looks like me—so much like me—but it was ridiculous to think I could fool her for even a second. I may look like Philip Petersen, know how to move like him, talk like him, but you can't reproduce the essence of a person. You can't fake soul. The man in that photo is dead, and no one will ever see him again.

My knee and elbow joints give a dry click when I get up. I stretch, circle my shoulders, ignore the pain. Then I cross the living room and go upstairs as quietly as I can. I make no noise—I'm practised at that. This time I'm careful to skip the fourth stair from the top.

I stop for a moment at the closed door of the bedroom. I know before I open it that the room on the other side is empty, but I'm still relieved. Her presence is so repellent to me that I'm glad of a few minutes longer without her.

Sarah

Constanze's angry words are still ringing in my head when I park the car in Miriam's road. I put on the handbrake, rifle through my bag, take out my phone and ring Johann. My impatience is becoming shot through with worry. Johann is a workaholic who can't live without his phone and is usually available 24/7. What if something's happened to him?

A metallic clank accompanies the ringing tone—one clank, two clanks, three, four, five, six. No one picks up. Damn. Another two days and nights until Johann lands in Germany and can help me.

I put the phone away, get out of the car and walk the few metres to Miriam's house. I usually stop and admire the full-blown blooms in her garden, swarming with bees that whirr like nervous satellites, but today I spare no glance for them. I'm here to check on Leo, to make sure he's all right, and to work out what to do with him for the next few days. I can hardly take him home, but I'm starting to wonder if I should abandon the house to the stranger and stay in a hotel after all.

I draw up my shoulders and ring the bell.

When Miriam opens the door and sees me, she pulls me to her at once. She smells of food and clean sweat.

'You poor thing,' she says. 'Are you okay?'

'Of course,' I say. It bothers me that she thinks I need comforting. I'm a thirty-seven-year-old woman, and stronger than most people. I don't need anyone to comfort me.

I follow her into the kitchen.

'Is Constanze all right now?' she asks.

'Yes, she's fine.'

'Today was probably a bit much for her. And then seeing Philip again and—'

'Where's Leo?' I say.

'Upstairs.' Miriam smiles. 'You know, it's incredible how alike the two of them are. He really is the spitting image of your husband.'

'Who?' I ask dully.

'What do you mean, who?' Miriam replies in amusement. 'Leo, of course.'

I blink, puzzled, but say nothing.

'I was wondering whether you and Philip wouldn't like to come round for dinner one night next week,' Miriam says. 'We'd love to have you. But only if it's not too much for Philip, of course.'

I don't reply. Miriam babbles on. Strange, I think, sitting there with her as if nothing had happened. Inside, I'm a different person, but on the outside nothing's changed. For the first time in my life I realise that everyone I know is an iceberg. I see their tiny, gleaming white tips, but not the forbiddingly large cones lurking in the darkness beneath.

'It's wonderful to see the two of you together,' Miriam says. 'You look like a Hollywood couple.' She giggles, as if we were teenagers talking about boys. 'Although…to be honest, I only knew Philip from the photos on your walls, and if I hadn't known who he was, I definitely wouldn't have recognised him this afternoon.'

I take a gulp of the water she's put in front of me.

'Crazy how people change,' she says. 'I mean, don't get me wrong, age suits him. But he looks like a completely different person.'

I take another gulp.

'Do you know what it made me think of?' Miriam asks. 'Martin and I once went to this exhibition of photos of American soldiers who'd fought in Iraq. There were three portraits of each man— one from before the war, one from during the war and one taken afterwards.' She takes a sip of water. 'It was amazing. I remember standing there with Martin trying to reconcile the young, open faces from before the war with the marked faces from afterwards. Only a few years had passed, but I'm telling you, Sarah, those men were transformed. Philip's the same,' she concludes. 'As if he'd come back from the war.'

'It's not Philip,' I say, and drain my glass.

'Eh?' Miriam says. 'What do you mean?'

Just then, Leo appears in the door. His eyes are small and red.

'I don't want to go home.' He flings the words at me and then turns round and vanishes.

Miriam and I exchange glances, and I leave the kitchen and go up the stairs after my son. I find him in the guest bathroom. He hasn't locked himself in, at least—he must have wanted me to come and speak to him.

Leo is sitting on the edge of the shower cubicle and eyes me suspiciously when I come in. I settle myself cross-legged in front of him on the aquamarine bathmat. It's a small room. The tiles are decorated with stickers of brightly coloured fish. I hesitate. Am I really going to take my son to a hotel, leaving a strange man alone in my house? It seems absurd, but I don't know what else I can do. How am I supposed to explain it, though?

'I don't want to go home—I want to stay here,' Leo says.

'You can't stay here forever, sweetheart. Miriam and Martin have a little baby—they can't have you getting up to mischief with Justus all the time!'

'It's not that,' Leo says. 'And we don't get up to mischief.' He pouts and wrinkles up his nose, his adorable face all freckles and rebellion.

When I was pregnant with Leo, I taught myself all kinds of things so that I would always have an answer when my son began to ask questions—so that he would know his mother was clever, that he could rely on her. I didn't want to have to resort to Google every time my son had a question. So I learnt all about how cars and mobile phones work, how many planets there are in our solar system, what photosynthesis is, and what lime and beech leaves look like. I learnt about the passive offside rule in football and how you tell death cap toadstools from mushrooms. But Leo never asks any of that. He only ever asks about things I don't know—life and death and the big why.

He says nothing now. He's hoping I'll say something, but I wait.

'I'm not coming with you,' he finally blurts out, getting up.

'Why don't you want to come home, darling?' I ask, although I know the answer.

My son raises his eyes and looks at me as if I were the most obtuse person on the planet, but still he says nothing.

'What's the matter, Leo?'

'I don't want to go home,' he says in the end. 'I'm scared of…' He seems to be searching for the right word. 'I'm scared of that man.'

He doesn't say 'my father' or 'Father' or 'Daddy' or 'Dad'—he says 'that man'. For a second or two I stare at Leo. Then I take him in my arms. He doesn't really like being hugged—not, at least, if anyone's looking, because it's uncool. But just this once he lets me. I wonder feverishly what to say to him. The situation is so fraught. I don't know what to tell Leo about the stranger. I only know that, apart from me and Constanze, my son is the only person who seems capable of seeing through the stranger's friendly facade. Leo has no memory of Philip, so he can't know that the stranger isn't his father. But he senses that something isn't right with that man. He has sensitive antennae. Like me.

I sigh and let Leo go. I think once more, fleetingly, about moving into a hotel with him until things sort themselves out— but things won't sort themselves out, and I know it. It's up to me to take action. In the meantime, I'm not going to leave my house to the stranger—no way.

When you're up against something you're afraid of and don't know how to escape, you should take a step towards it. Most monsters are as scared of you as you are of them. I learnt that from my wise grandmother.

'Come on,' I say to Leo, holding out my hand to him. 'Let's go and ask the M&M's if you can stay a bit longer.'

The stranger

She still isn't back. I wonder what she's doing. She must be up to something—she's always up to something.

I get up, suddenly too restless to sit still.

Once again I replay the day's events in my head. Then I take my phone out of my bag and switch it on. My hands begin to shake slightly when I see that Grimm has rung me back. I check my voicemail for a message, but there's nothing. I call him at once. It rings, but he doesn't pick up. I feel like hurling the phone at the wall. But I'm not going to. Control yourself. Keep going.

I take a deep breath and press redial. Again, the ringing tone sounds. I let it ring for a long time, but no one picks up. Sarah could come back at any moment. I put the mobile in my jeans pocket. Just as I'm wondering what to do next, the phone downstairs begins to ring. There's no number on the display, only the word *private*. I pick it up—it's not impossible that Grimm should try me on the landline.

I have to think for a moment before answering. 'Petersen?' I say.

'Hello.' A female voice comes down the line. 'It's Miriam.'

I don't immediately respond and there is a pause.

'I'm a friend of Sarah's,' she says. 'We…' She hesitates. 'We met briefly today.'

The kind-looking woman with the ash blond hair and round glasses.

'Yes, of course,' I say. 'Hello, Miriam. I'm very pleased that—'

'Me too!' she says nervously. 'It's so good that you're back. I'm so happy for Sarah.'

Interesting, I think. Sarah hasn't told her friend that the man in her house isn't her husband. Very interesting.

'Yes,' I say.

Miriam doesn't reply. Neither of us speaks.

'Sarah's not around,' I say at length.

'Oh, yes,' Miriam replies. 'I know. She was here until just a minute ago. I wanted to take advantage of the time she'll take to get back. I'd like to talk to you.'

That wakes me up.

'Well, yes,' Miriam begins. 'To be honest I'm worried about Sarah. She's been acting strangely lately.'

I suppress a cynical laugh. Yes, I think. I can imagine.

'And I know you've only just arrived yourself,' Miriam goes on, 'but…'

She lets the sentence trail off.

I wait. I can feel my headache stirring.

'I keep trying to talk to her—to ask her if she's okay—but she shuts down every time. And after what happened today…'

'Don't worry,' I say automatically. 'The last few days have been a bit much for my wife. For all of us. She needs to get some rest. She'll be all right then.'

'Is there anything I can do?' Miriam asks.

Leave me in peace, I think. For God's sake, just leave me in peace. But I know it can't hurt if Miriam likes me—if she pities me a little—if I come across as loving and concerned. She may be useful to me in some way.

'Just be nice to her, if she drops in again,' I say. 'And patient. And give me a ring if you need to. Okay?'

'Okay,' says Miriam.

'What about Leo?' I ask, on a hunch. 'Has Sarah picked him up?'

'Leo's going to stay with us a bit longer,' says Miriam, sounding a little cagey.

'Oh.'

'Yes,' she replies. 'It is the summer holidays, after all. And I'm sure you and Sarah could use some time alone. You've both been through so much.'

I'm running out of things to say. 'Thank you for ringing.'

'Yes. Not at all. And good that you're back. Really good.'

'Thank you,' I say again.

'Yes,' says Miriam. Now she seems embarrassed. Maybe it's dawned on her that it's not very nice to talk to your best friend's long-lost husband behind her back. But that's not my problem.

I've only just hung up when I feel my mobile vibrating. I whip it out of my pocket and take the call.

'This is Harald Grimm,' says a dark voice.

Sarah

Summer in Hamburg—the swifts are calling. I throw back my head and watch the aeroplanes carving up the sky, surprised that it doesn't shatter and fall to earth with a crash.

I'm sitting in the car. After leaving Miriam's neighbourhood, I drove a few streets and then stopped again. I'm nearly home—Miriam doesn't live particularly far away—but I don't want to get there yet. I need a moment to collect myself.

I can't get Constanze's words out of my head. They hover over me like a curse muttered in the dark. 'My son is dead,' I repeat softly. 'My greedy, deceitful daughter-in-law killed him. Everyone in Hamburg knows that. Everyone.'

I close my eyes in exhaustion, just for a moment—just a moment's peace. At once I feel myself slipping away—feel sleep stalking up to me with long stealthy strides. Silence. Peace. Just for a second…

No. I can't fall asleep now. I open my eyes. With a shudder I remember the dreams I've been having lately. The beginning isn't new. I've been dreaming about that door for years. It's always the same: I'm standing outside a closed door and an eerie rumbling sound is coming from the other side. I stare at the door, and then, although I want to run away, I open it. Then I wake in blind panic. But lately I've seen what's behind the door: a dark road, gleaming black as licorice. Philip is with me, his eyes vacant. I stand on the asphalt, looking down at my hands—and my hands are covered in blood.

That part of the dream is new. The blood on my hands is new.

My friends urged me to see a therapist when Philip went missing—a beefy man, who would, it seemed to me, have been less out of place at a rock concert than in a psychotherapist's practice—and I wonder now what he'd have to say. He was, in fact, a very nice man, but I only went to one session. I don't like talking about myself. I prefer to sort things out on my own. Philip often criticised me for that. I can hear him say it now, only half in jest: 'My beautiful, silent wife.'

Again my thoughts return to Constanze. Does she seriously believe I killed Philip? And if so, are there others out there who think the same? I suddenly see the face of the stranger, who is probably still in my house. I lean my head against the headrest and my thoughts go haring all over the place like young dogs.

It's all about money, I tell myself. Forget the rest—forget the threat, forget the goddamn dream and your own guilty conscience. Don't let him in your head. Don't let him manipulate you. It's all about money.

An impostor who resembles Philip—who has been chosen

precisely because he resembles him—passes himself off as the millionaire and entrepreneur Philip Petersen, cleans out all his bank accounts—and disappears again. Again I hear Johann's voice in my head: It always comes down to money in the end.

There was once a rich king, I tell myself, who was beloved by all the world. But his queen was full of envy and wickedness, and she poisoned the king with an enchanted potion. The good king was never seen again, nor could anyone say for certain what had become of him. Rumour spread, however, that the queen had had a hand in it, and the king's trusted courtiers determined to avenge his murder. But they could not prove it was the queen who had killed the king, for no one had ever found the king's dead body. And so they conceived of a plan and searched the land high and low for the man who bore the greatest likeness to the missing king. From all four corners of the kingdom, young men came to present themselves, and for seven days the king's trusty courtiers examined the faces of these young men, until at last they found one whose resemblance to the missing king was extraordinary. This man was taught to talk like the king, clothed in sumptuous robes, and brought before the wicked queen. Knowing the king had been poisoned by her own hand, the queen had a fit. 'It's a lie! It's a lie! You're dead and buried!' she cried, and so great were her fear and rage that, before they could stop her, she had thrown herself off the highest turret of the castle and plummeted to her death.

I open my eyes and blink—the sun is dazzling. What am I thinking? I don't have the time for such nonsense! Would I have spent seven years wondering what had happened to Philip if I'd killed him myself? I rein in my wild thoughts and start the car.

The stranger

After the phone call, I have a long shower and get changed. I immediately feel better.

The phone rang several times when I was in the shower, and it's ringing now. It rings for a long time, stops for a second or two—and then starts again. I follow the sound downstairs, into the living room, and hesitate only briefly before picking up.

'Hello?'

No reply.

'Hello?'

Somebody clears his throat. Then I hear a man's voice.

'Yes, um, hello. Sorry. This is Mirko. Mirko Blücher. I'm a colleague of Sarah's.'

I say nothing.

'Well, I, er, just recently heard that you're back,' the man says. 'I saw you on television. At the airport. Amazing story. Congratulations. Or whatever you say in such a situation.'

'Thanks.'

'Yeah,' says the man.

I say nothing. I never was one of those people who feel the need to fill silence with chatter.

'Is Sarah around?' the man asks.

'No,' I reply. 'She's out.'

'Oh, okay. Thanks,' he says and hangs up.

I stare at the telephone a moment, then step out into the garden and sit under one of the apple trees. I can't let myself sleep, but I can at least get a little rest. She will be back. It's her home, after all, and she's hardly going to go off and leave it to me. I know enough about people—about her—to be sure of that.

I had imagined that everything would be much more straightforward. But life's not like that. It's a great many things, but it certainly isn't straightforward. My thoughts drift back to the camp, to the arguments we used to get into—always over little things. Who got to wash first, who hadn't left enough food for the others, who snored or talked too much—or laughed too loud. But such things didn't bother me. What I couldn't bear was the lack of privacy. I freaked out completely if anyone went near my things—I couldn't help myself.

I think of my best friend in the camp who, like me, had a wife and child at home. Over the years, we grew to be like brothers, sharing a lot, reading the same books, discussing the same topics. I loved him—he was a good man. I won't break the promise I made him.

Stay strong, I think. Keep going. Keep going. Keep going.

Sarah

As I walk in the front door, I can sense that he's here. His presence is like a low note that you hear not with your ears but your belly.

I close the door noiselessly, lean up against it and shut my eyes for a moment, going over in my mind what I know. His vanishing act this morning, his foray into town, the fact that he knows so much about Philip, that he has acquaintances here in Hamburg he goes to meet, that he slips men money at the station—that he's even prepared to do a DNA test to buy himself time. My thoughts wander back to our talk with Barbara Petry. The stranger knows so much about us. He must have known Philip well. He has had time to study him.

I consider calling Petry again, or perhaps—remembering the

debacle my last encounter with her turned out to be—I should call Bernardy or Hansen instead. I have nothing new to tell them, though. It's hardly likely to impress anyone that I've seen the stranger walking around town, talking to people.

The stranger is extraordinarily convincing. To be that convincing, you have to believe in yourself. It's not at all easy to wear a mask every second of every day, never taking it off. It isn't enough to tell others who you are now—you have to keep telling yourself as well. If you want to be plausible, you have to be eternally on your guard. You can't risk a single wrong word, or even a single wrong thought. You have to keep repeating it to yourself: I am innocent. I am innocent. I am innocent. Tell yourself every second of every day that you are innocent and you will be innocent. You'll be able to convince anyone, any lie detector—even yourself. Tell yourself every second of every day that you are called Philip Petersen and you *will* be called Philip Petersen.

I push myself away from the door and set off in search of him. After I've checked the kitchen, living room, dining room and all the bedrooms, I glance out of the terrace door and spot him in the back garden. He's leaning up against a tree in the shade, his legs stretched out in front of him. He's changed his clothes and is now barefoot in jeans and a white T-shirt.

I have to change my tactics, I think. The aggressive questions I've been asking so far haven't got me anywhere. If the stranger really did know Philip, perhaps there's a way to get him to talk.

He's noticed me standing at the door and gives me a wary look. It's almost evening, but still warm and humid. I cross the lawn and sit down next to him, careful not to come too close, then pick a daisy and twirl it between my fingers.

'When Philip went missing,' I say, 'my son was just a year old.'

The stranger doesn't look at me.

'Leo was our third try, our last try.' I swallow. 'I had two miscarriages before Leo.' I look at the daisy in my hand, then cast it aside. 'It's so easily said,' I say. 'As if it were no great matter. Like hiccups—mishap, miscarriage. Nothing serious.'

The stranger still doesn't look at me.

'After my first miscarriage, we were devastated, Philip maybe more so than me. We were told it was for the best and that we should try again straightaway, so we did. I was soon pregnant again, and at first everything seemed to be going smoothly. Why shouldn't it? I was young and healthy. I'd just graduated. I—'

I interrupt myself, stop and think before I go on.

'Philip loved children—he'd always wanted his own. Some people can't be happy without children. Philip was like that. After my second miscarriage, after we'd buried our second baby, I was scared. I wondered how we could put ourselves through all that a third time. Three's a kind of magic number for me, you know. Somehow I always have the feeling that if something doesn't work out the third time round, it never will.'

I feel a bead of sweat run down my neck.

'I was scared that was going to be my life—getting pregnant and having miscarriages, over and over—three times, four times, five times, ten times, until neither of us had any strength left. One evening, I found Philip in the room we'd decorated together for the baby. He was staring into the empty cradle and turned round when I went in. He seemed embarrassed that I'd caught him there. That evening I told him I was ready to try again, and he said no. I couldn't believe my ears—I knew how much he wanted a baby. I asked him why not, what was wrong? And he said he'd hardly been able to bear our last failed attempts—and that it must have been much worse for me. He didn't want me to put myself through that again.

'You see?' I say. 'That's the kind of man Philip was.'

I swallow again and glance apprehensively at the stranger. He's staring straight ahead, and it's impossible to interpret his expression.

'But I insisted,' I say. 'On a third and last attempt.'

The stranger is silent.

'You knew my husband, didn't you?'

Still the stranger is silent.

'If you know Philip, then you know what a good man he is.'

Something stirs in the stranger's face. Something is working in him—a new thought, perhaps, or a half-forgotten memory that has been washed to the surface. Then I see his Adam's apple jump. He turns to face me, looks me in the eye. I have trouble holding his gaze, but I don't look away.

'I am Philip Petersen,' he says. He doesn't bat an eyelid. 'I was born on a rainy day in Hamburg. My father was called Philip, like me. My mother's name is Constanze. I am married. I have a son called Leo.'

He reels it off like a dull poem.

I jump up. I can't listen to any more of this con man's parroted lines.

'Everyone thinks we named our son after Leonard Cohen,' the stranger says. 'But in fact he's called after my wife's great-grandfather.'

I pause, mid-step.

'We got married in Las Vegas,' he says. 'You wanted tattoos instead of wedding rings, but I talked you out of it.'

I turn round.

'You like Radiohead because it makes you sad, and the Beatles because they make you happy.'

I stare at him.

'Once we were out jogging in the woods and had to climb a tree to escape a herd of wild boar.'

I crouch down in front of him.

'We once raised a young swift that had fallen out of its nest.'

I stretch out my arms.

'We promised each other we'd go to the woods at the next eclipse of the sun to find out whether the birds stop singing.'

I take his face in my hands.

'I'm sorry I wasn't there, Sarah,' he says. 'Forgive me.'

I put my face very close to his. I feel my throat seize up. I swallow.

'Please,' I say. 'Please tell me where my husband is.'

There is a long pause. The stranger looks straight at me, and only at me.

'Are you even sure you want him back?' he asks.

'Of course I am!' I swallow the gall that has risen in my throat. 'I loved my husband,' I say. 'More than anything else.'

'Sarah, please,' says the stranger, his eyes cold and dark. 'We both know that's not true.'

'Please,' I repeat. 'Stop it. I can't take any more.'

Again something stirs in his face, and for a brief, irrational moment, I think he's going to burst into tears. Instead he gives a short, bitter laugh, shakes off my hands and gets up.

'You want to know where your husband is?' he asks.

I nod. Idiot that I am, I'm still hoping there's some way of softening this man.

'He's standing right in front of you,' he says, with an ugly smile that sends shivers down my spine. Then he turns and walks off.

I jump up, livid with rage, and set off after him, into the house. I catch up with him in the kitchen.

'I was right,' I say, when he turns to face me.

He looks as if he's on the point of losing his patience.

'You did know Philip. How else could you know such a lot about us?'

He sighs as if he were as fed up with all this carry-on as I am.

I walk round the kitchen table and come to stand in front of him. I think to myself that if I laid my hand on his chest, my cheek wouldn't fit exactly into the hollow of his neck—that it wouldn't feel right.

'You're shorter than Philip,' I say. 'Not a lot—only a few centimetres. But still, noticeably shorter.'

I look him in the face. Something flashes in his eyes—something hard and dangerous.

'Your eyes are quite different from Philip's,' I continue. 'You're doing a pretty good job, I must say—you've fooled a lot of people. But how long do you think you can keep this up? How long before it all comes out?'

He says nothing. There is no stirring of emotion.

Surprise him, I think. 'Let's assume I'm prepared to believe you,' I say.

He gives a snort.

'No, really,' I say. 'I'm prepared to believe you. I only ask one thing of you first.' Soon I'll have him.

He looks at me quizzically.

'Only one thing,' I repeat.

'What?'

'I'd like to see you stripped to the waist.'

'Stripped to the waist?'

I nod.

'What for?'

'I want to see your chest,' I say, ignoring his question.

'What for?' he repeats. 'What are you playing at?'

'All I want is to see the little birthmark on your chest,' I say teasingly. 'That's not a lot to ask—is it, Philip?' I raise my eyebrows expectantly. 'Well?'

'No,' says the stranger.

'No?' I echo scornfully. 'I ask this one little favour of you, and you say no?'

The stranger doesn't reply.

'I thought as much,' I say, angry now. I move quickly, surprising him. I give his T-shirt a yank, pull it up a little. He shrinks back, but I have already seen the scar tissue covering his skin.

This throws me for a moment. The stranger's glare is savage, like a wounded animal's. He looks more dangerous than ever.

I glare back at him, then turn on my heel to leave the kitchen. In the doorway I pause.

'I'm going to ring your good friend Barbara Petry now,' I say. 'It's time you took that DNA test.'

'There won't be a DNA test,' the stranger says.

The stranger

She's wearing me down. She's been talking at me ever since she got back. She doesn't let up—follows me all over the place, pesters me. It's too much. I don't know when I last slept. My headache is now so intense that little flashes of light keep flickering across my field of vision. My nerves are in shreds. I can feel myself cracking up.

I look at her—she's exhausted, but her tired face is contorted with anger, with hate, and for a moment I think she's going to set on me. I feel something that scares me: joy. No, not joy. That's not the word, even if it feels similar. What do you call it?

That's right: glee. I feel malicious, sweet-tasting glee.

Gradually it dawns on me: I'm enjoying this.

I didn't come here to torture her. That wasn't the plan.

I'm here to do what has to be done. I need to put an end to all this as soon as I can.

But it pleases me to see her so desperate.

It frightens me, too.

Next time I lose control, it won't just be a little table that gets broken.

Sarah

don't know why I'm so shocked. I should have been expecting it—and yet a single sentence from the stranger has thrown me completely off balance. I feel myself sway and have to steady myself against the doorframe to stop myself keeling over.

'Say that again,' I manage to get out.

'There won't be a DNA test,' the stranger says.

Then he turns away as if the matter were settled, opens the fridge door and takes out a strawberry yoghurt. Philip hates strawberry yoghurt. The stranger fetches a clean spoon from the dishwasher, opens the yoghurt pot, sits down at the kitchen table and begins to eat.

'Oh yes, Mirko rang,' he says, in between spoons. 'Kiss kiss!'

Then he resumes eating. Cool as a cucumber, as if I weren't there.

Furious, I storm out of the kitchen and up the stairs to my bedroom, lock the door behind me and throw myself on the bed. I'd like to cry, but I can't—I'm too tired or too angry or both. Then my anger prevails and I'm on my feet again, unlocking the door and flinging it open so that it slams into the wall. I hurry back down to the kitchen and find the stranger with two empty yoghurt pots in front of him, about to start on a third.

'Tell me what you've done to my husband,' I demand.

'I *am* your—'

'Then show me the birthmark on your chest!'

He shakes his head.

'I'll answer any question you like,' he says. It sounds almost conciliatory, but his eyes flash scornfully.

'Okay, tell me your name,' I demand.

'Philip Petersen,' he says.

I grab a coffee cup from the dresser and dash it against the wall. It shatters noisily and the pieces fall to the floor. 'For Christ's sake!' I shout. 'Tell me what you've done to my husband! Is he dead? Is he? Is my husband dead? Have you killed him? Talk to me, you bastard!'

He can see it in my face, I can tell. He can see that I'm about to lose all control, wild with rage. He can see it and he smiles.

'But Sarah, darling,' he says, relishing each word. 'I *am* your husband!'

'You are not!' I shout. 'You're nothing like Philip. You're the complete opposite of Philip!'

The stranger gets up, throws away the empty yoghurt pots and puts his spoon in the sink. He crouches down and gathers up the pieces of broken cup and throws them in the bin too. When he's done, he leaves the kitchen without a word.

I stand there for a few seconds, then storm upstairs, throw

myself on the bed again and press the pillow down over my head. But I find no peace—even the silence is loud. If he's trying to drive me mad, he's succeeding.

I take the pillow off my head, roll over and stare up at the ceiling. A big fly keeps bumping against it with a strange, soft thump, and as I watch it I wonder how many people before me have lain in this room staring at the ceiling.

Directly above my head I notice fine cracks I've never seen before. I've made those cracks with my thoughts, I think, averting my gaze. I see Philip and Leo and me together in this bed and close my eyes.

I hesitated for a long time about whether or not to have children. Philip didn't have any doubts—he told me very early on in our relationship how much he was looking forward to being a father. I wasn't lying to the stranger on that count. Any scepticism was on my side. Philip thought I was afraid of forfeiting my independence, but it wasn't that. And it wasn't—or at any rate, not only—that I was worried I wouldn't be able to protect my child from the world. I wasn't afraid I'd be a bad mother—I was afraid he'd be a bad father. Philip hated his father. Petersen Senior was a cold tyrant. In his eyes, Philip could do no right, and he ended up shunting him off to boarding school. Philip never forgave his father for sending him away, unable or unwilling to suffer his presence for more than five minutes at a time. And don't we all turn into our parents in the end?

It was a long time before I was able to talk to Philip about it.

How do you tell your husband you don't think he's fit to be a father? It was unfair of me—I know that now. But it was the way I thought at the time.

I'll never forget that conversation—it's branded on my mind.

'What if you turn out like your father without meaning to?' I'd asked, fearful of how he might react. Philip laughed, but not at me—he just laughed his typical optimistic laugh.

'I've wondered that too,' he said. 'It's what they say, isn't it? That women turn into their mothers and men into their fathers.'

To this day I don't know what he found so funny about that, but after a while he grew serious.

'I promise you, I'd rather die than turn into my father.'

I try to read his expression.

'You'll be patient with our children?'

'As patient as a saint.'

'You'll like having them around? You won't ever send them away?'

Philip took my face in his hands and looked me in the eyes.

'I swear that I will never send any child of ours away. Hell will freeze over before that happens. I promise you.'

He promised and I believed him. My husband may have had his faults, but one thing you could rely on: he always kept his promises.

I think of Mirko and my hard-heartedness towards him.

I think of Leo.

I can't work out how it all hangs together. But I'm going to find out. All roads lead to Philip. Maybe I've been trying to approach things from the wrong angle. In a few hours, when it's morning, I'll get in touch with the police and the Foreign Ministry and try to find out as much as possible about Philip's kidnapping. I still know far too little. The file I've started hardly tells me anything that might get me anywhere, but I grab it all the same and put it on my desk. Then I boot up my laptop, open a Word document and begin to type up what few relatively uncontroversial facts I know.

In 2008, Philip went to South America on a business trip.

The trip was to last five days.

Philip was often in Colombia on business.

The trips were routine.

I said goodbye to Philip at the front door.

He promised to be in touch every day as usual.

A bare twenty-four hours later, Philip sent me a text telling me he'd landed safely and all was well.

That was the last time I heard from him.

A colleague who had accompanied him to Colombia said that Philip had set off alone for a meeting with a potential investor.

He never turned up at the luxury hotel in Bogotá where he was expected.

Somewhere between his hotel and his business partner's hotel he went missing.

There was nothing to point to kidnap, although apparently with a rich man like Philip that can never be ruled out.

There was no letter claiming responsibility.

There was no ransom note.

There was no evidence of any kind. Nothing.

And then, seven years later, almost to the day, a man turns up claiming to be Philip, and I am fed a story which is, rationally speaking, utterly implausible. I am told that Philip was kidnapped by guerrillas in Colombia and taken to a camp in the jungle. It is assumed that the first ransom note somehow went astray, and that the kidnappers didn't make a second attempt. Nobody knows exactly why, but it's sure to come out—internecine conflicts, perhaps, something of that sort. Whatever happened, the kidnappers didn't kill their hostage. They simply waited—for years. And I'm supposed to believe that, after seven years, nearly a dozen hostages were suddenly released and the German entrepreneur Philip Petersen happened to be among them?

I scan the room for my handbag, find it, open it, rummage around in it for my phone. Johann, I think. I need to get hold of Johann. It can't wait any longer. Johann has influence—he can help me unmask the impostor and get rid of him. No one will dare call *him* mad. When I find my phone, I stare in alarm at the display: thirty-eight missed calls. One from Miriam and thirty-seven from a withheld number. I frown. Just as I'm about to check my voicemail, the phone starts to ring in my hand. I stare at it: another withheld number. It's late. Hardly anyone has this number. Who could it be?

'Hello?' I say.

I hear someone breathing, feel them waiting. Then whoever it is hangs up.

I drop the phone on my bed as if it might bite me. What's going on? I close my eyes for a second. Then I force myself to pick up the phone again and dial Johann's number. I let it ring for a long time, my heart thudding hopefully against my ribcage, but again I have no luck. I hang up and check my voicemail—nothing. While I'm at it, I check my emails too, something I've done my best to avoid so far. In my inbox are a newsletter, an advertisement, a message from my boss with information about the new school year—and an email from Mirko, sitting there with no subject line and staring at me reproachfully. I log out. Then I check my texts and find three unread messages from Miriam.

My pulse immediately shoots up. Please let Leo be all right, please let Leo be all right. I open the first text, from 8.30 pm.

All well, sweetie, but give me a ring when you get this. Miri.

I click it away and open the next one.

Sarah, I can't get hold of you. I'd hoped to speak to you before I started putting Emily to bed, but there's something you ought to see.

Link to follow. Read the comments. They're all over the net—under all the articles about Philip. This is just an example. Miri.

I don't understand a thing, click this text away too and open the last. In it is only a link and the words: *I'm so sorry. Hope you're OK. Let's talk tomorrow. I'm sure something can be done. Miri.*

My first impulse is to put the phone down and ignore the whole thing. Whatever Miriam may have come across, I'm sure I have worse problems. But my curiosity gets the better of me and I follow the link. I jump when I see where it leads. A photo appears on the small screen of my phone: the stranger—a smile on his face, Leo in his arms—and me beside him, looking vacant. That was at the airport yesterday. No, the day before yesterday.

'Hamburg Man Home at Last', it says above the photo. I feel sick to my stomach and decide to spare myself the ordeal of reading the article. Following Miriam's instructions, I scroll down to the comments and read a few. I can't at first find anything out of the ordinary, but then I see it. I blink. I am, apparently, an opportunistic whore who married Philip Petersen for his money, trapped him with a child and slept with half the town in his absence.

I'm flabbergasted. Aren't online comments supposed to be moderated? Who would leave such vile slander, such foul abuse, up there for the world to see?

If Miriam's right—and why would she lie?—there are comments like these posted everywhere, under every article about Philip Petersen's homecoming. This isn't just some troll making a random attack—this is a targeted campaign. Someone is trying to drag me through the mud—to destroy my credibility.

What if Leo finds out? Or the neighbours? My colleagues? My pupils?

Is this what the stranger meant when he said I'd lose everything if I didn't keep quiet? Is this the first step of his plan?

I take the vase from my bedside table and hurl it at the wall, then watch with a feeling of satisfaction as it smashes to pieces. I kick the wardrobe and feel a sharp pain in my foot. I throw books and pillows and pens about the room—whatever I can lay my hands on. The little lamp from my bedside table shatters against the wall. I rant and shout and rage. Then I sit down on the bed, a bundle of fury and headache and confusion. And at last the tears come.

The stranger

I'm sitting on the floor outside her bedroom door, listening to her cry.

She is producing deep, theatrical sobs and throwing things around the room.

It is by no means clear to me whether she is trying to manipulate me or is truly distraught. Both are possible, but I'm hoping, of course, for the latter.

If this is a moment of genuine weakness, I really ought to take advantage of it.

Just now it is particularly annoying that Grimm had to put me off—that he didn't have any useful information for me.

I am suddenly hit by the fear she might harm herself. I wouldn't want that—not for the moment, anyway. I get up and stand at the door, my arm raised to knock. I hesitate, let my arm fall again. No. Let her rage and weep a little longer. She's not going to slit her wrists or hang herself—she simply isn't the type.

She'll have a good cry. Then she'll sit up, blow her nose and wipe her eyes. She'll be annoyed at herself for giving in like this, tell herself she's strong and has to get a grip. That's what she's best at—getting up again, no matter what. So she will. She'll get up, and then she'll act.

And at last things will come to a head.

I back away from the door. I'm going to stretch my legs a bit—get some fresh air.

I leave the house and go out onto the street. Chestnut trees. An elderly man walking his alsatian, children out on their bikes, birds twittering.

I take a few steps. I have certainly felt fitter, but I'm all right. Just need some sleep.

Stay strong.

The man with the dog is closer now. I give a start when he speaks.

'Is Mrs Petersen at home?' he asks.

'Sorry?'

I'm momentarily thrown—I hadn't reckoned with questions from prying neighbours.

'Mrs Petersen,' he repeats. 'Is she at home? You've just left the house, haven't you?'

'Yes,' I say. 'She's at home.'

The old man eyes me with mistrust.

'Lauterbach's the name. I live a few houses further up.' He sounds hostile. 'And who are you?'

'I'm Philip Petersen,' I reply. 'Sarah's husband.'

The old man laughs. 'But I'd recognise Philip,' he says. 'I've

216

known him since he was a little boy.' He leaves me standing there and goes off after his dog, who's already making a beeline for the next tree. 'Some people have a funny sense of humour,' he mutters to himself.

Instinctively I glance up at the house, at her bedroom window. There's no sign of her.

I go back into the house and take up my post at her door again.

Sarah

Though night has fallen, it's hot in here. I can feel fine beads of sweat on my forehead. A drop runs down between my breasts and seeps into the waistband of my trousers. A little fresh air would do me good. I open the window, expecting to feel a breeze on my face, but all that is waiting for me out there in the night is silence, velvety darkness and a few never-tiring bats. Not a breath of air—no respite for my overheated brain. A storm was forecast, but hasn't come. I step back from the window and sit down again.

I have so much to think about, I don't know where to begin—but the stranger has to go. Everything else is subordinate.

I try Johann again. It rings once, twice—and he answers. I'm so surprised I can't at first react.

'Hello?' he repeats. 'Sarah?'

'Johann,' I say, 'I've been trying to get hold of you for so long!'

'I know,' he says. 'I've been abroad.'

His voice sounds as cool as ever. Doesn't he know?

'Have you heard—?' I venture.

'I can't believe it,' he says, interrupting me. 'They've found him. They've actually found him!'

Oh God. How do I tell him?

'I've been trying to get hold of you all this time,' I whisper.

Johann doesn't hear me. 'I couldn't believe it at first,' he says. 'After all this time.'

'It's not Philip,' I say.

I can almost hear Johann frown and blink in confusion, as if I've played a prank on him and he's waiting for me to say 'April fool!'

'I don't understand,' he says.

'The man they've found isn't Philip,' I say.

Silence.

I swallow, forcing myself to keep calm.

'What do you mean, it isn't Philip?' Johann asks.

I grope about for words.

'I saw you on television,' Johann says into the silence. 'I have a newspaper here in front of me with a photo of the three of you.'

'Johann, look closely at that photo,' I say. 'Look at the man. Remind yourself exactly what Philip looks like—his build, the way he holds himself, the way he moves. The shape of his eyebrows. The dimples on his cheeks. His hairline. His eyes. Especially his eyes. And then look at the man in the photo. You can't seriously believe it's Philip.'

Johann is silent again for a moment. 'You can only see his profile,' he says, 'but—' He breaks off, mid-sentence.

'I understand your confusion,' I say. 'I've tried to get hold of you so many times in the past few days because I wanted to spare you just this.'

Johann is silent.

'Of course you think it's Philip,' I add, placatory.

Johann still says nothing.

'Context. It's all context.' I smooth an imaginary strand of hair out of my face. 'You'd heard Philip was back. Maybe you cried. Maybe you laughed uncontrollably. Your fingers shook. You thanked God, although you don't really believe in him. I know you did. I know, because I felt the same.'

Still Johann says nothing.

'And then you open the paper and see a man the age Philip would be now, a man of about Philip's height and build who also happens to look very much like him. Of course you think it's Philip.'

Silence.

'It's all context,' I say again.

'Sarah, what is this nonsense? If it isn't Philip, who else could it possibly be?'

'A stranger. A fraud.'

'Are you serious? Why on earth would you think such a thing?'

I don't know what to say. I open and close my mouth, but I can't speak. A strange, strangled sound escapes my throat.

'My god, you're serious,' Johann says. 'Where is Philip—I mean, this man—now?'

A wave of relief crashes over me. Johann believes me. He'll help me. 'I don't know exactly, somewhere downstairs,' I say.

'He's in the house with you?'

I nod, pointlessly, but nothing comes out of my mouth.

'If it isn't Philip,' Johann says, with studied restraint, 'then who on earth is it?'

'I don't know,' I say. 'Believe me, that's something I'd—'

'If it isn't Philip,' Johann says again, interrupting me, 'what is he doing in your house in the middle of the night?'

'I've tried to—'

'If it isn't Philip,' Johann says, almost shouting now, 'why haven't you rung the police?'

'I was going to! But he said—'

'If this man isn't Philip, what the hell is he doing holding Leo in this photo?'

I'm speechless. This isn't going the way I'd imagined.

'Listen, I spoke to Constanze,' I say. 'She agrees. This man—'

'Dear Lord! Constanze? Constanze is ill, she—'

'For God's sake, let me finish,' I cry. 'If you'd only listen to me for a moment, you'd understand! He's clever! He—'

'Now you listen to me, my girl,' says Johann. 'I don't know what's wrong with you, but you need to pull yourself together.'

He no longer sounds confused—he sounds cool and menacing. I knew he could be like this, but I've never witnessed it.

'I don't know what's wrong with you and I don't want to know. I don't want to know whether you're screwing some other man, whether you've got used to the idea of being a filthy-rich widow, or whether it's just too much like hard work having your husband back in the house when you're using to having your own way. I'm not interested. But you're damn well going to pull yourself together now, have you got that? Think of your child, for God's sake!'

He hangs up.

I am cold. Icy cold.

Think of your child, for God's sake, Johann had said. Did I hear right?

Was that an unspoken threat to take my son away from me?

221

What the hell is going on?

I have no time to draw breath, let alone digest the phone call. Just moments after I've hung up, my mobile starts to ring again. And again, it's the withheld number. The phone rings and rings—goes quiet—rings again.

Suddenly it's all too much for me: the stranger's cruelty, Leo's confusion, Constanze's poisonous remarks, the threats, the fear, the lies, my nightmares, the blood on my hands, this grim night, the whole bloody mess. I curl up on the bed and give in to my tears.

My phone rings and rings and rings.

Then, all of a sudden, it stops, and at last I can think again. Finally, I see it. I understand.

Johann.

The fact that I couldn't get hold of him.

His company's financial difficulties.

His repeated attempts to access Philip's money through me—to have Philip declared dead, although it was far too early.

Johann.

It was Johann all along.

With the help of the stranger, he is trying to lay his hands on Philip's millions.

When Barbara Petry asked us to come up with someone who knew Philip, it was the stranger who suggested Johann. Why would he have done that, if Johann were not on his side?

I have an answer, now, to the disturbing question of how the stranger got hold of so much information about Philip and me—about our past, our life together.

Or am I being unfair to Johann? Is he simply determined to believe that Philip is back? After all, he hasn't yet met the stranger in person…

My thoughts are interrupted by a soft creak outside the door.

I clear my throat and swallow. And as soon as I feel sure that my voice won't sound afraid or tearful, I say loudly, 'I know you're there.'

There's no response. I'm beginning to think I've made a mistake when I see the doorhandle move. A moment later, the stranger is in my bedroom.

'What do you want?' I ask.

'Just making sure you're okay.'

I am so sick of his little games.

'No one can hear us,' I say. 'You can stop this nonsense.'

The stranger opens his mouth, then shuts it again.

'You must have known my husband very well,' I say, 'if he's told you so much about us.'

The stranger doesn't reply.

'Or did you get your information from someone else?'

The stranger doesn't reply.

'Where's my husband?'

I hear the stranger breathe. I hear the tick of the clock on the wall.

'I'm going to give you one last chance to tell me what I want to know,' I say. 'Then I'm going downstairs and ringing the police to press charges.'

The stranger doesn't move a muscle. Maybe he thinks I'm bluffing.

I swallow drily. 'What do you want?' I ask.

The stranger is silent.

Slowly, I count to ten in my head, then I jump to my feet and make for the door. But the stranger grabs my arm. I start. He pulls me back to the bed, grasps me tightly by the shoulders and puts his face very close to mine. For a crazy moment I think he's

223

going to try to kiss me. His face is so close I can feel the warmth of his breath on my skin.

'Not a word,' he says. He almost whispers it. 'If you say so much as a single word about this to anyone, you're done.' He gives me a brief, penetrating look, then lets go of my shoulders. 'Do you understand?'

His threats no longer frighten me.

'You're not my husband,' I hiss.

'No, I'm not.' He spits the words at me. 'Thank God for that. The poor bastard. But believe me, I still know more than enough about you—more than you can imagine. Don't test me.'

I can feel my mouth hanging open.

At last, his mask has dropped.

The stranger

The words just tumbled out. A slip.

All I'd wanted—because she hadn't stopped crying—was to make sure she wasn't going to harm herself.

I turn away. The dull pain in my head is back, swelling and ebbing. That's good, I think. Pain is good. Pain keeps you awake, tells you that you're still alive. What was it one of the boys at the camp always said? Pain is just weakness leaving your body.

My gaze is drawn outside to the garden and the neighbouring houses. A summer's night in Hamburg. A soft jumble of voices comes in at the tilted window. Somewhere out there, people are having barbecues, sitting outside enjoying the balmy evening. It all seems utterly surreal to me—in my life there are no garden parties, no after-work beers with friends. Where I've come from, none of that existed. I know no normality. Not that I can remember, anyway.

What if I were to follow the sound of the voices and go out, I wonder. What if I went off and left her? Does it really matter whether or not she rings the police? Does anything matter anymore?

I run my hand over my face. No. I'm familiar with these thoughts—they have often stalked me. It isn't bad to think them. Thoughts are only impulses sent from synapse to synapse. Thoughts aren't a problem. It's only when you give in to them that they become a problem.

I pull myself together. I can't allow myself to be tired, can't allow myself to think of my pains. I made a mistake. I let myself get carried away. But this is not over yet. All is not lost.

I turn back to her. This is like a game of chess, but I never have more than a few seconds to work out my next move. And she is a completely unpredictable player. Hard to say whether my threats are still making an impression on her.

I have to stop her, whatever it takes—but I don't like resorting to violence unless it's necessary.

Sarah

Terror, fear, relief—my emotions come thick and fast. At last he's confessed—that's something, at least. I was on the verge of losing my mind. The tension that falls away from me is so great I almost burst into tears again.

The stranger has gone out and left me in my bedroom. The crash of the door as he slammed it shut behind him is still reverberating in my ears.

I'm dizzy, my mouth dry. I desperately need to drink something. I glance out of the window. It's dark outside now, late evening. I open the door and look down the passage. I'm about to go downstairs and fetch myself a glass of water from the kitchen when I hear the stranger's voice, low and muffled. Is someone with him? I creep down without a sound. The voice is coming from the living room. I step nearer, careful not to make a noise. The living-room door is ever so slightly ajar. A floorboard creaks as I approach. I give a start and stand still. Did he notice? I hear his voice again, and then silence. He's on the phone! I listen. At first I hear nothing. I'm beginning to be afraid that he knows I'm listening and has hung up, but then I hear his voice again.

'I don't think so, no.'

Pause.

'I don't think she'll go to the police.'

Pause.

I swallow.

'I don't know!'

My throat seizes up.

'I find it very hard to say.'

Pause.

'If she does go to the police, she's doing herself more harm than anyone else…'

The hairs on my neck stand on end. Gooseflesh spreads over my body.

'I don't think that will prove—'

Pause.

'I'm not going to—'

Silence.

'Who do you think you're talking to? I wouldn't do a thing like that!'

Pause.

'Forget it. I wouldn't dream of it!'

Pause.

'No violence, that was the deal!'

Pause.

'I'll see if I can reason with her.'

Pause.

'It's worth a try, isn't it?'

Pause.

'You promise me that Sarah and her son will come out of this unscathed, if I manage to pull it off?'

Pause.

'Promise?'

Pause.

'Okay. Okay, thanks. Yes. Goodbye, then.'

I hear him replace the phone in the charging dock.

It's not so much his words that drive cold sweat out of every pore in my body—it's his tone. It was different from the tone he's been using with me. He still sounded angry and exhausted, yes, but there was something else in his voice, something that puzzles me.

Fear.

I move away from the living room as quickly and quietly as I can and creep upstairs and into my bedroom, closing the door behind me. I sit down on the bed. I have to think, to make sense of this latest development, but before I can even get started, I hear footsteps again.

The stranger knocks and then lets himself in without waiting. He stands there silent, as if searching for words, shoulders drooping, avoiding my gaze. Then he turns and looks me in the face.

'Okay, listen,' he says. 'If you think I'm your enemy, you're wrong.'

It's so absurd, I almost have to laugh. 'If you're not my enemy, what are you?'

He doesn't reply.

'You're an impostor!' I cry. 'You've wormed your way into my house, you've threatened me. What else are you?'

'I didn't choose to play this part.'

'Do you think that makes it any better?' I ask, but I don't wait for an answer.

'I know you're in cahoots with Johann Kerber,' I say.

Suddenly I have his full attention. He blinks at me, his dark eyes alert.

'I can give you the money he's promised you,' I tell him. 'There's no need to hurt me or Leo to get it.'

For a moment it's quiet again, then the stranger shakes his head wearily. 'It's not quite as easy as that.'

I remember the tone of his voice when he was on the phone—the fear. 'Why not?'

He doesn't reply.

'You said you didn't choose to play this part. I'm prepared to help you.'

He laughs. 'You want to help me?'

'I want you out of my house,' I say. 'And I'm prepared to pay you to go. I'm not bluffing.'

'That's not the point.'

'What's the point then?' I ask.

He hesitates. My nerves are quivering with tension.

'May I give you some advice?' he says. 'Be patient. This business will soon be over.'

'What do you mean?'

He sits down. 'Only two more days,' the stranger replies, without looking at me. 'Two days and you're rid of me—if you don't lose your head.'

I look him in the face—and against all reason I have the feeling he's telling the truth.

'I want to know what's happened to my husband,' I say.

'You'll know everything soon enough. Give me two days.'

I don't understand what's going on—why the stranger is suddenly so cooperative, or why those two days are so crucial. Why should I trust him? I want to believe him—hope gleams red and sweet and enticing as a toffee apple. But what if I put everything on hold for two days, only to find that he's cleared off, taking with him all he knows about Philip?

He's averted his eyes again.

'What's going to happen in two days?' I ask.

He doesn't reply. I think of the man I saw him talking to in town.

'Is Philip alive?' I ask.

The stranger doesn't reply.

'Is my husband alive?'

Silence.

'Please,' I implore him. 'Just tell me that.'

'Two days,' says the stranger. 'Give me two days, and I'll give you all the information you want.' He turns to look at me. 'I promise,' he says.

I let his words sink in. 'I believe you,' I say, but I'm not sure that I do.

We are silent for a while.

'Two days?' I ask.

The stranger nods.

I think for a moment, then come to a decision.

'If I'm going to be spending another two days under the same roof as a man I don't know, you could at least tell me your name.'

Again, it falls quiet in the room, the ticking of the clock on the wall the only reminder that the world is still turning. I've already decided the stranger isn't going to reply when he clears his throat.

For the first time, he sounds sincere.

'Vincent,' he says softly. 'I'm Vincent.'

The stranger

S ilence descends on the room. She stares at her knees.

That was the right thing to do, I think. The right thing.

When I saw the exhaustion in her face, I realised it was time to change tactics. Hope, I thought. If I can bait her with anything, it's hope. I decided to try something new: reassurance instead of provocation.

After talking to Grimm, I realised that I'd have to buy myself some time. It's crucial that she doesn't panic and take off, and I was worried that she might.

I think of the phone call.

I registered with annoyance how violently my hands were shaking as I asked him my most pressing question.

'I can't tell you for certain yet,' he said, 'but—'

'When can I expect an answer from you, then?' I asked. 'A definitive answer?'

Grimm was silent. 'Give me two days,' he said at length.

'Two days? How am I to keep this up for another two days?'

'I don't know what else to say to you,' he replied.

Then I heard her at the door. I decided to take the opportunity to improvise a bit. 'I don't think she'll go to the police,' I said, loudly and clearly.

'I don't understand,' said Grimm.

'I don't know!' I said.

Grimm said nothing, confused.

'I find it very hard to say,' I added.

'What do you find hard to say?' asked Grimm.

'If she does go to the police, she's doing herself more harm than anyone else…' I said. There seemed little doubt that she was still eavesdropping.

'I see,' said Grimm, who had finally twigged. 'You can't talk just now.'

'I don't think that will prove—' I said.

'All right then. We've settled everything anyway,' Grimm replied.

'I'm not going to—' I said.

'Goodbye,' said Grimm.

'Who do you think you're talking to? I wouldn't do a thing like that!' I said loudly.

There was a click. Grimm had hung up.

'Forget it. I wouldn't dream of it!' I said.

Dialling tone.

'No violence, that was the deal!'

I gave my voice a hint of moral indignation, then left a pause for my imaginary interlocutor.

233

'I'll see if I can reason with her.'

Pause.

'It's worth a try, isn't it?'

Pause.

'You promise me that Sarah and her son will come out of this unscathed, if I manage to pull it off?'

I wondered whether I was laying it on too thick. Never mind.

'Promise?'

Pause.

'Okay. Okay, thanks. Yes. Goodbye, then.'

I hung up.

How harmless she can look. But I feel no pity for her. She can shed as many crocodile tears as she likes—I won't be taken in, and I won't turn my back on her for a moment. I'm not that stupid. I know her so well now—maybe better than she knows herself.

In two days I will know everything. And then, if things turn out as I suspect they will, God help her.

Sarah

I look at him long and hard. He's certainly managed to take me by surprise. Vincent, then. I remember seeing the name written in the book I came across when I was going through his things.

It doesn't matter whether or not his name really is Vincent. The fact is, he's clearly determined to make sure I keep my mouth shut for another two days—even if he's not prepared to whack me over the skull and leave me in a pool of blood somewhere that I won't be found until he's well out of the way. Oddly enough, this realisation doesn't reassure me in the slightest. My mind only returns over and over to the same question: *What is going to happen in two days?*

'Two days,' he says again. 'Okay?'

I don't reply.

'Okay?'

I nod.

'Good.'

I hear the phone ringing again downstairs and frown. I don't want to answer it, but then I think of Leo, and of that tree house he loves so much. I think of cuts needing stitches, of broken bones, of all kinds of catastrophes. I leap to my feet and hurry to the phone, the stranger trailing behind me.

'Hello?' I say.

I hear breathing.

'Hello?' I say again.

Nothing.

'Who is it?' I ask.

There's a click down the line. Whoever it was has hung up.

'Who was it?' asks the stranger.

'Wrong number,' I say.

Then the phone starts up again. That withheld number. Quickly I pick up.

'Hello?'

Again the breathing. Again the caller hangs up. Furious, I replace the phone in the charging dock. Is the stranger playing games with me again?

He looks at me questioningly. I just shrug.

'Try to get some sleep,' he says. 'Tomorrow's another day.'

Philip hated such platitudes and always made fun of me if I used them. *Good things come to those who wait. It takes two to make a quarrel. Truth is stranger than fiction. Tomorrow is another day.*

'You look pale,' says the stranger. 'Can I get you anything? Glass of water? Cup of tea?'

I force myself not to laugh at the fact that this Vincent, or whatever his name is, has offered to make me a cup of tea. Besides,

I'm glad of the opportunity to get rid of him.

'A cup of tea,' I say, sinking onto the sofa and watching him disappear towards the kitchen.

I can't carry on like this. How many sleepless nights have I had now? I should at least eat something. Have I eaten since throwing up my breakfast yesterday when Barbara Petry was here? Was that yesterday even? Or was it the day before? Never mind, none of that matters. Concentrate, Sarah. What matters is this: are you going to go along with Vincent's game and trust that it will all be over in two days? Or are you going to call the police?

The first option is pretty appealing, I think.

Make up your mind, woman. Trust him or call the police. But if you're going to call the police, do it now.

I get up and take the phone from the charging dock. I hesitate. Then I enter Miriam's number. I have to tell somebody. I have to talk to somebody.

I don't hear the stranger return.

'What are you doing?' he asks, and I drop the phone, panicked. 'What is this, Sarah?' he says. 'I thought we had an agreement. What are you going to tell the police anyway? That your husband has a doppelganger? Or a wicked twin? Listen to yourself. Look at yourself. You're crazy. Who's going to believe you?'

I can only stand there and stare at him.

'Think of the way you've been carrying on in the past few days—do you realise you've been running about like a raving lunatic? Capering about on the road at night, shrieking. Telling staff at the Foreign Ministry some crap about an impostor. And then you have the nerve to drag a poor sick old lady into your paranoid schemes.' His voice was cold and flat at first, but now he's almost shouting. 'You're out of control. Maybe I'm the one who should call the police! How do I know you're not going to creep into the kitchen in the middle of the night and fetch yourself a big knife? Eh? Yes, maybe I ought to make a few phone calls— and have you committed!'

I'm so angry that everything goes black, just for a moment. At last it's out. At last, he's admitted it. That's what it's all about then. That's what it's been about all along—having me committed. I reach for the phone, on the floor at my feet, but he is quicker, and I try to tear it from his hand. We wrangle over it, but he won't let go—he clutches it tight. I give up—let go— stagger backwards.

'Do you really think you can get rid of me?' the stranger gasps. 'Drive me away? Do you?'

I turn and leave the room, but he comes after me. 'You're crazy!' He flings the word at me, then pauses briefly—catches his breath. 'Who's going to believe you, Sarah?' he asks. It's more of a statement than a question. And again, maliciously: 'Who's going to believe you?' His face is red with fury. 'Let me tell you one thing,' he says. 'I don't buy your masquerade. You'll pay for what you've done.'

He turns to go and I watch him, perplexed. Then suddenly he stops in his tracks and I see him turn back to me in slow motion. Something in his face has changed. His anger has vanished—he seems quite calm now. The frown line bisecting his forehead is gone, his mouth no longer contorted with hate, his face like the smooth surface of a lake. I feel scrutinised, have trouble holding his gaze.

He stands like that for a long time.

'What's the worst thing you've ever done?' he asks eventually.

And suddenly time stands still.

Something is there. Big and heavy and forbidding.

I can only make out shadowy outlines in the dark, like the

silhouette of a tower emerging from the darkness, as if out of nowhere. Yes, there's something there.

The door from my nightmares is opening.

Headlamps in the darkness.

Moths on the windscreen.

The rumbling noise.

Philip and I.

Blood.

At first it's only fragments, disconnected images.

The stranger continues to stare at me for a moment. Then, without a word, he turns and plods upstairs. I hear a door click shut. I don't care. I don't care about him. I suddenly know that I have to face up to my past if I'm to carry on in the present.

I run my hand over my eyes, trying to turn my gaze inward, but my memories elude me, again and again. My attention is caught by a soft papery noise. I can't immediately work out where it's coming from, but then I see a big moth beating its black wings against the wall. I remember Philip once catching a moth in the hollow of his hands and releasing it into the darkness, and I remember us driving through the night once with all kinds of nocturnal creatures—moths and beetles and who-knows-what-else—making ugly cracking sounds as they smashed against the windscreen. I remember.

Past and present touch, as gingerly as young lovers.

And now the pieces come together to make a whole—haltingly at first, as if my memory wanted to spare me. But soon everything has fallen into place.

Asphalt.

Darkness.

The two of us.

Blood.

It's as if a spell has been broken. The dream images that have been dogging me in recent nights have overcome the barrier between sleep and reality, and now haunt my waking moments too. Impossible to sweep away, they cling to me, wrapping me about like a cocoon.

I close my eyes.

I hear the noise of the engine.

Before me lies a dark road.

The road gleams black as licorice.

I know this place. I'm not alone here—Philip is with me.

All around us is darkness. Woods.

I'm afraid of the woods, always have been—afraid of their silence, which reminds me of that moment of silence before something terrible happens. They are so old and, ultimately, so alien. Inscrutable. I can imagine nothing creepier than wandering through the woods at night. Who knows what's hidden there—what might suddenly murmur in your ear.

I put my foot to the floor and the car ploughs through the darkness. The beam of the headlamps grazes the edge of the woods: dense undergrowth, tree trunks and sometimes a pair of shining eyes—or at least that's how it looks to me. Whenever a bend appears in the milky glow of the headlights, I'm forced to brake abruptly to avoid coming off the road.

Philip objects to the way I'm driving, but I ignore him. If he hadn't insisted on getting his own way, we'd be at home with our son now, not driving through these woods, their hostility almost palpable.

We're on our way home from the house on the lake that once belonged to Philip's parents and is now his. A romantic evening—just the two of us. It's the first time since Leo was born that we've left him with a babysitter overnight. Philip's idea, not mine.

The evening wasn't a success. We circled each other like stars whose paths will never cross. Once Philip made an awkward attempt to kiss me and I turned away. He said it was more than a hundred days since we'd last kissed—a hundred and five, to be precise. I suppressed the urge to make fun of his obsession with counting days and said instead that kissing was meaningless, only biochemical processes being played out, a way of sounding out your partner for genetic compatibility—that was all there was to it. Philip looked at me dumbly and then opened the second bottle of wine.

We'd both put away a fair amount by the time the call came from the babysitter: Leo had a high temperature and wouldn't stop screaming. What should she do?

We got in the car immediately.

And of course, we argue, the way we have done ever since my first miscarriage, when Philip accused me of not taking it easy enough—it was my fault the baby had died. Constanze must have put that idea in his head, but I'll never forget the moment he hurled those words at me. How do you forgive a thing like that?

I say we should never have left Leo. I certainly hadn't wanted to. This stupid 'date night', as Philip called it. Ridiculous. As if I'd ever enjoyed myself in that stuffy bourgeois house on the lake, where the ghosts of Philip's embittered parents hovered over our bed at night and watched us argue during the day with their gloating grins. The thousand-eyed woods all around us.

Philip says I always liked being there in the past. I tell him it's not true—I may have pretended I did, but I always loathed that house on the lake, just as I loathe our villa in Hamburg—its cold elegance, Constanze's creation and her legacy, that chill that's worked its way into my marrow.

Philip says he doesn't recognise me—I'm no longer the woman he married.

For a moment I see myself from the outside, yelling and cursing, striking the steering wheel with the flat of my hand, very angry, very unhappy, but inside I'm thinking that I don't recognise myself either. Not me, not you, and certainly not us.

We drive in silence for a while. I turn the radio on. Philip turns it off again even before I've worked out what song is playing. I say nothing. My thoughts stray to Leo again and automatically I rein in the speed. Of course I want to get back to him as fast as possible, but I should drive carefully for that very reason. It is quiet in the car. It smells of the damp earth on the soles of our shoes. I take deep breaths until I'm calmer. It's quiet now, the only sound the rush of asphalt under the tyres.

Babies often run a temperature, says Philip after a while. Leo is sure to be fine again in the morning. I snort—as if I didn't know all that myself.

I tell Philip that, after the shock I've had, I definitely won't be coming with him to his mother's birthday party the next day—that we'll have to see how Leo is first, anyway. Philip answers that he hadn't been expecting it—I always found some way of wriggling out of my family duties.

I've forgotten what I replied. I only remember that Philip spoke those fateful words which sent everything spinning out of control.

'Sometimes I think my mother was right.'

I remember the roadside blurring, my field of vision narrowing until I could only see what was immediately in front of me. I looked at Philip—his self-righteous face—and I shouted something and

243

Philip shouted back at me, and then he cried, 'Look at the road, for God's sake!' and there was a strange rumbling and I braked instinctively and came to an abrupt halt. The car stopped with a jolt and then it was suddenly very, very quiet.

I hit something, I thought, glancing across at Philip, who was staring at me, his eyes wide with horror.

'Was that a deer?' I asked.

'I don't know. I didn't see.'

I swallowed heavily. I looked in the rear-view mirror, but couldn't see anything behind us. I got out of the car and heard Philip do the same. I walked round the car. Then, in the red glow of the brakelights, I saw it.

A person. A man? A woman? I didn't know. But I knew at once that whoever it was was dead.

I surface from the memory, gasping for air, stunned.

How could I have forgotten?

How could I have forgotten what happened?

What kind of a person am I?

How could I blank out such a thing?

What's the worst thing you've ever done?

I curl up on the kitchen floor like a wounded animal mustering its last strength to drag itself back to its lair.

I ran someone down.

I killed someone.

The rumbling.

The shock.

The blood on my hands.

I remember.

have no idea how long I lie there.

I don't seem able to get up. The memory weighs too heavy. It's all come rushing back to me, not just the night itself, but what came afterwards—the guilt, the pain, the weeks after, when I went about feeling as if I was shrouded in cottonwool. Even now, that time is a strange blur—only one moment stands out sharp-edged.

Philip and I are sitting opposite one another at the kitchen table. Leo is asleep, Philip is drinking wine, I'm crying into my glass.

Philip says, 'You do nothing but cry—stop crying all the time.'

I say nothing. We sit and drink in stubborn silence.

Then he says, 'Do you remember the night before our wedding? You asked me what the worst thing was I'd ever done. Because you wanted to know what kind of a man you were going to marry. Do you remember?'

I nod.

'I didn't have an answer,' says Philip. 'Do you remember?' He drains his glass. 'Today I'd have an answer,' he says.

Another tear drips off my chin into my white wine.

This woman who goes to school day after day to hold forth on English grammar and German literature to teenagers—this woman who jogs through the local streets, helps out in the refugee hostel and does the shopping for her elderly neighbour—this single mother who so touchingly attends to all her son's needs and manages everything so admirably, although life has been so hard on her—this woman is a murderer.

Leo's mother is a murderer.

I look about the kitchen, and it's as if I were seeing everything for the first time, as if I could suddenly perceive the true essence of things. Everything here in the house has a soul, I realise all at once. This house sees and hears and feels everything—it soaks up love and tears, anger and forgiveness like a sponge. I frown. Was Leo's lunch box always such an intense blue? Did the basil on the windowsill always smell so pungent? Was the light of the kitchen lamp always so bright? Weren't the fridge and the table further apart? Not much, but enough to make a difference? I blink, but the strange sensation remains.

Something has shifted.

Again my eyes fall on the moth, now perched calmly on the white wall.

A bloodstain, I think. The moth is the shape of a bloodstain.

I start—I can hear footsteps.

Is that it? I wonder. Is that why the stranger is here? What does he know about that night?

How *could* he know? Did someone see Philip and me? Did we leave something at the crime scene that gave us away? Was Philip right? Was I wrong to call him paranoid and ridiculous—to say he was a coward?

Less than two seconds later, the stranger appears in front of me again. He looks down at me lying on the kitchen floor, my face streaked with tears, and he shakes his head as if contemplating something at once repugnant and fascinating.

'Self-pity!' he says sarcastically. 'How touching!'

And he laughs.

I sit up—it's as much as I can manage.

'Do you know,' he says, 'I don't have a crumb of pity for you. The person I really feel sorry for is your son.'

I wipe the tears from my face.

'How old is Leo again?' he asks. He pretends to think it over. 'Eight, isn't he? That's right, eight. At that age you have some idea of what's going on. What do you think—how long will it be before he works out what kind of a person his mother is?' He stares at me, as if he were seriously expecting an answer. Then he shrugs and, with perfect sangfroid, turns to pour himself a glass of water.

He's right, I think. Poor Leo. But he must never find out. I'm all he has.

I look up. The stranger has his back to me. His T-shirt has slipped slightly, and I see the sharply drawn line between the tanned skin of his neck and the paler skin below. Amazing, the way he can turn his back on me like that—entirely at his ease. He knows he has me round his finger. He's known all along.

I leave the room and trudge up the stairs, my body moving on autopilot. There's only one thought in my mind: Leo must never find out. I go into my bedroom and open the wardrobe door. I have to go up on tiptoe to reach the top shelf where the case is hidden. I push the T-shirts aside and grope around to the left and right, but I feel only cloth and the back wall of the wardrobe.

The gun is gone.

Fear grips me like a fever. I close my eyes for a moment. Then I take the piles of clothes down from the shelf one by one and almost laugh with relief. The case is still there—of course it is. I hid it too well, that's all.

I open it, look at the gun and force myself to take it in my hand. I tuck it in the waistband of my jeans, then open the bedroom door, step out into the passage and set out in search of the stranger. I'm no longer frightened, no longer crying.

Out on the landing, I feel a bead of sweat run down my forehead, feel my clothes sticking to me, but there's a chill deep in my bones. The screams of the last swifts of the evening come in at the upstairs windows, and I remember that in an earlier life that noise was the soundtrack of my summer. The gun is pressing against the base of my spine. It is cold, but feels alive. Time to go.

The kitchen. The intense blue of the lunch box on the counter, the brightness of the lamp, the narrow space between table and fridge, the smell of the basil. The stranger. His back.

'I'm not going to play this game for much longer,' I say loudly.

Slowly he turns to face me. He's holding a glass of water in his hand. He raises it to his mouth and drinks in slow gulps, his eyes fixed on mine. Then he puts the glass down.

'Get out of here!' I say.

He sits down. 'Where's Leo, by the way?' he asks.

I can only stare at him.

'At Miriam's, right?' he says.

'Leave my child out of this,' I say, my voice cracking.

'Don't worry,' the stranger says. 'If anything happens to you, Leo has me now.'

I feel like pulling the gun and shooting him, just like that. But what would become of Leo then? What would become of my child if I lost my head now? I can't let myself be so easily provoked.

'At least tell me what you want from me!' I cry, although I'm afraid of the answer.

The night. The road…No. He can't possibly know. This is all about money, no matter what he says.

I cling to this belief like a drowning woman.

The stranger folds his arms behind his head. I spot an inexpertly pricked bluish tattoo on the pale skin of his sinewy upper arm.

'You know exactly what I want,' says the stranger. 'I want the truth.'

The dark road appears before me. The lifeless bundle.

Is it possible?

How can he know?

'I don't know what you're talking about,' I say.

I'll deny it to the end. He's shown me how it goes.

'We both know exactly what you did.'

'Stop it!' I cry. I make a last, desperate effort. 'You want money, right? Why all this carry-on if I'm prepared to give it to you?'

The stranger stares at me.

'It isn't a problem,' I say. 'Money isn't a problem. I've already told you that. You can have all you want.'

I hear his breathing.

I hear the ticking of the clock on the wall.

The stranger says nothing.

'How much do you want?'

The stranger says nothing.

'I don't know what your plans are, or how you're thinking of getting hold of my husband's money. But none of this is necessary. You can have the money. Everything I can lay my hands on. Everything I have.'

This is a bluff. Of course I'd pay to get rid of this man and resume my everyday life, but I don't know if I can. I never took an interest in Philip's money—I have no idea how it's invested, and I don't know if I could get hold of really large sums just like

249

that. And of course I think of Leo. How could I ever forget him? That money is his—it's his future. If anything ever happens to me, he'll need it.

Say yes, I think. Please say yes. Say you'll take all my money and leave me in peace.

'You really don't get it, do you?' the stranger says. 'You still have no idea who I am.'

He sounds almost sorry for me, but I'm not going to be taken in by him again. The pistol is pressing into my back. It suddenly scares me, as if I had no control of it—as if it had control of me. It whispers to me how easy it would be to drive him away if I had it in my hand—so easy. I shake off the thought.

'You're not my husband, that much I do know,' I say, as calmly as I can.

'No,' he says darkly, 'I'm not your husband.'

'Who are you?'

'I'm your past,' he says, getting up. He bows his head, muscles tensed, then looks up, looks me in the eye. 'What's the worst thing you've ever done?' he asks.

Hate blazes in his eyes—or something else, something more primitive.

But I no longer feel fear. Something inside me shuts down, and I watch what comes next as if I'm watching a film.

The kitchen is lit up like a stage set. The kitchen paraphernalia serves as props, and the sound effects are prerecorded. The man stands there like an actor waiting for his cue.

'What do you want?' I ask, giving it to him.

'The truth.'

No, I think.

'Just tell me the truth.'

He can't know.

'What did you do?'

He can't possibly know.

'What did you do, Sarah?'

I say nothing.

'It was you.'

How can he know?

'You did it.'

How is this possible?

'It was you.'

We were alone.

'You know it was.'

No!

'Tell me!'

I don't want to.

'Tell the truth!'

I can't.

'It was your fault!'

That isn't true.

'Tell me. Tell the truth for once in your life!'

'I don't know what you want from me!' I cry.

A chasm opens. Everything goes white—not black, this time—and then it all comes crashing down around me: the call from the Foreign Ministry, my nightmares, the airport, the stranger by my bed, the driver of the sedan, the taste of vomit in my throat, Constanze calling me a murderer, my bloody hands, the rumbling, Leo's voice—*I'm scared of that man*—the ammunition in my wardrobe, the stranger's eyes.

I no longer see anything, no longer hear anything—all I feel is panic, blind panic. I don't know where I am. I tear open my eyes, but there is nothing, only glaring white. I'm blind, but a terrible rumbling sound fills my ears, and I don't only hear it—I feel it all through my body. I feel the car jolt when I brake, the adrenaline coursing through my veins. Past and present mix like toxins. I take a step backwards and then another—blunder into something— crash to the floor. Then I feel a hand at my shoulder and break away from it. I feel something hard against my back. I knock into something and a sharp pain stabs my elbow. I crawl on. I blink—I can see again. Vaguely, very vaguely, I make out the contours of the kitchen. My face is wet, and I realise I'm crying. I put my hand to my face, clumsily wipe away the tears—I can't let myself go now.

The stranger is a hazy figure, slim and dark, staring down at me. Panic swallows me like a gelatinous mass. I'm dying—this must be what it feels like to die. The dark figure comes nearer and nearer. The funereal smell of lilies is in my nose. I pull the pistol from my waistband and heave myself up, the metal cold and heavy in my hand.

'Stand back!' I gasp.

But the dark figure keeps coming towards me.

'You won't get rid of me,' it says. 'Never. Not as long as I have breath in my body.'

It comes nearer.

And nearer.

I taste blood in my mouth. I cough. My heart is pounding, there's a rushing in my ears, the world is red—bright red—and I'm dazzled, my entire body numb, fear whispering in my ear, and I raise the gun, the way Philip showed me, in both hands. I take aim and pull the trigger. Twice. I pull the trigger twice.

No sooner have I pulled the trigger the second time than I wish I could turn back the clock. I know at once that I've done something irreversible—that for the second time in my life I have done something that cannot be undone.

Angry, I take my eyes off the road for a moment.

Panicking for a split second, I raise the gun.

His arms flailing, the stranger falls back and lies motionless on the polished floor of my dazzlingly white kitchen.

The stranger

She pulled the trigger, I'm thinking, as my body hits the floor. My God, she actually pulled the trigger. I can't believe it.

I knew she was dangerous, I think. But I underestimated her all the same.

She pulled the trigger, for Christ's sake.

Sarah

It is quite still in the room. I stare at the figure lying at my feet and stumble back a few steps, as if to distance myself not only from the figure itself, but also from what I have done. I knock into the dining-room table, banging my thighs, and lay the gun carefully on the tabletop, as if in slow motion. For a moment I stare at it lying there like an ugly black animal, and it's a while before I realise that something's not right.

Shouldn't there have been—

The hairs on my neck stand on end.

That means—

I swallow drily. My brain is working painfully slowly.

I pulled the trigger twice and the stranger fell over backwards.

But I didn't feel any recoil.

And the shots didn't make a noise.

And there are no bullet holes, no blood.

I stare at the stranger, lying twisted on the floor. He is very still. Then suddenly I see his chest rise and fall, and before my brain can catch up, I hear a roaring noise.

The stranger is laughing.

He opens his eyes, sits up, gets to his feet and looks at me, shaking with laughter. He laughs and laughs for what seems like an age while I look on aghast.

'Of course I unloaded the gun,' he says.

My mouth is hanging open.

'But interesting,' he adds. 'Interesting that you pulled the trigger like that.' He pauses briefly, as if replaying the moment in his mind. 'Not once, but twice.'

I don't know what to say.

There is contempt in the stranger's eyes, and his mirthless smile is a sharply pencilled dash.

'Do you know what that's called?'

I shake my head, bemused.

'Killer instinct,' he says, with a hint of respect. 'That kind of thing can't be taught.'

My face is numb.

He gives a derisive laugh when he sees my expression.

'*I don't know what you think you know about me, but you're wrong!*' he shrieks in a high-pitched voice, and it's a moment before I realise he's mimicking me. '*I'm only a mother! A teacher! I wouldn't hurt a fly!*' His look is black with disgust. At the same time he seems quite calm.

I'm stunned.

I was in a panic, it's true. But I pulled the trigger. I pulled the trigger. Twice.

My legs give way again and I keel over backwards. I end up sitting on the bare boards, no strength left in me.

'Killer instinct,' the stranger repeats. 'Here she is at last. The *real* Sarah Petersen. Who does what has to be done…'

I swallow.

'…regardless of the consequences.'

He spits the words at me.

'Your husband may be a coward,' he says. 'But you're not.' He looks down at me. 'Yes,' he says. 'You're different. You're made of sterner stuff.' His eyes are devoid of anything human.

'You're wrong,' I whimper.

He shakes his head. A cynical smile appears on his face. 'Really, Sarah? Are you going to keep this up forever?'

'What do you want to hear from me?' I scream—or at least I mean to scream, but what comes out of my mouth is more like a whimper, feeble and pathetic.

'You haven't been paying attention,' he says. 'I want the truth.'

'What truth?' I ask. 'The truth about what?'

'The truth about you and Philip,' he says, slowly and deliberately, as if he were talking to a stubborn child.

'The truth about that night,' I say.

That night. Oh God.

He doesn't reply.

'Where's my husband? What have you done to him?' I ask. I try to heave myself up, but my limbs won't obey. 'Where is Philip?'

'You know that.'

'No, I don't!'

What on earth is going on?

'You do know. Tell me.'

I can't take any more.

'I don't know!' I sob.

'You do know. Tell me.'

It is suddenly quiet.

Nothing.

Only my breathing.

His breathing.

The creak of the boards.

'You killed him,' I whisper.

My body is light.

The stranger looks at me calmly. '*You* killed him,' he says.

'Why are you doing this to me?' I whisper.

'You know why.'

'Because of what happened back then,' I rasp. 'Because of what we did.'

With a sweeping movement, he bends down to me. 'What's the worst thing you've ever done?'

My stomach lurches. Light flickers in front of my eyes.

'What did you do?' he asks.

A chasm opens.

'What did you do? Tell me!'

I can't.

'Tell the truth!' he shouts.

I open my mouth—

I can't.

I'm fainting.

The stranger

Careful now, very careful.

I approach her slowly. At first I think she's only shamming. This woman is no timid creature, easily spooked. She just shot at me at close range. In cold blood.

But she really has passed out. I feel her pulse and she doesn't stir. I don't have to think for long. I can't let her attack me again, can't let her escape.

I open the back door, grasp her beneath the arms and begin to drag her out to the garden.

As I reach the terrace, she lets out a whimper, like a frightened child. I almost feel pity, but get a grip on myself. Philip Petersen has paid for his sins. There's no reason his wife should get off scot-free.

Sarah

When I come to, I don't immediately know where I am or what's happened. All around me it's dark—I can't see a thing. At first, I only hear noises—horrible and very close. A screech, and then a deep, primeval snarl, such as children might imagine coming from the devil. I try to open my eyes, but it's an effort. I see something—a movement—and try to focus on it. The snarling stops, and there is silence. My consciousness scrapes along the edge of reality, making sparks like metal against metal, but then it slides off and I have to grope my way back up. I blink. It is no longer light but dark, and the ceiling above me is moving—no, that isn't the ceiling—someone has spread a dark cloth over me, and the cloth is full of holes, and there's light shining in at every little hole and—nonsense, it isn't a cloth—it's the night sky. I'm outside.

I hear the noises again, fiercer and more aggressive, but I can't work out where they're coming from. Are they meant for me? Where am I? Why do I feel so nauseous? Why is everything spinning? Am I drunk? Am I sick? I'm moving. There's the Plough—Philip once showed me how to recognise it. Where am I going and why? I blink, and a stabbing pain in my shoulder brings me back to myself and I understand. I'm not walking— someone has hold of my shoulders and is dragging me across the grass. Am I injured? Is it a paramedic? Where is he taking me?

Then everything comes back to me.

The stranger is dragging me across the grass. My clothes are wet with dew and I can hear him panting. I screw up my eyes and try to move, but I've lost all control over my body. Has he drugged me? No, I can feel my limbs, move them—I only passed out for a moment. What is he going to do? Where is he taking me?

The shed, I think—he's taking me to the shed. I'm suddenly icy cold and have to tense all my muscles to stop myself from shaking uncontrollably. Again I hear the eerie noises and realise that it's cats fighting in a nearby garden, but that hardly makes the noise less frightening.

Then the stranger stops. He's dragged me right to the other side of the grass.

I suppress a whimper when I realise what he's planning.

The stranger

Keep going.

Focus on the task in hand.

She has caught me off my guard—again. Now I must take back control.

The caterwauling has stopped. I deposit her body on the grass and open the shed door. For a moment I stare into the darkness. It's not much more than a wooden box—no windows. I can vaguely make out the shapes of garden tools: spades, rakes, a roll of hose on a hook, watering cans. It smells of timber and soil.

I lean against the doorframe to recover, breathing in and out, slowly and deeply, eyes closed, concentrating on the rise and fall of my chest until my heart finally stops pounding and the panting subsides. I'm running my hand over the metal bolt, trying to gauge its strength, when I glimpse movement at the other end of the garden, hear a rustling by the fence. I squint into the darkness, almost expecting to see a figure emerge from the shadows, but there's nothing there.

Am I seeing things? Hearing things? Keep going, I tell myself. Do what needs to be done.

I take a deep breath, then turn to pick Sarah up, bundle her into the shed, lock her in.

I freeze.

She's not there.

Adrenaline floods my system. There's only one thought in my head: catch her, catch her, catch her.

She can only be in the house. I'm back inside within seconds, looking left, looking right, calling out. 'Sarah!'

The kitchen's empty. She's not in the hall, not in the living room. I feel a draught and, following it, I realise the front door's open.

She's gone.

Damn.

I stare out onto the street—nothing.

Furious, I close the door and turn round.

It hits me full on.

Pain explodes in my eyes and throat. I can't breathe, can't get my bearings. I put my hand to my face. I try to get some air in my lungs, try to open my eyes, but they're burning. I press my fists into my eye sockets. I gasp and fall to my knees. I cough, I gag, I retch.

I can't see her, but I can hear her. She's close. For a moment I think she's going to seize her chance and kick me—in the head, in the belly. I'm utterly defenceless. I raise my arms to shield my head. I steel myself, prick my ears, hear her footsteps dying away. Then silence. Then the front door. Then nothing.

Sarah

The moon is full and red as blood, the street ahead empty. There are people all around me, behind walls and windows, even if I can't see them—but I might just as well be on Mars. I am alone. A cacophonous symphony clangs in my head. I run and run. My handbag, which I had the presence of mind to pick up, is knocking against my hip and I'm shod only in flimsy pumps which, in my blind panic, were all I could find in the hall. If he catches you now, he'll kill you, says a voice in my head. If he catches you now, he'll kill you, if he catches you now, he'll kill you. The voice is high-pitched and frantic and I believe it. When I come to the end of the street, I duck into a doorway and look back. He hasn't followed me—how could he? I'm still amazed at the devastating effect of the pepper spray I'd been carrying around in my bag for months.

I can still see the stranger's face, contorted with fear. I hear his gasps, see him collapse to the floor, coughing and cursing. I have to cough too and my eyes are smarting—I got a tiny whiff of the pepper spray myself.

The images flood my mind again: the dark road, my anger, Philip's face, the rumbling, the black bundle on the asphalt lit only by the red of my tail-lights.

The two of us driving away.

As I'm trying to get a grip on my senses, a big black car comes whizzing round the corner and zooms past me. I know that car. I watch it stop outside my house, watch the door open and a man get out. It's like a slap in the face. The noise of the car door slamming echoes in the night. Johann—the man I would have trusted with my life until recently—walks up to the front door without glancing left or right and raises his arm to ring the doorbell. As the door opens, a shaft of light falls on him, illuminating his face. I watch from a safe distance. The men exchange a few words, inaudible from where I'm standing. I don't know what I was expecting. Maybe I was still hoping that Johann was on my side.

My limbs feel so heavy, it's as if I were lugging lead weights. Johann's betrayal cuts me to the quick, but it's really something else that is preying on my mind.

I feel my finger crooked on the trigger, feel the resistance as I squeeze it—reluctantly the first time, automatically the second.

I see the stranger keeling over backwards, his arms flailing.

I hear his laugh, echoing in my ears, the sound of his voice.

Killer instinct.

The *real* Sarah.

Again I hear his voice.

You know why.

His words.

265

What's the worst thing you've ever done?

For years, that fateful night was erased from my memory, locked away deep down inside me. Now a single question has washed it to the surface. I hear the stranger's voice as if on endless loop: *What's the worst thing you've ever done?*

Killed someone, I think. I killed someone. That's the worst thing I've ever done, the worst thing anyone has ever done, the worst thing you can do on this earth.

I breathe deeply. The tickle in my throat from the pepper spray has gone—only my eyes still smart.

What do I do now? Where do I go now?

I can't go back to my house.

I stand in the middle of the road, shaded from the moonlight by the canopy of trees. Out of the corner of my eye I see something move. I give a start and, spinning round, find myself face to face with a fox, frozen mid-movement and staring at me, barely ten metres away. Its eyes shine in the darkness, and I think I can make out the red of its coat, although it's so dark I see the world only in greys and blues. A fox—Philip would have liked that. Philip loved animals, whereas I prefer to admire them from a distance. Cats, wolves, foxes—I find their eyes unnerving. They look as if they know something I don't.

This creature stands quite still. It looks as if it's thinking. Nonsense, I tell myself. Animals don't think. They act from instinct—a bit like you these last few days.

I too stand quite still.

I've often read that German cities are full of foxes, but the sudden appearance of this sly-faced animal makes it seem more like an apparition—the fox from the fairytales and fables Leo is so fond of, the wily fox and his tricks. What is it trying to tell me? Maybe because I knocked my head when I fainted, or maybe because I've barely eaten or slept for days, I almost expect the fox to open its mouth and talk to me.

We look at each other for a moment, then the fox scampers off.

The stranger

For some minutes I lay on the hall floor in a pool of my own sweat and saliva and vomit, thinking I was going to die. Then, very gradually, the cramps eased off, the coughing subsided and I could breathe again. I dragged myself to the bathroom. It wasn't until I had rinsed the snot off my face that I was able to think straight.

By the time the doorbell rang and I saw the old man on the doorstep, I was ready to keep going.

That woman took everything I had. I'm not going to let her go unpunished.

Sarah

The night city has never seemed so hostile. The dark is darker than usual, the light of the street lamps dimmer. Everywhere shadows reach out for me, everywhere loose cobblestones wait to trip me up.

My thoughts take a while to settle. I walk on blindly, not noticing where I'm going, until I find myself at the nearest underground station. What am I doing here? The digital display tells me there's a train leaving for the city centre in just under half an hour. I sit down, glancing across at the escalator that carried me down and has now come to a standstill. I'm sure the stranger didn't follow me—I'm sure no one followed me. But I have to be careful. Now that I know so much about Johann, and especially if my suspicions are correct…

Gooseflesh spreads over my arms as I hear Johann's voice in my head: 'You could do good things with Philip's money. You could help people if you wanted.'

Yes, I think. And when you say 'people', you mean yourself, don't you, Johann? You and your company, which the papers say is close to bankruptcy—and which you are determined to save, because it means everything to you—because it is to you what Philip was to me.

But if it all boils down to money, I suddenly think, what's all this talk about truth?

Then it dawns on me.

Diversionary tactics. It's so simple. I thought there was some clear motive for the stranger's threats and insinuations. But in fact they were extremely vague—nothing about anyone being knocked down, or about a hit-and-run, or about me at the wheel. He was simply trying it on and happened to hit the mark. How did he know I had something to hide? Well, don't we all? Don't we all feel guilty about something? Only with me he really hit the jackpot. Or did he?

Did he?

That terrible night.

Don't think about it now—not now.

Don't go to pieces.

Johann and 'Vincent' were trying to divert my attention from what was really going on—just until they had carried through their plan. And, idiot that I am, I was taken in.

Johann is right. It always boils down to money in the end—certainly with people like him.

The ground beneath my feet is pitching as if I were on a ship. I close my eyes, but it only makes the dizziness worse. I'm having trouble concentrating.

I see before me the face of the man the stranger spoke to the other day—the man who struck me as so familiar. I have to talk to that man. Maybe he can answer my questions. At last I have a goal. At last I'm not just running away.

The underground station is deserted and has a ghostly feel, like all places absolved of their function—the dark aisles of a supermarket at night, lecture theatres, swimming pools, law courts after hours. Who knows what goes on in such places when the last person has left and the lights have been put out—or, indeed, what goes on anywhere when we're not looking?

My eyes fall on the stairs next to the escalator, where someone has sprayed a message in red paint, one word to a step:

MONSTERS
DON'T
SLEEP
UNDER
YOUR
BED
THEY
SLEEP
INSIDE
YOUR
HEAD

I hear the escalators start up and see them roll down, step by step by step. Maybe I should jump to my feet, maybe I should hide, maybe I should run towards the other exit—but I'm too tired. I stare at the clanking escalator, and for a few seconds there's nothing to be seen. Then a pair of shoes appears, trouser legs, a male torso in a black T-shirt, a neck, a head. The man glances briefly in my direction, then walks past me and sits down some way away. I wonder where he might be heading—it's too late for the night shift and too early for morning shift. He takes his phone from his trouser pocket and begins to swipe. I heave a sigh of relief.

It's still a while until the train is due and I have nothing to do but wait. I look at the graffiti on the wall opposite. Next to huge silver letters that make no sense, a stylised bee is hovering with a fierce look on its face and a nasty-looking sting. It reminds me of something I read about bumblebees recently. That's right, bumblebees and lime trees. Distractedly, I take my phone from my bag, unlock it and type 'dead bumblebees' and 'lime trees' into Google's search field.

I read that huge numbers of bumblebees die under lime trees every year, but that it has nothing to do with toxins or pollution or anything like that. The bumblebees apparently fly off in search of food with almost no energy reserves, and because the lime trees don't have enough nectar, the bees simply starve to death. Scientists sometimes find more than a thousand starved bumblebees per tree.

As I'm reading this, the train draws into the station. I am amazed that the half-hour has passed so quickly—did I drop off for a few minutes? I get up. My body feels very light. I am, by now, no longer alone with the man whose arrival gave me such a fright. A small group of late-night revellers—seven, no, eight, people—also get up from their seats and cross the platform. No one gives me a second glance. The train comes hurtling towards us—its doors open, swallow us up and close again. The people in my compartment dig out books or phones, or simply lean their heads against the windows and close their eyes. Their weary faces are painted yellow and grey by the fluorescent light.

Blinking to keep my tiredness at bay, I work out where I need to change trains. My brain longs for silence, for oblivion. The gentle rattle and shake of the carriage begins to lull me to sleep. No, I think, not yet.

I get up. Grab hold of a strap. Stay awake. Think of Johann. Want to cry. Don't cry. Stare out of the grubby train window and watch the stations flying past. We stop again, just as another train stops on the opposite platform—and for a brief, surreal moment I think I see Philip through the window as we move off.

Impossible.

An illusion.

Really?

Yes, really.

How can you be so sure?

Because Philip would look older. The man I saw looked the way Philip used to, seven years ago. It's my mind playing tricks on me, like when he first went missing and the city was suddenly full of his doppelgangers and hardly a day went by that I didn't run after some stranger and grab his shoulder—only to be disappointed time and time again.

I leave the underworld, escaping the flicker of the fluorescent light into a velvety darkness broken only by a few street lamps and the occasional neon ad. It takes me a moment to get my bearings, then I remember the way. I picture the stranger, see him before me, crossing the road, vanishing briefly and then re-emerging and ringing at the door of number forty-one.

I trace his steps, then stand on the footpath a moment, looking up at the house. It's the middle of the night—you can't ring on strangers' doors at this time of night—but I can't bother myself with that just now. Still, I hesitate. Perhaps I should be afraid of the man who lives here—but no, I'm past being afraid. I ring the doorbell, leaving my finger on the button for a long time—three seconds, four, five. Then I wait. It is silent. Nobody comes. No light goes on in the house. I try to be patient, try to imagine someone being torn from sleep—taking time to work out that it was the doorbell that woke him. I try to imagine this someone sitting up dazedly, realising that he's naked, that he left his pyjamas off because of the heat—that he can't go to the door like that. I imagine him groping for something to put on, hurriedly pulling on a pair of trousers and—

The door opens with a jerk. I give a start and find myself face to face with the man the stranger came to see. He's wrapped in a dressing-gown and looks irate. His irritation morphs into something else, not easily definable, when he sees me. He knows me, I think. He knows who I am.

The man swallows. His voice, when he finally speaks, is thick with sleep. 'I thought you'd show up at some point,' he says. 'But I hadn't expected you in the middle of the night.'

And at that moment, I know who he is.

The stranger

I'm roaming around a city whose rhythm, language and people are foreign to me. My body is aching all over.

I ought to be systematic about this search, but I don't know where to begin.

I almost had her—I was so close. Then she went and gave me the slip. Since then I've been acting haphazardly, not pausing to think things through.

I force myself to stand still. Enough of this rushing into things. I stop and think. I wipe the sweat from my forehead. I turn round. I set one foot in front of the other. I return to the house.

I look for her mobile number. I can't find it. I look for her address book, but without any luck. I boot up her laptop. I was positive the password would be the boy's name, or perhaps his date of birth, but I was wrong. Once again, I have misjudged her.

I go in the kitchen. I look at the notes stuck to the fridge with magnets, rummage through the drawers, open all the cupboards— nothing. I don't know what to do next.

Suddenly I'm tearing drawers out of cupboards, shouting and swearing and smashing my fist into the wall.

It shocks me to realise how thin the membrane is separating me from total lunacy.

My knuckles are torn. There's blood on the whitewash. I focus on the pain, the way I did when I was captive. I was captive for a long time. I've had plenty of practice. My hand is throbbing. I'm bleeding. I go into the living room. I sit down on the sofa. All I can do is wait. So I wait. She'll come back.

Criminals always return to the scene of the crime. Especially when the scene of the crime is their own home.

Sarah

Exhausted, I stare at the man who has opened the door to me. He's wearing white boxer shorts and a baggy AC/DC T-shirt beneath the dressing-gown. His hair is grey and has thinned since I last spent any time with him. He's put on weight, too, but his face is the same—a kind, soft-eyed, slightly doughy face that robs his hulk-like form of its menace. Right now it's creased with sleep. In the hall behind him I can see a child's red sit-on car.

I realise I'm staring at him mutely.

'What did you say?' I ask.

The man gives a groan of annoyance.

'What do you want?'

I blink.

'Have you come to make accusations against me?' he asks.

I stare at him, not knowing what to think.

'Do you know what time it is?' he says. 'It's the middle of the night.'

I don't react.

'Come back some other time.'

He slams the door in my face.

I'm confused. I had reckoned with everything, but not that.

I ring again, half-heartedly. I have a feeling Bernd Schröder isn't going to open the door to me this time. I wait all the same—no luck.

Bernd was one of Philip's colleagues—the last person to see Philip alive. What does it all mean? Why did the stranger go to see him this morning—no, yesterday morning?

I remember the last time I saw Bernd Schröder. It must have been at the summer party, that stupid summer party a good year before Philip went missing. Bernd was there with his wife, who was pregnant at the time. I've forgotten her name—Bianca, Beate, Bettina? I only remember that it was the first time I drank alcohol since having Leo, and that I danced, first with Philip's PA, whom I'd always liked, and then with Philip. I see his handsome face, always rather too boyish for his age, smell the warm scent of his skin. Philip didn't like dancing, but sometimes he danced all the same. For me.

Confused, I drop down on the doorstep and try to think. For some reason, Bernd Schröder is important. Why?

I run through everything again.

In 2008, Philip went to South America on a business trip.

The trip was to last five days.

Philip was often in Colombia on business.

The trips were routine.

I said goodbye to Philip at the front door.

He promised to be in touch every day as usual.

A bare twenty-four hours later, Philip sent me a text telling me he'd landed safely and all was well.

That was the last time I heard from him.

A colleague who had accompanied him to Colombia said that Philip had set off alone for a meeting with a potential investor.

He never turned up at the luxury hotel in Bogotá where he was expected.

Somewhere between his hotel and his business partner's hotel he went missing.

Bernd Schröder was the last person to see Philip before he disappeared.

What does it all mean?

It's too much. I don't know what conclusions to draw—I'm not up to it.

I get up and set off. I look at the sky, but see no stars, no moon—only hostile black. I walk down the street, dig in my bag for a tissue, blow my nose, switch off for a second and don't see the man coming the other way until it's too late. He bumps into me, I mumble an apology, and he gives me a dirty look, hisses, 'Watch where you're going!' I cross the road against the lights and a taxi driver hoots at me. Two young girls, both blond, both in miniskirts, whisper and giggle as they pass me. I dodge a dead pigeon lying between the kerb and a manhole cover. The faces of the people coming towards me are blank and shuttered. Someone has been sick on the asphalt.

I walk. No one pays me any attention. The buildings I pass look down on me, indifferent, my surroundings as hostile as if I were in the death zone.

Then my phone rings. I don't have to look at it to know it's the withheld number.

I struggle inwardly. Should I take the call? I psych myself up.

'Hello, Mirko,' I say, without knowing I'm about to.

At first the line is silent.

Then I hear, 'Hello, Sarah.'

The stranger

The hand I bashed against the wall is throbbing. I found a first-aid kit on the shelf under the towels in the bathroom and have made myself a makeshift bandage.

She'll come back, I'm sure of it. I saw in her face that she had understood. She'll come back and we'll see this through.

I give a start when the landline begins to ring. I'm so sick of the noise that I almost unplug it, but I force myself to take the call.

'Petersen.'

'It's Grimm.'

I swallow.

'Your mobile was off,' he says. 'That's why—'

'No problem,' I say.

My voice suddenly sounds hoarse. If he's ringing me at this hour, it must be something important.

'I've done as you asked,' he says.

'Wait,' I interrupt him. 'Before you say anything—are you sure?'

'Quite sure. It was easier than I thought.'

'All right then,' I say. 'Let's have it.'

He talks, I listen.

'Okay,' I say, when he's finished. 'Thank you for letting me know.'

A pause follows.

'There's another thing,' says Grimm.

And he tells me something that makes my world collapse.

Sarah

The noise of traffic coming from the busy road in spite of the late hour suddenly seems to swell: the driver of a convertible is leaning on her horn because a double-parked VW campervan is blocking the way. Pressing my phone to my ear, I hurry away from the main road and into a side street. It's busy even here, but at least I can hear what Mirko's saying.

'Sorry,' I say. 'Can you repeat that? It's rather loud here.'

Mirko curses. 'I said I'm not really like that. I'm not even particularly jealous. And I'm certainly not the avenging type. I'm honestly not—you can ask anyone.'

'I know,' I say. 'I know you aren't.'

I lean up against the brick wall of a house with a laundrette in the basement. Beautiful young people are streaming past me towards the trendy bars and clubs I haven't taken an interest in for at least ten years. I watch a couple pass, hand in hand, and cross the road before coming to a beggar who's sitting dozing in front of a rancid old rancid hat. They stop to ruffle the coat of his shaggy dog.

'I already had the ring in my pocket,' says Mirko and I feel myself go cold.

Christ, I didn't know that.

'Everything was going so well in the last few months—perfectly, even,' he says, and it's only now that I realise he's so drunk he can hardly speak without slurring his words.

'I mean, sure, she has a son from her first marriage. And she'd probably always wonder what had happened to her husband.'

I realise that when he says 'she', he means me.

'But when I started teaching at that school and saw her for the first time—there was something between us. I felt it instantly. *Instantly*. The beautiful, single mother who does triathlons. So vulnerable and yet so strong.'

I know that in other circumstances the hurt in his voice would pierce my heart.

'I'm sorry, Mirko,' I say dully.

And it's true. I'm sorry that I'm not capable of feeling anything right now. Least of all for Mirko. I realise at once what I've gone and thought and I'm horrified. What kind of a person am I? I killed someone. I used Mirko to get over Philip and then dropped him when I no longer needed him. Just like that. And Philip...

Philip, I—

Mirko has noticed at once that my thoughts are wandering.

'You kept refusing my calls,' he says. 'I don't understand. Cutting me off like that for no reason.'

I say nothing.

'Without any explanation. And then you wouldn't even come to the phone when I rang you at home.'

He curses again.

'I only knew your husband was back because I saw it in the newspaper!' he shouts. 'That's no way to treat anyone, for Christ's sake.'

I am silent.

'I don't know,' Mirko says. 'I can't make sense of it.' There's a pause. 'Are you still there?' he asks.

'Yes.' I say nothing else. What can I say?

'Fuck you,' Mirko says, and hangs up.

I feel nothing—I'm too tired. But my urge to see Leo is suddenly overwhelming. All at once I have a goal again: to get to Miriam's as fast as possible. I set off at a run, and the people coming towards me give me funny looks—there goes another weirdo in this crazy city. At the next crossroads I take a left and pass a group of young men. I ignore their lewd remarks and their cans of beer, and run and run and run.

Although it's very late when I get to Miriam's, she's awake, breastfeeding Emily. I'm incredibly glad to see her. She may not be influential or powerful like Johann, but she's on my side and that's all that counts just now.

I'm going to take her into my confidence at last—I should have done it ages ago.

'Sweetheart,' she says, when she opens the door to me, the baby on her arm. 'I'm so sorry.'

For a second I don't know what she means, but then I understand. She thinks I've come because of the online comments—as if I care about that.

Miriam thrusts Emily into my arms and puts water on to boil for tea. She chatters away, telling me about the barbecue they had yesterday—how the children were allowed to help Martin and stuffed themselves with barbecued meat and potato salad. I can't get a word in edgewise. The baby stares wide-eyed at my face and I can't help but smile at her. It seems to me it's only a few months since Leo was that small. I swallow my sentimentality and sit down at the dining table with Miriam, who takes Emily from me again and puts her to the breast. The baby immediately starts to drink in greedy gulps, and I hesitate. Is this really the moment to tell my friend what's going on? In the middle of the night, when she's breastfeeding? On the other hand, she didn't seem surprised to find me on the doorstep at this hour.

'I have to tell you something,' Miriam blurts out. She looks guilty. 'I talked to Philip,' she says.

I feel the colour drain from my face.

'We're both very worried about you,' Miriam adds.

'What?'

'You've been acting so strangely for weeks.'

I feel sick.

'Can I be straight with you?' she asks.

I can't get a sound out, but Miriam seems to take my silence as a yes.

'I remembered what you told me about your mother's death.' She clears her throat. 'Her suicide,' she adds.

I can't believe it.

'You told me it had been such a blow that you'd had to seek help.'

My best friend's betrayed me.

'And, well. Maybe the present situation is similar. Maybe you need help again. It's nothing to be ashamed of. Philip says—'

I can't take any more. Miriam sucks in her breath in alarm as I leap to my feet. Emily sets up a wail.

'You talked about me behind my back?' I ask.

Miriam opens and closes her mouth.

I storm out of the room, without even waiting for her to reply.

'Sarah,' Miriam calls out after me. 'Wait! Where are you going?'

I run upstairs to the first floor, where the children sleep. I'm fetching Leo, I think. I'm getting out of here.

Cautiously, I open the door to Justus's room. The beds are empty. At first I get a fright, but then I see a big tent in the middle of the room. I almost burst into tears—how idyllic, I think. How lovely it must be to sleep in a tent. For some strange reason, I'm reminded of the bumblebees and the limes. Carefully I unzip the tent and poke my head in. I see Martin lying in the tent and Justus snuggled up to him and it pierces my heart. They look so alike, Justus a smaller, younger version of his father. I let my eyes wander over the alpine landscape of quilts and sleeping-bags, looking for Leo's face, a foot, a hand, anything. Then it hits me—there's no Leo. He's not here.

Again I hear the stranger's voice.

You'll lose everything. Your son. Your whole beautiful life.

Frantically I hare back down the hall. Miriam is waiting for me at the foot of the stairs.

'Where's Leo?' I shout.

She only looks at me. 'Isn't he up there?' she asks mildly.

I storm past her and am almost out of the door when I stop.

'I need your car,' I say.

'What on earth's the matter with you?'

'The car keys!' I shout at her.

Miriam looks shocked, but she fetches her keys and gives them to me.

'Where are you thinking of going?' she calls out after me,

while baby Emily screams and screams and screams in her arms.

The baby's wails are still ringing in my ears as I get in Miriam's car and drive off.

The stranger

I am standing on the threshold, bag over my shoulder, staring into the darkness—trying to come to a decision.

I'm not a bad person, I think. I'm not a bad person.

I keep thinking it until I almost believe it.

I may have completely misjudged Sarah, but I do know myself.

I close the door.

I set down the bag.

I can't run away.

Sarah

The moon is glowing an intense orange and looks very close, as if it weren't in the sky but hanging just above the houses, waiting to be plucked by the first late-night reveller who comes along. To me it seems a bad omen. Ravens, dead bumblebees—and now a bloody moon.

The roads are empty, but still I can't get along fast enough, have to force myself not to jump the red lights. The whole time I'm aware of the phone in the pocket of my jeans, fervently hoping that it will start to ring—that Miriam will call to say that Leo's turned up, that he's okay, that he was only hiding, that he had wanted to punish me, or whatever. But my phone is silent.

I feel as if I'm in a tunnel, oblivious to what's going on to the left and right of the road. Strips of darkness and light. I drive, stop, release the clutch, drive off, floor the accelerator, stop, drive off again, speed through the darkness. Then I turn off onto our street.

The sense that everything is conspiring against me is now so overpowering and intense that I almost have the feeling I could bite into it like a ripe, poisonous fruit. The faint headache I've had for a while has given way to almost unbearable tension, as if my head were in a vice and someone were trying to make my eyes pop out of their sockets. The pain feels like a punishment.

Together with the lack of sleep, the pain makes everything around me seem strangely surreal, as if reality had slipped ever so slightly, revealing a fairly precise but still imperfect copy of itself in which the entire world is a little bit different—blacker, deeper, duller, more alien, more menacing.

Before me lies the road I took when I ran away from the stranger. I skirt the fences that border my neighbours' gardens, and when I come to mine I squeeze myself through the hole again.

The house looms up before me in the darkness, a haunted castle. A solitary light is burning in the spare room.

He's here.

He's awake.

Is he waiting for me?

I cross the garden, giving a slight start when a sudden crack breaks the silence. I turn my head and see something dart off, maybe a cat—or the fox. I feel myself shiver, but I keep going, towards the house. The terrace door is slightly ajar; I open it noiselessly and slip inside. The house and its rooms are so familiar that I don't need any light, moving with the sureness of a sleepwalker. I listen out—no sound to be heard.

I assume the stranger is in the spare room. The gun, which must still be somewhere in the house, flashes into my mind—then

291

the big block of knives in the kitchen. But the time for games is over. I inhale deeply, cross the ground floor and mount the stairs without a sound, instinctively skipping the creaking step. On the landing I stop and listen. I look down the passage leading to the spare room, but there is nothing—only darkness. Suddenly I think I hear a rumbling. The hairs on my neck stand on end; my heart beats faster. But no, it was only my nerves. Silence. I go down the passage towards the spare room. Outside the door I stop and steel myself. Then I press down the handle and push open the door. The room lies in darkness. I turn on the light—blink—swallow. I see in a split second that the room is empty. Where is he?

Without stopping to think, I head back to the kitchen. I'll wait for him there—he'll turn up sooner or later. I think of putting the light on, but something stops me. I give a start. I freeze. The stranger is sitting in the dark at the kitchen table, motionless. He looks at me. I flick the switch.

'There you are,' he says.

He gets up and comes towards me. Now he's right in front of me, his dark eyes gleaming.

I take a step back. Get me away from this man.

'Where's Leo?' I ask. 'Where's my son?'

'Sarah,' he says. 'Calm down. Leo's safe at Miriam's.'

'I've just come from Miriam's,' I say. 'He wasn't there.'

For a moment that throws him—he doesn't seem to know what to say next—but he's quick.

'Miriam rang just now,' he says. 'She said to tell you that Leo's turned up, and he's fine.'

I give a bitter laugh.

'Sarah, listen,' he says. 'I've made a terrible mess of things. Please let's talk this over sensibly.'

He astounds me, really he does. Behind every mask is a new mask.

'What exactly do you want to talk about?' I ask. 'My husband's murder or my son's kidnapping?'

He splutters at that, feigning shock.

'Where is my son?' I shout. 'Does Johann have him?'

He frowns. 'Johann?'

What do I do now?

'Sarah,' he says. 'Sarah, please listen to me. I don't have Leo. He's at Miriam's. Why would I kidnap Leo?'

'To frighten me,' I say. 'To make me do as you say.'

'That makes no sense, Sarah,' he says. 'Think about it. If I wanted to use Leo to make you do as I say, wouldn't I admit that I had him?'

He's right. Is he right?

'Why should I listen to anything you say?' I ask.

'Because it's the truth. I'd never do anything to harm the boy. What I said is true—Miriam really did call just before you got back. She's found Leo. He's fine.'

'You killed my husband,' I say.

'No,' he says, 'I didn't.'

'You said it yourself.'

'I was testing you!'

I laugh again. 'Great excuse!'

'It's true!'

'Why would you need to test me?'

He's about to reply, then stops. 'You can see for yourself that Leo isn't here,' he says. 'He's at Miriam's.'

'But she'd have rung me!' I say.

'She did,' says the stranger. 'But the call went straight to your voicemail. The battery's probably flat.'

293

I can feel my eyes narrowing to slits. I grope in the back pocket of my jeans for my phone, careful not to take my eyes off the stranger. I take out the phone with my left hand and glance at the display—

'Sarah, I'm sorry,' says the stranger. 'I'm so sorry—about everything.'

He takes a step towards me. I back away instinctively, but he comes after me and takes me in his arms. I gasp and push him away. The kitchen counter is only a step away. I stop thinking and act—pull a knife from the block, hold it out in front of me.

In a flash he has grabbed my wrist and is trying to wrest the knife from me. My phone clatters to the floor. I resist him with all my strength and manage to struggle free.

The stranger gasps and jumps back.

I don't hesitate for a second, but swing my arm wildly and slash him across the chest. He cries out in alarm and backs away, his shirt hanging open, blood welling up, soaking the cloth red. I blink. I too take a step backwards. The stranger presses his hands to the wound, but it's too late.

I've already seen it.

I drop the knife.

There's only one thing I can do—have to do. I muster what little strength and courage remain to me and go up to the man.

He doesn't back away, doesn't resist.

I yank off what's left of his shirt—and I see it now. All of it. The scarring. He is covered in scars. But they can't hide it. There it is, directly beneath the cut I have inflicted on him. There it is.

Philip's birthmark.

've been dreaming of this for years.

It is night. We are standing facing one another. The world is deserted—there is no one but us. Adam and Eve. All the rivers, all the mountains and lakes, all the meadows and woods and streets and fields and orchards and circus tents and oceans—all ours. I daren't move, I daren't say anything, because I'm afraid of breaking the spell, of bursting the cocoon around us that's keeping the world at bay. I almost flinch when Philip raises his hand and gently, very gently touches my cheek. It is as if he wants to make sure that I'm real. I close my eyes and try to get it into my head that I am standing here and that Philip is stroking my cheek, the way he's stroked it hundreds of times before. I open my eyes again. The spell breaks.

He pulls back his hand like a child who's suddenly remembered that it's dangerous to push your hand between the bars of a cage.

I stare at Philip; Philip stares at me. I back away—I can feel myself shaking my head, hear myself saying something, but I don't know what. I clutch the arm of the sofa to stop myself from falling into an abyss. The boundary between dream and reality has blurred, all certainty flown out of the window. I understand nothing, and at the same time I know everything.

I keep backing away. One step, another step. A choked cry leaves my throat. I want to turn round, I want to run away, but I'm in such shock, I can hardly move.

'Sarah, please stay!' says the stranger—Vincent—my husband—Philip, reaching for my hand. I pull it away.

My eyes fall on the phone lying on the floor. I stoop down and pick it up—something to do, a way of holding off thought. I tap away at the screen, trying to unlock it, but the display won't light up. Is the battery really flat or was the phone damaged when it fell on the parquet?

'Sarah,' says Philip.

The sight of him pains me. I can't bear to look at him and see a stranger.

Spurred by a sudden thought, I go off and leave him, walking like a clockwork toy—as if there's a key sticking in my back, as if someone's wound me up.

Leo. I need to know that Leo is safe.

I walk stiff-legged into the living room, take the telephone and dial Miriam's number. I blink in confusion when the engaged tone sounds, hang up and stare at the phone in my hand, fighting the urge to try again, wanting to keep the line free so Miriam can call me. I count to ten, but it doesn't ring. I curse and redial and breathe a sigh of relief when I hear the ringing tone.

It rings once, twice, three times without anyone answering. Then someone picks up and I hear Miriam's worried voice. 'Sarah, thank God!' she says. 'I've been desperate. Is everything okay?'

I say nothing—I feel numb.

Leo.

'Is he at yours?' I croak.

'Yes. I found him—didn't Philip tell you? He's absolutely fine. It's *you* I'm worried about!'

'Say it again,' I demand.

'Leo's absolutely fine,' Miriam repeats. 'You took off so suddenly that I couldn't even tell you he was probably—'

'Miriam?' I say, interrupting her. 'Where was he?'

'He was only in the bathroom!'

He was only in the bathroom, I think, dully.

'Didn't Philip tell you? I spoke to him earlier. Sarah, are you okay?' Miriam asks. 'You know I'm here if you need me.'

'Thanks, Miriam,' I say and hang up.

I turn round, still in a complete daze—and there he is, standing in the door. Philip. Not the husband of my memories, but my husband. Seven years older, seven years different. I know it must be him—his birthmark is unmistakable—but I still don't recognise him.

Philip. I see us, hardly more than children. It's summer and we're standing in a sea of people and Radiohead are playing us a song; we're sitting by the Elbe at night and Philip has his hand in my wet hair and our lips meet; we're standing on the Elbe Beach and Philip goes down on his knees and I pretend to be surprised; we're in Las Vegas and the fat Elvis impersonator is singing us 'Love Me Tender'. I see Philip's face when I tell him I'm pregnant again and that it's going to work out this time; I see him checking his bag for the hospital—cameras and batteries enough for an entire camera crew; I see him with Leo in his arms; I see us arguing and making it up and—

In front of me is a stranger.

In front of me is my husband.

It is night.

There is no longer past and future.

Just us.

Us, now, this moment.

I ought to say something, I know, but I have no words. Everything is blood and pain and guilt—a carpet of starved bumblebees.

'I didn't recognise you,' I say, when I can talk again, and my voice sounds old and rough.

I don't know what else to say.

I struggle for words.

'I'd forgotten,' I say.

'I know,' he says.

We look at each other, but without recognition.

The devil, I think, once fashioned a mirror that made all the beautiful things reflected in it dwindle to almost nothing, while all the bad things reflected in it got worse and worse. But one day the mirror shattered, and the little splinters went flying and anyone who got one in his eye saw everything twisted, or only had eyes for twisted things. Some people even got a splinter from the enchanted mirror in their hearts, and those people's hearts turned to lumps of ice.

I think of the characters in Leo's beloved 'Snow Queen'—of Kay who gets a splinter from the mirror in his heart, so that it turns to ice, and another in his eye, so that he no longer recognises his dearest friend, Gerda. And of Gerda herself, who goes out in search of Kay and travels halfway across the world to look for him—but when she finds him at last, he is cold as ice and doesn't recognise her.

How often have I read Leo that story? Fifty times? A hundred times? I used to wish for a life like a fairytale. I'd forgotten how brutal so many fairytales are.

Summer 2015

The plane was on its final approach to Hamburg. He watched the earth speeding towards him and for a moment it felt as if the plane was going to crash. The thought didn't frighten him. He sat there, motionless, watching as the houses and trees and everything else which went to make up the world grew bigger and bigger.

The last few days seemed unreal to him. Everything had gone so fast—being released, saying goodbye to the others, getting out. Out of the damp, filthy camp that had become his home and into hospital, then out of hospital into a limousine, and out of a limousine into a hotel lobby—all in less than twelve hours. He'd tried to get his head round it, tried to feel happy. But there hadn't been time. There had always been something needing to be discussed, somebody wanting something of him. It was only now on the plane that he had a moment's peace. The people accompanying him on the flight had gone quiet. They were looking out of the windows, watching the earth come closer, or reading the paper. He saw his home town hurtling towards him, his old life, his old loves. It was going too fast—he was still at the camp, with his companions, still in the filth and the damp. He didn't know what was waiting for him. Did he still have a home?

When he thought of home, he always thought of one particular day—he didn't know why.

A Saturday at the height of summer, the garden full of flowers, the swifts giving a farewell performance. Sarah had suggested a picnic in the garden, and so there they were in the shade of the old cherry tree, with strawberries and rapidly melting vanilla ice-cream, the occasional unhurried bumblebee buzzing past. Leo lay between them on the rug, babbling contentedly and staring at the light that shone through the branches of the trees and made the cherries Sarah would pick for the children next door sparkle like tiny toffee apples. Now and then Leo would crawl off into the grass in search of adventure, snatching at butterflies, chuckling at the blades of grass that tickled his bare arms and legs. Now and then they would get up and bring him back to the rug.

Sarah had twisted her hair into a simple knot at the nape of her neck. She was barefoot in her pale yellow summer dress, her left foot swollen—she'd trodden on a bee earlier in the day. Philip had pulled the sting out of the sole of her foot and fetched ice to cool it. She was sitting cross-legged, a book in her lap. He'd have liked to know what she was reading, but didn't like to interrupt her, afraid that the moment would take flight like a startled bird if he made any sudden move. Leo dragged himself off in pursuit of a particularly plump bumblebee that dropped down behind the gooseberry bushes like a helicopter gunship, then came up again, buzzing loudly, and vanished into the blue of the sky. Philip was amazed at how quick little Leo was now. If you held his hands he could even take a few wobbly steps. Sarah looked up and put her book down—he saw she was reading Hemingway, probably for the English class she'd soon be teaching again. She was with the baby in a step or two and swung him high above her head, making him laugh. Philip picked Sarah a daisy. She accepted it graciously, then ate it, and he laughed.

Later, Sarah went in to get the supper and Philip stayed in the garden a while longer. He was eating gooseberries from the bush when he heard something rustle in the grass in front of him. Soon afterwards a small ginger and white cat emerged, swiftly followed by a second, with brown patches. They stopped a little way off, waiting and watching. Philip smiled.

'Hello,' he said, watching them trip towards him, then back off and come to a standstill again. They meowed softly and at last overcame their hesitation, tumbling towards him.

The cats seemed to be brother and sister. They had no collars and one of them had a cloudy eye. Philip wondered whether they were strays.

A high-pitched voice came from the garden next door. 'They're so adorable!' A little red-haired girl with a ponytail was looking at him through the fence. He glimpsed shorts and a football shirt.

'Are they yours?' he asked.

The girl shook her head. 'They're quite timid,' she said. 'One of them has a bad eye. Maybe someone was nasty to him.'

Philip nodded gravely. 'Shall we give them names?' he asked.

'They must already have names.'

'But we don't know what they are.'

After they had named the kittens and the girl had gone away,

Philip followed his wife into the house. When he entered the kitchen, she jumped out at him and covered his sunburnt forehead with painful kisses. They fell to the floor together, laughing.

That was home.

Did it still exist?

Today is my fourteen thousand four hundred and fortieth day on earth, he thought. Fourteen thousand four hundred and thirty-nine times he had woken up and opened his eyes, lived through the day and gone to sleep again. Fourteen thousand four hundred and thirty-nine times he had lain and dreamed.

He hadn't stopped counting—had so often wondered whether he would ever be free again. And if so, on which day of his life? The thirteen thousandth? The twenty thousandth?

He looked out of the window and wondered where he stood. He didn't know. Everything he'd once thought of as his life, everything that had made up his identity was so far away—childhood, youth, love, university, marriage, fatherhood, work. He'd spent the last seven years in a limbo of waiting and survival.

When, in the hotel in Colombia, he had seen himself in a mirror again after so long, he'd been afraid of himself. He'd stared at his face and found not the slightest resemblance to his old self. No, he had thought eventually, I'm not that man anymore. Not at all. Not even his own mother would recognise him. The carefree idiot he'd once been had vanished. His appearance reflected his inner self.

He remembered his first shower after he'd been freed, remembered how he'd stood in the bathroom with a razor and all the necessary equipment set out in front of him, and how he'd peered into his bearded face and hadn't been able to bring himself to shave. He'd hidden behind that beard for so long—almost seven years. He couldn't part with it. It was doubtless best to be a little on his guard still.

Part of him just wanted to be left in peace. He'd sent away the psychologist who had offered to talk to him. Was it so hard to understand that he wanted to be left in peace? Yes, apparently it was. Apparently his behaviour was not normal. So he decided to stay strong. He could do that by now. Stay strong and keep going. Not get into any unnecessary discussions. Not until he was home—it wasn't long.

The beard remained. And the desire to retreat into the solitude of his house until he had worked out who he was and what he wanted to do with the rest of his life—that remained too.

He'd imagined things differently. It was nothing like the movies, where the kidnapping victim comes home, embraces his family and all is well. It wasn't that straightforward.

What he needed more than anything was an answer.

And maybe also revenge.

For seven years he had been tormented by the question of whether his kidnapping had been ordered by someone he'd loved and trusted.

There were three people on his list, and in the pale, wasted days and wakeful, desperate nights in the camp, he'd spent a great deal of time hating those three people. If there was anything he'd had plenty of during his captivity, it was time. He'd sworn that if ever he made it out of that hole at the end of the world and into the light of day, those people would pay for what they'd done. He used to wish they'd drop down dead—sometimes one, sometimes the other, sometimes all three, depending on which of them he thought guilty just then.

There was his fatherly friend, Johann Kerber, who had urged him to make this trip, supposedly because it would do Philip good to get away from Sarah for a bit. 'Absence makes the heart grow fonder,' Johann had told him. As if he'd ever given a damn about Philip's marital troubles.

Then there was Bernd Schröder. Bernd should have been with Philip in the car that morning—the car from which he'd been kidnapped. But Bernd had been taken ill at the last minute and couldn't leave his hotel room. That's what he'd said, at least. Ambition-crazed Bernd Schröder pass up a crucial meeting because of a slight cold? Hard to believe.

Last of all there was Sarah. Had his mother been right? Had Sarah only been after his money? He regretted never having asked her if there was any truth in his mother's constant hints— that she had been prepared to accept money to leave him. He had once trusted Sarah blindly. Once.

Because of course he'd had good times with her too—it was just that his memories of them had largely faded, like photographs in an old newspaper that have been too long in the sun. All he'd been able to think about during his captivity was the fighting, the bitterness—admittedly his as well as hers. Towards the end, before that fateful trip, he'd sometimes thought there was no love left between them—only blood and tears. Could he really blame that one terrible night by the side of the road in the woods? Or had it merely laid bare what had long been there beneath the surface—that they were too different to love and understand one another? He remembered begging her to talk to him, saying all those stupid, desperate things that people said in films—that women said in films.

'Please talk to me…'

'What are you thinking?'

'I can't bear your silence anymore.'

'If you've ever loved me…'

Was it only that terrible night? Or would their marriage have collapsed anyway? Had it ever stood a chance? He tormented himself with these questions, turning them over and over in his mind, until he'd convinced himself that Sarah had never loved him.

His guard had told him often enough. 'You become vegetable here, rich man,' he'd say in his broken English. 'No one want pay for you.'

Now the plane was about to land.

Barbara Petry had told him that his wife was coming to the airport to welcome him. Of course she was.

The ministry officials hadn't yet been able to give him any details about the investigation into his kidnapping. Harald Grimm had asked him to be patient. He and his team and their colleagues in South America wanted to get to the bottom of things, but it would take time. Grimm was confident he could find out whether or not Philip's wife had ordered his kidnap, but he'd need a few days to make his inquiries.

Philip couldn't believe he'd have to go home with her, not knowing if she'd done it.

Could it really have been Sarah who had tried to get rid of him? Was she capable of such a thing? Psychologically? Logistically?

Yes, a lot had happened. Yes, Sarah had spent a few weeks in a psychiatric clinic as a teenager after her mother's suicide when she'd lost touch with reality. But that was a long time ago. Yes, she might have been unstable in the past. Yes, she might at times have had a tendency to extreme behaviour. But treachery? Was Sarah really capable of treachery?

Philip realised that his thoughts were going round in circles again, like goldfish in too small a bowl. Only one thing had changed.

He was free—free to act, free to see them. Johann. Bernd. And her—Sarah.

Only a few minutes to go. Then he'd look her in the eyes. He'd stare into her face and he would *know*.

Suddenly he thinks of their wedding.

Las Vegas, a sparkling mirage in the middle of the desert.

Sarah had almost got cold feet, only minutes before the wedding.

They were roasting in the sun, waiting their turn outside the little white chapel with the enormous sign saying 'Wedding Chapel: America's Favorite Since 1940'. They'd just seen a couple of newlyweds come out and zoom off in a huge pink Cadillac.

He was excited and full of happy anticipation—the mood of this strange, loud, bright, hyperactive city had infected him. Sarah, however, seemed pensive, quieter than usual.

'Are you okay, Princess?' he asked. Sarah loved it when he called her that, but she didn't react now. 'Is something worrying you?' he said.

Sarah ran her hand through her hair, which fell loose over her white dress.

'What if we turn out like all the other married couples?' she asked. 'If we end up arguing all the time?'

He realised that she was thinking of the fight they'd had a few days before—he'd already forgotten what it had been about.

'Then I guess we argue,' he replied. He smiled at Sarah, stroked her cheek, ran his fingers through her hair.

She looked at him doubtfully.

'We just have to go back to loving each other again afterwards as quickly as possible,' he said. 'That's all.'

But she didn't seem satisfied.

'We love each other,' he said. 'That's enough.'

'All couples love each other when they get married,' she said. 'But that doesn't mean they all manage to stay together.' She hesitated. 'The problem is that when we argue like we did the other day, I completely forget that I love you and that you love me. It's not as if we even had anything to argue about. If we fight over little things like that, what will happen later? When we have children or…' She let the sentence trail off. 'When I'm as angry as I was the day before yesterday, I don't care about anything, I'm capable of anything at all,' she concluded.

He looked at her in silence, not knowing what she wanted to hear from him.

'It scares me,' she said.

'What scares you?'

'When we're like that,' she said. 'When we lose control like that.'

'I'll never let you forget that I love you. I promise.'

Sarah's look darkened. 'Don't make promises you can't keep.'

From inside the chapel they heard music. They were next.

The chapel door opened and they were ushered in by the Elvis impersonator they'd booked to walk Sarah down the aisle and sing 'Love Me Tender' during the ceremony.

How we changed, he thought, in the time between our wedding and our botched goodbyes. He saw it all like a film montage: the night they met, their first date—on the Elbe Beach—their first kiss, their first fight. His proposal—that, too, on the Elbe Beach, *their place*—and then the wedding, the baby, the drifting apart.

Their goodbyes had haunted him for seven years. Did she no longer love him? Had she inflicted all this on him? Or was he being unfair to her? Did she still love him? Would she wait for him?

Seven years had not been enough to solve the mystery.

My fourteen thousand four hundred and fortieth day on earth, he thought. The day I return home—if such a place exists.

Then everything went very fast—the landing, the crowds of people. Philip felt like a mole being dragged out into the light.

Keep going, he told himself.

He had, in any case, eyes for one person only. He would look Sarah in the eyes—and he would *know*.

Sarah

Philip is sitting opposite me at the kitchen table in silence. He's not an arm's length from me, but still he seems impossibly far away.

We are as alien to each other as two people can be. He has an entire universe in his head—I will never begin to understand him.

On the windowsill is an old photo of us. We look so ridiculously young and happy. Now he looks the way I feel—ready to die of exhaustion. I let my gaze wander about the kitchen. The brightly coloured flowers on the table are hanging their heads, the spherical lamp hovering over them like a languid moon.

We've been sitting here for ages. It's going to take me some time to get my head round things. First I have to conflate the stranger with Philip.

I feel porous, and fragile as an empty snail shell. I look at Philip. I don't know what to say.

I think back to the time before Philip went missing. To our fight the day he left, and the one the day before and the day before that. I've forgotten the flimsy reasons, the tenuous arguments. It wasn't over anything particular—we argued for the sake of arguing, for the sake of proving ourselves right, of winning, of hurting one another.

There was a time when I cried every day, which drove Philip mad. What he didn't know was that I wasn't crying because I was sad or helpless or desperate or trying to make him feel bad, but because I was angry. I cried because he made me so furious that I sometimes didn't recognise myself—so furious that I felt like taking something heavy and bringing it down over his head.

It wasn't until he suddenly disappeared that I realised it wasn't because I no longer loved him that I got so angry, but because I loved him still.

In the space of a single day, my life was reduced to hopes and fears—and questions: Where are you, Philip? Why have you left us? What's happened to you? Are you still alive? Are you well? Do you still think of us—of your wife and son? What happened? Were you murdered? Kidnapped? Did you have an accident? A stroke? A brain haemorrhage? A heart attack? Did you die somewhere and nobody found you? Have you lost your memory, as I'd like to imagine? Or have you run away? Are you in hiding? Have you started a new life? Are you somewhere out there? Are you happy? Would I sense it if you were still alive? Would I have sensed it if you'd died? Where are you, Philip? Where are you? Will you ever come back?

How can you have disappeared without trace? How does anyone disappear without trace? Did you do it on purpose? Have you gone underground? Did you have secrets from me? Were you the man I thought you were? Or are there things I don't know—undreamed secrets in that rich old family of yours, in that family business? Did you have enemies? Were you an enemy to anyone? Did you have a lover? Was there someone you loved more than Leo and me? Because believe me, that would be fine, absolutely fine. I just want to know. I have to know what's happened to you.

What has happened to you?

And now?

For a long time I believed there was nothing I wanted more than to get Philip back. And now I think of something my grandmother used to say to me: be careful what you wish—it might come true.

We sit in silence. The fridge hums. Outside, a night bird calls. The floorboards creak, as if the wise old house were trying to lighten the silence between us. I turn away from Philip's face and focus on the grain of the kitchen table. I run my hand over it, unsure what to think or do or say. Rationally, I know that the man at the airport and in the car and in my house—the man who followed me and whom I followed—the man I hit and screamed at—the man who threatened me and whom I threatened—I know that man was Philip. I know it, but I can't get my head round it.

It's all so surreal. I feel like a character in a play—as if any minute now I might go crashing through the papier-mâché and discover that the table I'm leaning on, the kitchen, the house, my whole world are nothing but a stage set.

I look up; our eyes meet. A small smile plays briefly on Philip's lips, and he almost looks the way he used to. Then a shadow flits across his face, sweeping the smile away, and once again he is the stranger who got off the plane the day before yesterday—or was it the day before that?

The wrinkles in his good-looking face have grown deeper in the past few days.

My voice sounds rough when I manage to speak at last.

'I just couldn't,' I say. 'I couldn't recognise my husband in you.'

'Couldn't?' Philip asks, 'or wouldn't?'

I don't reply. I don't know.

But I remember. I remember the seven years without him, the eclipse of the sun, those few secret nights with Mirko, my goodbyes. And then this strange man with the hard eyes, who stepped out of that plane and burst into my painstakingly rearranged life. It was like when I was seventeen and found my mother hanging in the kitchen. The altered colours, the chill in my bones, the feeling of being swathed in cottonwool.

'Something in me shut down,' I whisper. I struggle to find the right words. 'It was too much,' I say. 'It was just too much.'

Something in me shut down.

I can't put it any better than that.

That is the truth.

Philip has a lovely face. I've always thought so. He is dark-haired and pale and has big brown eyes, which sometimes, when he's happy about something, have an almost childlike expression. But when he raises his eyebrows, they form little triangles, like Mephistopheles' eyebrows in a traditional performance of Goethe's *Faust*. Philip's lips are thin, but his upper lip has an attractive curve to it, which I fell very much in love with many years ago.

If you look closely, you can still see all that. If you know what you're looking for.

How amazing that we all look different, I think. Over seven billion people on the planet and no two faces are the same. And we are capable of perceiving each one as unique.

Most of the time.

Philip raises his eyes and sees me scrutinising him. I look away.

There are so many questions in my head that I can't get a grasp on even one.

For a long time Philip says nothing. Eventually I can stand the silence no longer.

'You must have thought I was doing it on purpose,' I say. 'That I was only pretending not to recognise you.'

Philip nods.

'Yes,' he says, 'I thought you were doing it on purpose. I thought you had a plan, that you were trying to get rid of me for good.'

'Why would I have done that?'

He shrugs.

'No idea, Sarah,' he says. 'Seven years are a long time. How was I to know what kind of a life you'd led in that time, what you thought, what you wanted, what you were prepared to do to get it?'

'When did you realise?' I ask.

'That you genuinely hadn't recognised me?'

I nod.

'I'm not sure. Probably when you followed me into town,' he says. 'That struck me as strange. That's when I began to suspect something.'

He considers.

'And then when you brought my mother round.'

The memory is like being winded.

'My mother, of all people. That's when I knew.'

His hand moves to his chest, where the knife grazed him, and I think of the meeting with Barbara Petry.

'When I asked you to show me your birthmark,' I say, 'why didn't you just do it?'

Philip drops his hand, but he doesn't answer. Finally I understand. The scars. Dear God.

For a while we sit in silence.

'I thought you had a guilty conscience,' he says. 'I thought that was the reason you refused to recognise me. I thought it was you.'

I go cold.

'That *what* was me?' I ask, but I already have some idea.

Philip looks me in the eyes. The hatred, the anger, the malice, the nastiness—suddenly it all makes sense. But I'm bewildered all the same. How could he think such a thing?

'You thought I was involved in your kidnapping?' I ask tonelessly.

He doesn't reply.

I think of the time before he went missing, the daily bickering, the ugly remarks. I think of that terrible night, after which nothing was ever the same again—the night we were driven apart once and for all—the night I had done such a good job of suppressing.

'You thought that?' I whisper. 'For seven years?'

Philip shakes his head. 'I didn't know what to think.'

'And what do you think now?'

He swallows audibly. 'That I simply had bad luck. That I was in the wrong place at the wrong time.'

'Do you know that for sure?' I ask.

Philip nods. 'It was confirmed earlier today.'

Silence.

A long silence.

'I still don't understand why you did what you did,' I say. 'None of it makes any sense.'

'I only wanted one thing,' says Philip. 'The truth. And I…'

He shrugs.

'You…took advantage of my confusion,' I say, finishing his sentence for him, 'to put me to the test. And to punish me—to scare me.'

He nods hesitantly. 'I thought it was you,' he repeats. 'When I got off the plane and came towards you, I saw right off that you weren't pleased to see me. Far from it—you were appalled.'

I say nothing.

'And Leo—Leo was frightened of me. I wondered what you'd told him, why he'd be scared. I thought you'd tried to turn my own son against me. He was terrified. Then, when I began to provoke you…when I asked you what the worst thing was you'd ever done…when I told you to tell the truth…you had guilt written all over your face.'

It's only now that it dawns on me. 'You meant the kidnapping,' I say.

Philip nods.

'And I thought you were talking about that night. About the accident. The hit-and-run. The man I killed—the man we killed.'

Tears well up in my eyes.

The fridge hums a tune.

'What did you do in town?' I suddenly ask, wiping the tears away.

'In town?'

'Yes. That strange tour of Hamburg.'

A crooked smile appears on Philip's face. 'Exactly that,' he says. 'I went on a tour of Hamburg.'

'Hmm,' I say.

We're silent for a while.

'What was it like?' I ask.

'What was what like?'

'Walking around your native town. After all those years.'

Philip smiles. 'What got me most were the little things,' he says. 'I had a lot of time to think in captivity. I used to go on long walks around Hamburg in my head, trying to imagine everything precisely, to conjure every detail.' For a moment he seems caught up in his memories. 'I managed to remember a lot,' he says. 'But there were dozens or even hundreds of small details missing— what colour were the chairs the Italian put outside his corner restaurant in the summer? Black or dark green? How many steps were there going up to our neighbours' houses? What kind of trees grew on our street? There were limes, I knew that—limes that made the windscreens of the parked cars all sticky in the summer. But weren't there also some beeches among them? Or was that only in the street that ran parallel to ours? And what colour were the litter bins? I must have thrown things into them millions of times, but I couldn't remember—maybe orange, maybe blue, maybe metallic grey, I didn't know.'

He looks at me.

'I checked yesterday,' he says. 'They're red.'

We're silent. Outside, a car drives past with booming bass.

'And the man?' I ask.

'What man?'

'The man at the vending machine. I saw him slip you something.'

'There wasn't a man.'

I'm immediately alarmed—how can he deny it? Is he still lying to me?

'Oh, hang on. The man in the football shirt? He asked me if I could give him change for a note.'

So banal, so simple.

'Hmm. And the anonymous calls? The hate campaign on the internet?'

'What?' Philip frowns. 'Hate campaign?' he repeats.

It's suddenly clear to me that I miscalculated.

I think of Mirko and realise it's possible that he was responsible for all the calls from the withheld number—and, yes, all the awful online comments. It wasn't a conspiracy, wasn't a campaign— only an aggrieved man whom I shared my bed with for a while and then cast out of my life somewhat ungraciously. I realise what a lot of damage I've caused, how much is going to need salvaging and patching up over the next weeks and months.

'Forget it,' I say. 'It's not important.' I suddenly realise how incredibly tired I am. All I want right now is to sleep.

'I'm dog tired,' I say. 'I'm going to bed.'

'I have to tell you something,' Philip says quickly.

I look at him. 'Can't it wait till tomorrow?'

'No,' he says, 'it can't.' He stands up.

I'm too exhausted to contradict him. I get up and follow him, only stopping when I realise he wants to leave the house. 'You want to go out? Now?'

He nods. 'We have to.'

Outside, the shadows under Philip's eyes are so dark they almost shimmer purple. But while I stagger along, hardly able to stay on my feet, he moves with the same control and efficiency as ever. He has something of a soldier about him, I think. As if he's been in training.

It's still dark, but dawn isn't far off. Philip gets behind the wheel of my car and I sit in the passenger seat beside him. He starts up the engine—it stalls at first and he curses under his breath, but the second time he gets it to fire and we roll slowly down the road. I know at once where we're going, and I wish we could turn back—wish we could stop and sit in the car in silence until the sun rises and drives away the shadows. Philip gives me a sidelong glance. He probably guesses my thoughts, but he says nothing.

The streets are deserted—only half an hour later we are leaving the town behind us. Silence. Only the noise of the engine as it devours the road in front of us, the asphalt gleaming black as licorice. I'm driving right to the heart of my nightmares.

As Philip steers the car out of Hamburg and onto a remote country road, my thoughts begin to stray.

One night, many years ago. The stuff my nightmares are made of.

We're on the way home from the house on the lake. Something's up with Leo.

We get in the car immediately.

And of course, we argue.

I look at Philip—his self-righteous face—and I shout something and Philip shouts back and then he cries, 'Look at the road, for God's sake!' and there's a strange rumbling and I brake instinctively and come to an abrupt halt. The car stops with a jolt and then it is suddenly very, very quiet.

I've hit something, I think, glancing across at Philip, who is staring at me, his eyes wide with horror.

'Was that a deer?' I ask.

'I don't know. I didn't see.'

I swallow heavily. I look in the rear-view mirror, but can't see anything behind us. I get out of the car and hear Philip do the same. I walk round the car. Then, in the red glow of the brakelights, I see it.

A person. A man? A woman? I don't know. But I know at once that whoever it is is dead.

'Oh God,' says Philip. 'Oh God, God, God.' And then, 'Is he dead?'

So it's a man. I summon up all my courage and walk towards the body on the road. I can only vaguely make out the man's face—his eyes are closed. He's lying on his side, dressed in dark clothes. I almost expect him to reach for me, but he doesn't stir, and when I feel his pulse there is nothing. Nothing. It's only when I withdraw my hand that I notice it's covered in blood. I stare at it, then wipe it off on my trousers. I hear a whimper, look at Philip and realise that the sound came from me.

I back away from the dark bundle on the road.

'Yes,' I say, 'he's dead.'

I ran him down.

'Where did he come from so suddenly?' asks Philip. He sounds frantic.

'I don't know. He was just suddenly there.'

I peer left and right into the woods and see a path that the man must have emerged from. Why was I driving so fast?

'We have to call the police,' I say, noticing that my voice sounds tinny.

Philip digs out his phone.

'We've both been drinking,' he says, anxious.

I hesitate. The man's dead anyway, I think.

'Call them,' I say.

Philip taps around on his phone for what seems like forever. He holds it to his ear, looks at the screen again.

'No reception,' he says.

'What?'

'Dead.'

'You idiot! Do you think that's funny?'

'Sorry, I—'

'Okay,' I say. 'We'll drive home. We can call the police and an ambulance from there.'

We get back in the car and I carefully avoid looking in the rear-view mirror as we drive away from the site of the accident. Hit-and-run—the words hammer in my skull. Fatal accident. Drink-driving. Hit-and-run. Not a single car passes us on the country road. It's only as we approach town that the roads grow busier.

When we get home, Leo is already better. False alarm. I rock him to sleep in my arms. Then I sit down on the sofa. I stare at the phone, look at my sleeping son, look at the phone. I get up, still carrying Leo.

'Please don't,' says Philip.

I turn round.

'He's dead. You can't change that,' he says.

I leave the room without a word and put Leo in his cot. I sense Philip behind me, feel his hand between my shoulder blades. I have a strong urge to shake it off. What's the point? Is that supposed to comfort me? If he hadn't distracted me, then none of this—

'That fucking lakeside house,' I say. 'Such a stupid idea. I had a bad feeling about leaving Leo right from the start!'

'Oh, so it's my fault now, is it?' Philip fires back at me. 'I didn't force you to drink so much!'

'I was a damn sight more sober than you,' I yell. 'Otherwise I wouldn't have offered to drive.'

'But you did offer to drive! And of course I thought that meant you were fit to drive!'

'I was fit to drive! But you can't pay attention to the road when the person next to you is hurling abuse at you—nobody can! It's so typical of you to try and shift all the blame onto me—you're such a fucking coward!'

So it goes on until dawn. We argue. Leo screams.

When morning comes, we carry on. Philip repeats what he'd said in the car—that he's convinced his mother was right, that I don't love him—never did love him. And I say he's quite right—if I ever had loved him, it was all over now and I'd rather die than have to look at his face any longer. We hurl all kinds of impossible insults at each other, but one thing we don't do—we don't give ourselves up to the police.

Nothing is the same after that night. Everything around me seems to come to life, conspiring against me to make my life hard, to punish me—the woman who has so far escaped just punishment. I'm not to forget for a moment what I've done or that I'm now living in a hostile world. Drawers fall on my feet, roots grow out of the ground in front of me and trip me up, conkers pelt down on my head without warning.

In the bathroom I slip in a little puddle of shower oil that was waiting for me to come along and break my neck. I cut my calf shaving my legs and finally stub my toe on the corner of the shower cubicle, which is suddenly sticking out just a little further into the room than it used to. Somehow I make it out of the bathroom alive. I run into Philip—close to tears, that lifeless bundle always before me—and he looks at me and asks what's wrong and I say, 'Nothing.'

After we have made it up—for Leo's sake, we tell each other—and realised that we're not going to call the police now, so long after the accident, I tell Philip I never want to talk about that night again. He protests—he wants to keep talking about it, thinks anything else unhealthy. He's sick of my reticence, my taciturnity—sometimes he asks himself whether he married a woman or an oyster.

'You're like a man.' He says that too, half-jokingly, but I don't do him the favour of laughing.

I insist on not saying another word about that fucking night and that stupid wood and that damn rumbling, and Philip gives in. I keep silent and he keeps silent with me.

That goes on for weeks—until one evening when I'm feeding Leo, and Philip comes into the kitchen.

'I know we'd agreed not to talk about it anymore,' he begins, without even saying hello to me, 'but—'

I give a start and glare at him, gather Leo in my arms and leave the room.

'I don't want to hear it,' I call back over my shoulder.

'You have to listen to me!' Philip says.

But I can't. I won't. I can't stand him anymore.

He makes two further attempts to bring it up again—I have no idea why. Because there's something important I need to know, he says. Because he wants to torment me, I suspect. Either way, I don't listen.

He is furious. I don't care.

When he tells me soon afterwards that he's going to South America for almost a week, I'm glad.

Suddenly I'm snapped back to the present. Philip slows the car to a crawl and then stops altogether. We're on a secluded country road in the middle of the woods. There's no one in sight—we're all alone. I turn my head. Beside me is a stranger. Adrenaline shoots into my bloodstream and I suddenly realise that I've made a fatal mistake. Nobody knows I'm here. No one will find me. I'm unarmed—no pistol, no knife, no pepper spray is going to save me.

The stranger turns his head.

Philip sees the terror on my face. 'Are you okay?'

I take a deep breath. It's going to take me a long time to conflate the stranger—the man who's spent the last few days scaring me

323

half to death—with my husband. It is surreal to have him sitting next to me just like that. It will be a while before I'm used to having him back.

I look about me. Yes, I think, this was the spot. Why is he so cruel as to bring me here? Is he going to keep making me pay for what I did?

Philip gets out of the car. I do the same. The slamming doors echo in my head like pistol shots. My stomach seizes up. I look about me. The moon bathes the edge of the woods in a wan light barely strong enough to coax the blurred contours out of the darkness. The woods whisper. Philip walks towards the forest path and is swallowed by the blackness after only a few metres. I hurry after him.

A rustle and crack beside me make me jump. My head swivels to the right and I almost scream when I see two big shining eyes staring at me. I freeze, just like the deer standing there on its slender legs. It looks at me sadly before disappearing into the undergrowth. The rushing of the wind in the trees, the cries of the owls, the rustle of little birds in the undergrowth—these sounds are ominous, dark, far too close. The blood is roaring in my ears, soaking the night wood a deep red. The trees are murmuring—murmuring to me—and I want to clap my hands over my ears like a frightened child. I almost bump into Philip, who has suddenly stopped in front of me.

'It was here,' he says. 'The forest path. We thought he must have come from here, the man you ran over. Do you remember?'

Yes, I think, and nod. That must have been what happened.

'Why have you brought me here?' I ask.

'This is where it began,' says Philip. 'This is where we lost each other.'

I nod again, but at the same time I ask myself whether it's true.

I've often wondered when our troubles began. After the wedding or before? When Constanze really took against me? When we moved into that far too big, far too expensive house that I never liked—or earlier? After the first miscarriage? Or the second? When Leo was born? Or not until long afterwards? Or long before? Or was it here, in the woods? I don't know.

'What are we doing here, Philip?'

'I've been very lonely over the past years,' he says. He doesn't look at me. 'Sometimes I cursed you. Sometimes I longed for you. For us. For the way things used to be. Sometimes I thought we might be able to recover what we'd lost.'

Is that why he's brought me here?

'I envy the past—the people we used to be.'

Does he think we can start over?

'But it's not that easy,' he says. 'I see that now.'

'Is that what you wanted to tell me?' I ask.

Philip shakes his head. He takes a deep breath. 'How clearly do you remember that night?' he asks.

Too clearly, I think.

'Do you remember seeing the man suddenly appear in front of us?' he asks.

'No,' I say. 'How could I? I wasn't watching the road. Because we were arguing, as usual!' I'm close to tears.

'I didn't see him coming either,' says Philip.

So? What is this? I can't stand this place. I want to get away from here.

'I didn't see him either. We thought we hadn't seen him because he came from this forest path. But that isn't what happened. He didn't come striding out of the woods and in front of our car. He didn't come along the road towards us either. He was already lying there.'

I frown. 'What?'

'He was already dead when we ran him over.'

My knees turn to jelly. 'You're lying.'

Philip shakes his head. 'Norman K., forty-one years old, single, recently unemployed. The same evening we went to the house by the lake, he left his flat and walked along this road—almost certainly intending to commit suicide. He was hit by a car and died. The driver didn't stop.'

'Yes, that was me!'

'No!' says Philip. 'It wasn't you. I tell you, he was already dead! You ran over a dead man!'

'How do you know?'

'I couldn't get over the fact that we hadn't called for help that night. The way we drove off and left that poor man lying there—I couldn't cope with that. I kept scouring the papers for any reference to a fatality that night, and I came across an article about a driver involved in a hit-and-run who'd subsequently reported himself to the police. When I realised the man he'd hit must be our victim, I made inquiries. It turned out that the driver who knocked down Norman K. and abandoned him had passed the site of the accident a good half-hour before us. He turned himself in a few days later, but he wasn't sentenced—among other things, because there were indications that Norman K. was run over by several cars…'

The facts rain down on me like stones. I don't move for a long time after Philip has stopped talking. I am stunned. I cry.

'Why didn't you tell me?' I ask in the end.

Philip sighs. 'I tried.' He makes a helpless gesture. 'I tried two or three times, but you didn't want to hear anything more about that night. I was furious. Well, all right then, I thought. Live another few days in the belief that you've killed someone. I wanted to hurt you. I wanted to punish you. I wanted to punish myself. It wasn't right to keep driving. It wasn't right not to call the police.'

I close my eyes.

'Then there was the trip to South America,' Philip continues.

In the woods something snaps.

'I was going to tell you.' Philip lowers his eyes. 'When I got back.'

My body feels numb. We're in the car going home.

We drive in silence. Philip's at the wheel. I'm staring at the road in a daze.

The beam of the headlights. The grey woods. The engine's thrum. Drooping eyelids. Dawn.

'Who's Vincent?' I ask.

'A friend,' says Philip. 'My best friend in the camp.'

I nod.

We drive in silence.

I wonder whether Vincent is dead, but say nothing. Vincent is a topic for another night.

'Why were you so keen to stop me going to the police?' I ask. 'I'd only have made a fool of myself.'

'I had no idea what you were going to tell them. And I wanted to avoid a media circus. I wanted to be left in peace. That most of all. And then, what if you'd reported the hit-and-run after all these years? Can you imagine what would have happened then?'

I ponder this.

'And the two days? What was all that about?'

'I'd been told I would find out in two days whether or not my kidnapping had been organised and paid for in Germany.'

I need a moment to process this.

'You hoped you'd know in two days whether it was me.'

327

Philip nods.

There's a question on the tip of my tongue, but I don't ask it. I don't want to know what he'd have done if he'd been told it was me—that I'd inflicted such suffering on him.

'Why does your mother call you Green?' I ask instead.

Philip sighs.

'Long story. I'll tell you some other time.'

'You always say that.'

He gives a crooked smile. 'May I ask *you* something?' he says.

'Mmhm.'

'When we were sitting in the garden and you told me about your miscarriages and how perfectly your husband had behaved—do you remember?'

I nod hesitantly.

'It wasn't like that. I wish I had reacted like that, but I didn't.'

The city appears before us.

'Why did you say that?' he asks.

Hamburg grows closer.

'Because you remember it that way?'

We're on our way home.

'Or because you wish it had been like that?'

Together, after all these years.

'Or both?'

I don't reply.

We drive in silence.

The sun's coming up.

Summer 2015

'm ready for the march-off. I move slowly—don't want to wake Sarah, whatever happens. Have to get away, have to be alone. I don't yet know where I'll go. Vanish into the crowds of Tokyo? Seek seclusion in the forests of Canada? Stare at the sea in Thailand? I leave the spare key on the kitchen table where Sarah and I sat last night, hunt for something to write with and find pen and paper in a drawer. I sit down and look about me, pausing for a moment when I see Leo's drawings hanging on the fridge. Quickly I look away. So much lost time and no chance to make up for it.

I begin to write.

Soon afterwards I am standing at the front door, holdall over my shoulder, hand poised on the doorknob. I change my mind, walk back through the house and out the backdoor to the garden. I skirt the high grass that Sarah has allowed to grow, bend down to the currant bushes, pick a few of the gleaming red fruits, put them in my mouth and grimace when the tartness hits my tastebuds. It is absolutely quiet, as if the world were all mine. Summer isn't ready to step down yet, but the wind is back. Hamburg is Hamburg again.

I sit down on the grass for a moment, shivering when a few wet blades touch my bare arms. I ignore the wetness that soaks into my jeans, leaving dark patches—I simply enjoy the quiet.

Returning home after years in captivity is a positively supernatural experience. It's as if you'd died and then risen from the dead only to discover that the world is perfectly capable of turning without you. That no one really misses you. That you're not only dispensable—you're superfluous.

In the end it just isn't possible that I still love her. What I feel is probably only a kind of afterimage. Like the patch the sun leaves on your retina if you stare at it for too long.

I wish I could sit here forever, but I have to be on my way. I'm about to leave when the old woman next door calls out to me, and we exchange a few words before she disappears back into her house.

I head for the hole in the fence, the one I've slipped through more than once in the past few days, when I suddenly feel watched. I look about me, but there's no one in sight. I hope I don't run into Mr Lauterbach again, who laughed in my face when I told him I was Philip Petersen.

I bend down and crawl carefully through the hole, then straighten up and look down the road. I'll walk to the main road and hail a taxi. I take a few steps, breathing in the scent of the old lime trees—and then there it is again, that feeling of being watched. I stop and look about me more carefully this time. At first I think I must have been mistaken, but then I see it—a strikingly marked cat sitting by the side of the road, looking at me. I crouch down and hold out a hand. The creature hesitates, then begins to move, skirting the fence shyly, but giving me a wide berth. I watch it a moment longer—from where I am, I can't work out whether it has a blind eye and ginger patches like Schnapps or two good eyes and brownish patches like Schnitzel.

I turn away and set off, saying hello to a red-haired young woman going the other way, presumably on her way home from some party.

'You're being followed,' says the young woman, and she laughs.

I follow her gaze and see that the cat is coming after me.

'There used to be two,' says the young woman. 'I think they were from the same litter—they certainly looked pretty similar. But one of them got run over last year.'

I say nothing, only stare at her, because I realise we know each other—that we named those two cats together. Unusual names that you don't forget in a hurry: Schnitzel and Schnapps. But the young woman just shrugs and goes on her way.

I crouch at the side of the road and wait until the cat plucks up the courage to approach me.

'Hey, Schnapps,' I say when it's finally close enough for me to stroke its ginger-and-white coat. 'Sorry about Schnitzel.'

The cat rubs against my legs, then rolls in front of me on the asphalt and lets me give it a good stroke. After a while it gets up again and goes back to rubbing against my legs. You'd think it were greeting an old friend.

Sarah

When I wake up, something's different, and it's a moment before I work out what it is. The chill that had taken hold of me in the last days has left my bones. The colours, too, are different—it's as if the filter has been taken off my eyes. When I go out into the passage, I sense that I'm alone in the house. I listen to the silence—to its many voices. Most of what has happened in the last few days seems like a dream to me. It's time I found my way back to reality.

For the first time in weeks I tie my trainers.

The sun is still low in the sky when I set off. Wind plays around my bare calves. I register the absence of a ponytail bouncing at the back of my head as I trot along the pavement. The scent of the limes—the undoing of hundreds of bumblebees—still hangs in the air, and I inhale deeply. The summer has reached its height—the first signs of autumn won't be long in coming. I turn off towards the park, past the villas of the neighbourhood, getting into a rhythm, left-right, left-right. A doberman barks when I jog past him and his master into the park and I run off, leaving him and his yelping behind me. Suddenly everything is green. I run faster and faster, over the grass, towards the trees, until I'm sprinting. I feel strong. I relish the thud of my heart. I almost have the impression I can feel the blood flowing through my veins—and then, at last, I stop thinking.

I get back to the house over an hour later, exhausted and drenched in sweat, and go straight to the kitchen to get myself something to drink. I see the note on the kitchen table as soon as I enter the room. I pour myself a glass of water, take a few sips, collect myself. Then I sit down at the table. My legs are shaking—I don't know if it's exertion or nervousness.

When I was a little boy, maybe five or six, I would only eat green food. Nothing else. My mother couldn't get me to eat anything else. She tried bribing me, she tried threatening me—but nothing was any good. I refused to eat potatoes and meat and tomatoes. I wouldn't touch fish or sausages. No carrots, no bananas, no chocolate. Instead, I ate a lot of things that most other children turn up their noses at: lettuce and spinach and sprouts. Anything, just as long as it was green—green apples, green jelly babies, greengages. Curly kale, eucalyptus sweets. Of course it was only a phase. The whole thing lasted just a few weeks—a month at most. But my fad acquired me the nickname 'Green' in my family. It's not a name I like, because my father often used to beat me so hard that I'd be left covered in green bruises—and the nickname tends to remind me of those beatings rather than of a five-year-old's harmless fad.

I drain my glass, then turn over the note and find a postscript: *PS—I really did trick you out of your maiden name.*

I have to laugh in spite of myself. I know, I think. And I tricked you out of your son's name.

In the shower I scrub myself until my skin is red, then watch the water rinse away all the tears and dirt and ballast. Standing in front of the mirror wrapped in a white towel, rubbing my short hair dry, I feel lighter.

Then I set off. At the market I buy fruit, vegetables and a big bunch of sunflowers for Miriam. I apologise to her, thank her, promise her that we'll talk everything over in peace soon—maybe over breakfast at my house. I watch her arrange the flowers in a green glass vase and give her a kiss. I find my son in the tree house with Justus—he doesn't want to leave, but I ignore his protest, promising there is no reason to be afraid, that I will explain it all, and he trusts me enough to calm down and let me take him home. I ring Johann and explain everything to him as best I can. I apologise; he apologises. I know he hasn't understood a word of what I said, but we'll leave it at that for the moment.

With a heavy heart I sit down at the computer and look for the newspaper article about the suicide who ran into the traffic on a country road many years ago. I click my way through the archives of all the local newspapers, but I find nothing. Was Philip lying to spare me? I bite my lip.

I ring Barbara Petry. She doesn't answer. Ashamed, I hang up. Then I take myself in hand, ring again, and leave her a message. I ring the nursing home and am told that Constanze is well, and has been raving about my tea party to anyone who'll listen.

I talk to Mirko again. He admits he was behind not only the anonymous calls but also some of the nasty online comments. We apologise to each other. There's a silence. We say we'll stay friends. We know we won't.

Again I sit down at the computer. I prepare for the first week of school.

I make a pan of tomato sauce.

I take off my wedding ring again, wrap it in one of my grandmother's old cotton hankies and put it in my chest of drawers.

I try to find the article again. I find the website of a local paper I'd forgotten about. I have to log in to use the archive. Impatiently I set up an account. Username: Radioheadfan1978. Password: karmapolice. I enter search terms and click around a bit. It doesn't take me five minutes to find the article I'm looking for.

Philip was telling the truth.

Seven years ago, my husband disappeared without trace.

Then for a bare three days he reappeared in my life, only to vanish again.

Dust tickles my nose, making me sneeze. It's stifling hot here in the loft, which has stored up the heat of the day and held it for hours into the night. A time capsule. Sweat breaks out on my forehead as soon as I go in. I open various boxes, but without any luck. I push them aside and keep looking.

Where is Philip now? I wonder. Where did he go?

When we got back from our drive, we ended up in the kitchen again. We looked sheepishly at one another, not knowing what to say. A couple of strangers. We stood there for a while, then Philip said he'd spend the night in the spare room and make himself scarce in the morning. He needed some time to himself, and so, presumably, did I. Again, we looked at each other.

Then he took himself off. In the morning he was gone.

There it is, the box I was looking for. 'Sentimental Stuff' it says in big letters. I open it. The photo albums are right on top. The photos of our trip to Las Vegas, of our wedding. Pictures of the first months with Leo. Even photos of the barbecue one of our friends organised for our first solar eclipse together. I hold the albums in my hands a moment—I had intended to take them downstairs and look at them on the sofa—then I put them away unopened and close the box. The present is all that I have and it is *always*.

I leave the loft and go and sit on the sofa in the living room. My eyes fall on Philip's record collection and I get up and search through it, find the record I'm looking for, slip it out of its sleeve, lay it on the turntable that Philip bought himself not long before he went missing (the sound quality, he said, was so much better than on CD, which I thought a bit pretentious). I sit down again and the music swells—Nick Cave and the Bad Seeds, 'Do You Love Me?'

I manage to endure the tight feeling in my chest. I keep breathing.

I look about me and think of all that Philip and I have been through together in this house. All the arguments we've thrashed out, all the insults, all the nasty remarks, all the love—and Nick Cave sings for me. My thoughts drift as the singer asks the mother of all questions. Philip's face appears before me and my throat tightens with longing.

I get up as if to shake off the feeling, go over to the little bookcase where I keep only my absolutely favourite books, close my eyes and pull one out.

Everything Is Illuminated by Jonathan Safran Foer.

I remember something my wise grandmother once said to me: being happy is a decision. Maybe, I think, it's the same with love. Maybe love is a decision.

Number one, I think: Years ago, at a Radiohead concert, I almost got struck by lightning.

Number two: I've done five triathlons.

Number three: I don't love Philip anymore.

One of those is a lie.

I'm walking down the road, under the old lime trees. Their dreams smell of love-struck bumblebees and summers of long ago. With every step I take, I feel stronger. It is night. Some things are going to sleep, others waking up. I try to imagine that it's broad daylight on the other side of the world. I've often thought about that in my darkest hours, when I couldn't take it anymore: somewhere, it is light now. It's always light somewhere.

I know what to do. Where to go. And if it's meant to be, Philip will be there too.

The view from here over the Elbe at night has hardly changed in all these years. I've been running, and try to get my breath back as I stare out at the water. It looks like an enormous sinuous snake in the darkness. The water is black as crude oil, with only the occasional blurry yellow spot here and there where lights are reflected in the surface of the river. There is no one here except me. This is our place, this is where it happened—our first official date—and, years later, Philip's proposal.

I think of our first date—one night, many years ago. It was a new moon, which I thought a shame, but Philip said, 'New moon's great. You see the stars better.' A night picnic on the Elbe Beach, a rather drunk Sarah who thought it would be a good idea to go swimming in the river—and Philip, who thought it silly, but couldn't stop her.

'Don't go too far out. There are currents.'

'I'm just going to paddle a bit!'

I remember the undertow, my delayed reflexes. It was only when I could no longer put my feet down—when I'd been under and come up again, gasping for air—that I began to panic. The cold water had sobered me up instantly, but it was too late. I could feel myself being swept away and didn't want to be swept away—I wanted to get out—out of the maelstrom, to the safety of the bank, but it was too late. There were no riptides, it wasn't that—only a slow, patient, deadly undertow, pulling me further and further away from life.

But then he appeared. First his voice, calling from a distance, frantic, alarmed. And then somehow he was there, grabbing hold of me from behind, pulling and tugging, flailing and panting. And we struggled together, a little way at a time, groaning and gasping for breath, and cold—so cold. I could feel his hand grip mine but was so tired I couldn't carry on—I was wavering between fighting and letting go, but I knew that if I went down I wouldn't go alone, that he'd go with me, so I made up my mind to fight and gave all I had—and at last I could put my feet down again. There was still an undertow, pulling and tugging at me, but I didn't give in to it, I fought against it, until the water grew shallow and gave way to the shore and we could throw ourselves down. Breathe. Rest. Lie.

Philip's pale face, his dark eyes and hair. His dimples. Philip who liked football and surfing, which I thought was great. Philip who liked old gangster films, which I thought was great. Philip who was a vegetarian and loved not only Radiohead, but also Leonard Cohen, Nick Cave and Tom Waits, which I thought was amazing.

'That was a near thing,' he panted, when he could speak again.

'Yes,' I said, 'a near thing.'

'Not a good idea to go swimming here.'

'No,' I admitted, 'a very bad idea.'

We looked into each other's eyes and something happened to me—I didn't know what. The moment seemed to go on and on, and suddenly it held everything—everything that had ever happened and ever would happen. I saw with absolute clarity.

The trillions of coincidences, circumstances and events that had led to our being exactly the way we were, to finding one another, to being here together, at this precise moment, in this infinite universe—right here and not anywhere else, right now and not at any other time—the two of us. I saw us from above, minuscule and at the same time vast, and I felt everything from the inside and knew all that lay behind me and all that was yet to come. I knew that everything was exactly as it should be and, for a split second, it all made sense. I saw everything. I understood everything. I saw the quadrillions of cells that went to make up Philip, the cells that ensured, with their crazy, tireless dance, that he was just the way he was and not the least bit different. Madness, I thought. Utterly perfect and utterly mad. Then Philip's face came close to mine and our lips met and I stopped thinking.

Our dramatic first night, water all around us and stars overhead, my wet hair draped over my naked shoulders like a cloak. The strange boy with drops of water in his hair. Silence, apart from our breathing. Darkness. The world suddenly tiny, shrunk so small that there was no room for anyone but us. A cocoon of silence and stars. And then, very cautiously: a hand in my hair.

I jump, startled out of my reverie, when I hear a noise behind me. Philip, I think, turning round.

But there is nobody.

When I get home I thank Mrs Theis, who's been playing at babysitter, see her out and get ready for bed. I've just slipped under the quilt when there's a knock at my door.

I sit up in alarm.

'Yes?'

At first nothing happens.

'Hello?'

Then, unbearably slowly, the door opens. It's Leo.

'Darling!' I say, surprised. 'What's the matter? Are you having trouble getting to sleep?'

He nods.

'Come here.'

He avoids catching my eye.

'What's wrong, Leo? Do you want to sleep in my bed?'

Headshaking.

'Where's the man?' he asks. 'Is he coming back?'

'We'll talk about everything tomorrow,' I say. 'All right?'

He nods.

'Come on, I'll take you back to bed.'

After he's drifted off, I sit a while and watch him sleep. Then I go in the spare room and lie down myself. I take a deep breath.

My chest aches.

I have lost my love.

Maybe there are things that are stronger than love.

Fear. Pain.

Time.

But I have friends, I think. I have my marvellous child. I am healthy. I am alive. I am free. Free of the past, free of all secrets. *Everything is illuminated*.

And the world does what it always does.

It keeps turning.

Epilogue

The water glitters enticingly. I hear it calling to me the second I get out of the car. The Elbe Beach. Again.

There's even a new moon.

I linger a while.

I probably ought to stop coming here. I can't ask Mrs Theis to look after Leo every evening and I can't get to school dead tired day after day because I spend my nights hanging around the shores of the Elbe.

Apart from anything else, I'm making a fool of myself.

And yet I can't help it.

I look about me. I'm alone, just like every evening. He's not going to come. It was idiotic of me to think he would.

This, I tell myself, is the last time.

Then—contrary to my usual habit—I set off in the opposite direction, away from the water, towards asphalt, people, streets. I walk on and on, making for the centre of town. The streets get busier and busier, and I walk this way and that, wondering how I'm ever to find my car again, but I don't care—I keep walking. With every step, my thoughts become clearer, the heaviness falls away. I work my way through the blackness. Now and then late-night revellers emerge from the darkness and stagger past me—a few lone wolves, some closely entwined couples, the occasional noisy group. And then suddenly a light appears before me in the darkness. I look up. A pub, it's neon sign guiding me. I must have passed a lot of pubs without feeling the desire to go in. But this one is different. I don't know why. Maybe I like it because it's so empty. I walk in.

Behind the bar is a petite woman of about my age, pale skin, bright red dyed hair. She smiles and gives me a nod. I sit down at the counter and order a beer. She puts a bottle down in front of me.

'Hard night?' she asks.

I take a swig.

'I've known worse,' I say, taking another. 'But, yes, hard night.'

'A man?'

I shrug. I don't feel like talking.

'I sometimes think,' the woman says, 'how amazing we'd be if love didn't always get in the way. If we could take all the energy we put into finding or hanging on to a partner, and put it into other things—projects or art or whatever.'

I look at her more closely. She's younger than I thought. Maybe a student who's taken this job to pay for her studies. It's only her rough voice that makes her seem older. I look at the tattoos covering her arms. Philip hates tattoos. It was because of him that

I didn't get any more done after the little butterfly on my hip.

'Does it even exist?' I ask. 'Love?'

The woman frowns at me.

I take another gulp of beer, savouring the bitterness.

'When we think we love someone…do we really love that person? Or do we just love the feeling that person gives us?'

She considers.

'Both, I guess,' she says.

'But then how could we ever stop loving? If it's not the feeling a certain person gives us that we love, but the actual person, how could we ever stop loving him—just because he does something we don't like, for example?'

The woman shrugs and turns away. People probably rope her into discussions like this every night, and she's had enough.

I've had enough too.

I take the bottle of beer and go and sit at the window. The grimy panes look out onto the night street.

I wonder whether Philip is still out there. I wonder whether it's true that I still love Philip. Whether love exists.

I wonder where it goes when we stop loving. Does it fizzle out in the cold of the universe? Does it seep into our cells and change our DNA?

I think of Philip and I get that roller-coaster feeling in my stomach, and my eyes fill with tears and I think, Yes, damn it. Even now, after all that's happened.

I pay for my beer and walk back to the beach. Collapse onto the sand and am amazed at how cool it is. I feel the urge to sink back and lie down, to look up at the stars and think of nothing at all, to rest my eyes a little, here, by the water. I feel like waiting in the dark, on the verge of dawn, until the river has carried away all my emotions, swept them around the next bend, washed all my pain out of sight. I indulge the thought for a moment. I feel as if my body weighs a ton. I can't get up. I'm too tired, too wounded, too heavy.

But then I tell myself that it isn't over yet. That the sun's about to rise. That there's always something you can do. That things carry on somehow. That that's what I'm best at—getting up again, no matter what. So I get up. I brush the sand and the pain off my clothes and hands. I avert my eyes from the water, turn my back on it—and find myself looking into Philip's face.

We gaze at each other in silence.

I think to myself that love is not a state, not a feeling—it is an organism that hungers and thirsts, a living being that can grow and atrophy, fall sick and convalesce, go to sleep and die.

That can be resuscitated.

And at that moment the birds start to sing.

Acknowledgments

As always, I should like to start by thanking my family, especially my mother, father, brother and my wise and beautiful grandma Hilde.

Thanks are also due to the wonderful people at btb—and in particular to Regina Kammerer, who helped me bring *The Stranger Upstairs* to light. What a blessing to have you as my editor!

Warm thanks too to the fabulous trio Georg Simader, Caterina Kirsten and Lisa Volpp. (Grazie mille! What would I do without you?)

And then, of course, there are all the readers, booksellers, events organisers and lovers of literature who have seen to it that I can keep doing what I like doing best. Thank you!

Very special thanks to my inspirational friends, especially to Jörn. But also to Sonia, Frank, Alex, Lukas, Laura, Maria, Jörn, Heiner, Anne Sasha.

And to Radiohead, for the soundtrack.

extracts reading groups
competitions books new
discounts extracts
competitions
books new extracts discounts
events books events
extracts new title reading groups
interviews
events extracts
discounts
new books events
events new
discounts extracts discounts
www.panmacmillan.com
extracts events reading groups
competitions books extracts new

reading groups

reading groups